# Voracious

Books by V. K. Forrest

*Eternal*

*Undying*

*Immortal*

*Ravenous*

*Voracious*

Published by Kensington Publishing Corporation

# VORACIOUS

V.K. FORREST

KENSINGTON BOOKS
www.kensingtonbooks.com

KENSINGTON BOOKS are published by

Kensington Publishing Corp.
119 West 40th Street
New York, NY 10018



All Kensington titles, imprints, and distributed lines are available at special quantity discounts for bulk purchases for sales promotion, premiums, fund-raising, and educational or institutional use.

Special book excerpts or customized printings can also be created to fit specific needs. For details, write or phone the office of the Kensington Special Sales Manager: Kensington Publishing Corp., 119 West 40th Street, New York, NY 10018. Attn. Special Sales Department. Phone: 1-800-221-2647.



ISBN-13: 978-0-7582-5570-9
ISBN-10: 0-7582-5570-5

First Kensington Trade Paperback Printing: August 2012
10 9 8 7 6 5 4 3 2 1

Printed in the United States of America

# Chapter 1

*Rehoboth Beach, Delaware*

Aedan rested his forearms on the scarred bar top, barely hearing the chatter of the other patrons or the beat of the blaring music. He reached for his Guinness and took a sip, savoring the slightly burnt flavor of the dry stout he'd been drinking for the last two hundred years. It was late. Time he headed home. But not before he finished his beer.

It was always like this for him. When he was gone—working for the sept, living among strangers—he yearned to be home in Clare Point amidst his own. But when he finally did have the opportunity to return, he felt as out of place here as he did on foreign soil. At least at first. It always took a week or two and quite a few solitary nights on a barstool, nursing a beer, before he could assimilate again. Out in the world, he was a killer. He survived by keeping to himself, keeping moving, remaining a stranger to those around him. In Clare Point, with relatives and friends, it took some time to allow himself to feel that closeness he shared with them. The closeness he always yearned for when away, the closeness he feared when he returned home.

It hadn't always been that way. He'd once been a trusting soul . . . with his heart, at least.

Aedan took another sip of his ale. Someone bumped into him from behind. He turned around and glared, and the bearded offender in the Dogfish Head T-shirt threw up his hands.

"Sorry, man. My bad." The guy stumbled backward a step, obviously intimidated by Aedan's size. Or maybe it was Aedan's scowl.

Aedan eyed the drunk again, then returned his attention to his Guinness, memories tugging at his consciousness.

He had once sought out strangers. Particularly the pretty females.

The sound of the barroom patrons, the taste of his ale, the smell of the old bar top brought back flashes of memories like black-and-white images projected on a screen in his head. His memories were of another bar, life cycles ago. It was the nineteenth century, the south of France, in the little cliff-dwelling town of Beaumes-de-Venise near Orange. Madeleine had been her name. It was her father's pub; he let rooms above stairs, served food and drink below. Aedan had been there on assignment for the sept when he met the barkeep's daughter.

Aedan made a fist and then loosened each finger in controlled motions as he fought the bone-crushing ache he experienced every time he thought about her. Which was exactly why he tried his damnedest not to think about her at all. Even after hundreds of years, the memory of Madeleine hurt more than any physical wound—being stabbed, shot, garroted—he had ever suffered. He had loved her. It had been the kind of true love a man experienced only once in a lifetime.

And Aedan's lifetime was turning out to be pretty damned long.

Fifteen hundred years, give or take a few, he had lived on this earth. Once he had been human like Madeleine, before he had become vampire. As a human, he'd fought against St. Patrick in Ireland in the fifth century. He had defended his family and his pagan faith. And he had paid the ultimate price when God had cursed him and the rest of the Kahills. God had transformed them into vampires, forcing them to live lifetime after lifetime, immortal, their souls without hope of redemption.

Not much hope, anyway.

That, in a roundabout way, was how he had ended up at Madeleine's father's pub in Beaumes-de-Venise. How he came to be here now. He, and all the cursed Kahills, were trying to make amends for the sins they had committed against God. They now tried to protect His humans from the dregs of the earth, its most heinous criminals. Aedan's primary job was investigating serial killers. Occasionally, he assassinated one, but only after the order was passed down by the High Council. Who would die was not up to him. He was neither the judge nor the jury, only the executioner.

Aedan took another sip of ale, tasting a hint of bitterness on his tongue.

He had been young and foolish and full of hope when he met Madeleine. The ale she had served him that first night he met her had not been as well brewed as this Guinness. It had been homemade, brewed in her father's cellar, but it had tasted as sweet as honey on Aedan's lips because it had come from her hands.

Sweet Mary, Mother of God, he had loved her. Aedan tipped his glass and finished it. He had loved her, all right. . . . Then he had killed her.

"Another?" A female voice dragged him back to the present.

Aedan shook his head, not bothering to look up. After Madeleine, he'd lost interest in women. Not that he was celibate. He could always find one willing to join him in bed. But he'd lost interest in the magic of the feminine voice. Of the smoky look they gave you. The feel of their touch.

"Good, because I've served enough beer for one night. I'll get your check." Her voice faded as she moved away from him, dragging a bar mop past his empty glass.

Aedan didn't know what made him look up. *Fate?* He wondered later. He wasn't entirely sure, even at fifteen centuries old, if fate even existed. But something made him look up at that moment. Or someone . . .

Her resemblance to Madeleine was uncanny. She was pretty. Not gorgeous, but pretty. Tall and slender. *Willowy* was how his Aunt Peigi would have described her. Blue jeans slung low on her hips, and a tight black T-shirt revealed the tiniest sliver of abdomen when she moved. The shirt read BREW and featured a witch's bubbling cauldron. Her natural blond hair was pulled back in a loose ponytail, piled up on her head the way women did when getting in the shower. Her hair was long. He could tell by how many times it looped out of the elastic band. It was an amazing color, yellow blond, like sunshine. Her eyes were dark brown. She wore no makeup. She had a sprinkling of freckles across her nose that made Aedan want to touch them with his fingertips.

Or kiss them.

He was so shocked by that thought as it bounced around his head that he rocked back on his barstool. He stared at the barmaid, intrigued. And a little scared.

She apparently didn't feel the vibe; she had already walked away.

It was all Dallas could do to not look back over her shoulder at the hunky ginger as she dropped the bar rag and went to the register to ring up his tab. The bar was busy tonight, busy for a Thursday in April. Busy was *good*. Tall, seriously big, good-looking ginger on her barstool, with blue eyes that could pierce a girl's heart. *Bad*.

He was here alone. She'd been watching him for a

while. Trying not to, of course, which made it harder not to do. He'd come in alone two hours ago. He didn't speak to other patrons, not even the pretty singles cruising for men. He didn't glance up at the basketball game on the TV behind the bar. He just sat there, nursing one Guinness after another, his handsome face all dark and stormy and totally intriguing. She wondered, at first, if his girlfriend had just broken up with him and that was the reason for the morose face. But she decided, after a while, that that wasn't it; something more tragic than that simmered in those piercing blue eyes.

Dallas almost groaned aloud as she hit the total on the cash register and it spit out a little piece of paper. She checked it to be sure it was right . . . and to stall. She didn't want to speak to him, whoever he was, her tall, handsome . . . and tragic ginger.

Men were off-limits these days, especially the handsome ones. Definitely the tragic ones. She'd already had her share of tragedy and then some.

Dallas needed to just give him his tab and walk away. Make sure *he* walked away. Her bartender, Tat, waited behind her for the register. She couldn't stand there all night, and she couldn't afford to hand out free beers to every good-looking sob story that came into the bar. She'd sunk every dollar she had into this place when she'd bought it. It was all she and Kenzie had left; Dallas had to make it work.

She made a beeline for the redhead. She'd always had a weakness for guys with auburn hair. His was dark and thick, the same shade as his beard stubble. *Hot.*

Dallas didn't know what was wrong with her. It had been a long time since a pretty face had caught her attention. She slapped his tab down in front of him, purposely not making eye contact. "Have a good night. Be safe."

She almost got away cleanly, but he must have reached for the little slip of paper before she pulled her hand away.

His fingertip brushed hers. They barely made contact, but it was enough. . . .

What she felt . . . what she *saw,* when they touched, nearly knocked her on her ass.

Her visions often came to her choppy and fast like old movie reel images, streaked with time and age. They came one right after another: people, places. And emotion. That was the worst part.

Dallas gasped, pulling her hand away as if she'd burned it on the French fryer.

"You okay?" Tat called. Her bartender was a big guy with a shaved head and two full sleeves of tattoos; he looked like an ex-inmate even though he was the nicest guy you would ever want to meet. He glanced at Dallas as he walked away from the register. He was looking at her strangely.

So was the guy on the barstool.

"Closing in five minutes," she announced loudly. She made her way to the far end of the bar, as far from the ginger as she could get, and began to pick up dirty glasses. She was shaking.

The music was still playing over the loudspeakers. She'd invested in XM radio for the nights she didn't pay a DJ or a live band. "Can someone hit the radio?" she called. She dumped five dirty glasses into a dishpan and picked it up, heading for the kitchen. More like running for the kitchen. "*Someone?*" She hollered to no one in particular, probably sounding bitchier than she needed to.

Aedan watched the blonde push through the door into the back, carrying a dishpan full of dirty glasses. The door swung shut behind her.

What the hell had just happened there between them? His hand had barely touched her, but a jolt of what felt like electricity had arced between them, scaring the bejesus out of him. Which was hard to do. Vampires didn't spook easily.

He didn't know what had happened or how. The only thing he was certain of was that they had made some kind of metaphysical contact.

His first impulse was to follow her. She'd obviously felt it, too, the way she'd taken off. And something made him think she understood far better than he did what it was.

He looked at the kitchen door. Did he dare?

Aedan's phone vibrated in his pocket, which was totally unexpected. Everyone knew he was on sabbatical for the next three months. He rarely got calls that weren't work-related, and never this late. Aunt Peigi was long in bed.

Curious, he slid off the barstool and fished his phone out of the pocket of his jeans. He checked the caller ID. It was his cousin Mark . . . a state police detective. Aedan suddenly got a bad feeling. "Hello?" he said into the phone.

"Aedan?"

"Yeah?" He glanced around the bar. People were filing out. Someone had turned off the music and turned up the lights.

"It's Mark. Mark Karr."

He could hear the tension in his cousin's voice. Mark was one of them, a vampire moonlighting as a cop. Or maybe the other way around. Mark was a good cop. The best. "What's up?"

"I know you're on vacation. . . ." He hesitated. "Sorry to bother you, but—"

Aedan heard the sound of an intercom in the background. A Doctor Wilkes was being paged. Mark was at a hospital. "What can I do for you, Mark?"

"I'm over at SCH. In Lewes. You need to come here. Right now."

Aedan frowned. "Is everything okay? Aunt Peigi?" Of course, that didn't make much sense. Kahills didn't do hospitals. They had a doctor of their own, and their bodies almost always healed without any intervention. It was hard to kill a Kahill. The whole immortal thing. And when they *did* die, they rose three days later, in the body of a teenager, ready to begin another cycle of their cursed lives. Aunt Peigi couldn't be sick or injured, dying in a hospital.

"A case," Mark said cryptically. "Like I said, I know you're on vacation and you're technically off duty, but you're going to want to see this."

Aedan glanced at the door that led to the bar's kitchen. The blonde hadn't come back out. Which was just as well. "I'm on my way," he said, dropping a twenty and a five on the bar. "Give me twenty minutes?"

"Come in through Emergency. They haven't moved her yet. I'll be looking for you."

Aedan hung up, slipped his phone back into his pocket, and walked out onto the street. It was chilly. He shivered as he headed for his car. Maybe it was just the cold. Or maybe he already knew what waited for him.

Dallas stood in the kitchen, peeking through the crack between the swinging doors, watching the ginger go. For a second there, the way he'd been looking at her, she'd been worried he was going to follow her into the kitchen. She held the hand that had touched his to her chest, feeling her pounding heart.

What the hell had just happened? How was it even possible—what she had seen in his head during that brief second she had made contact with him. She'd had a lot of crazy experiences in her life, but this went way beyond crazy.

She had what her mother had called *the gift*. Dallas called it *the curse*. ESP, mental telepathy, mind reading . . . It didn't matter what label you attached to it, it was an intrusion on her life and on the lives of the people she touched. Literally. Since she had been a small child, Dallas had had the ability to see people's pasts, feel the emotions they had felt, just by touching them.

It was a curse, all right. One that had followed her through school, into college and now into adulthood. Over time, she had learned to turn it down, like the volume on a radio, but there was no mute button. And no matter what she did, she couldn't turn it off. Which meant she couldn't have normal relationships. At least not with anyone but her daughter, whose past she already knew. Whose past she had actively participated in. It was just too hard, seeing all the things other people saw. Feeling what they had felt. Knowing what they carried around inside.

So what was up with the ginger? How . . . why had she picked up on so many people when she had touched him? It wasn't just pieces of the guy's life, but of lots of people's lives. Lots. Which wasn't possible unless . . . unless maybe he had the same curse she did, and he was carrying all the people he had ever touched around in his head. Was that even possible?

Tat appeared in the crack of the kitchen door. He was a nice-looking guy, even with all the tattoos and the two-gauge, stainless steel ear tunnels. He had kind brown eyes. "Hey, you okay?" he asked through the door. " 'Cause you're acting weird."

As the front door closed behind the ginger, Dallas pushed through the swinging door. "I always act weird. We've already established that." She walked past him, grabbed a wet rag from under the counter, and began to wipe down the sticky bar. Bar patrons could make a pretty big mess in one evening, what with all the beer and bullshit they spilled.

He turned to watch her, nibbling on his lip ring. "Yeah, but you're acting weird, even for you."

"Can you herd the rest of them out?" Lifting her chin, she indicated a couple of guys standing around one of the two pool tables in a small room off the main barroom. Everyone else was either gone or headed that way.

"Sure," Tat said, but he still stood there. "That guy. The redhead. Was he bothering you?"

Dallas was dragging a wet bar mop over the polished wood and glanced up. "Nah, but if he was, I could handle it," she said lightly. "I hired you to tend bar; you don't have to be my knight in shining armor."

She wondered if the redhead was a tourist. It was early in the season for tourists, but he'd never been there before tonight. Not since January, when she had taken over the bar. She was positive. Otherwise, she'd have remembered him.

"I know." Tat hesitated. "But I would. I'd be your knight in shining armor. If you'd let me."

She smiled, feeling a little sad. That had to be one of the nicest things anyone had ever said to her. Tat had made it pretty clear the week he'd started working for her that he was interested in her, if she was interested in him. Her first thought had been just to get rid of him rather than have to deal with the complications of his unrequited love, but he was too good an employee to lose. Instead, she had told him the truth, flat out, that she wasn't interested. She'd given him the line about her dead husband, about it being too soon, and he'd said he understood. But sometimes she caught him watching her with a wistful look.

Tat didn't know about her curse. No one here in Rehoboth Beach knew. And she planned to keep it that way. It was all part of her plan for starting a new life, escaping the ghosts of her past and the witch hunt in New England.

Dallas turned back to mopping the bar, keeping her tone light. "Take care of the stragglers, Sir Lancelot."

"You bet your sweet tushy, Guinevere." Tat grinned and walked away.

As Dallas scooped up several dirty pilsner glasses, she glanced at the front door again. She'd half expected the ginger to walk back through the door. He didn't.

Which was just the way it had to be.

* * *

Aedan parked his car, thrust his hands into his jean pockets, and, with trepidation, made his way to the entrance marked EMERGENCY in glowing red letters.

Mark had said there was something there he needed to see. What could he possibly have been referring to? Right now, Aedan was stationed in Paris. He and his team were tracking the movements of two men, a serial killer and a pedophile, at the same time, gathering evidence to be presented to the High Council. But he was a continent away from Pierre LeCruex and Dominique Rue. This couldn't possibly have anything to do with those cases.

The pneumatic doors in front of him hissed and opened, and he stepped into the bright light of a waiting room. There were rows of chairs lined up in front of an admissions desk. A middle-aged woman in yellow Snoopy scrubs was registering a patient. More chairs and several vending machines ran along the back wall. A young Hispanic woman sat in the front row cradling an infant wrapped in a tattered blanket. Behind her, a guy sat reading a newspaper, his left hand wrapped in a bloody towel. Aedan spotted Mark standing near a vending machine, drinking from a Styrofoam cup. A toothpick protruded from his mouth. Mark had started chewing on cinnamon toothpicks a couple of years ago when he quit smoking. Aedan sometimes wondered if the toothpick habit was worse.

Mark looked up, sensing that one of his own kind had entered the room. It was some kind of vampire radar; it worked with zombies and werewolves, too, but not always as well. Mark nodded a silent greeting.

Aedan nodded in return. He could smell the cinnamon of Mark's toothpick. Must have been a fresh one.

*Get you a cup of coffee?* Mark sent telepathically. When in close proximity, most Kahills could speak to each other without speaking aloud.

*Nah. Not much of a coffee drinker. Had a couple of beers.*

*Not too many to be driving, I hope.*

Aedan frowned. *What have you got for me?*

Mark caught the attention of the woman in the scrubs at the front desk. He pointed to the set of double doors marked STAFF ONLY. She nodded. A buzzer sounded, and the doors swung open toward Mark. Mark tossed his cup into a trash can as he walked through the doorway. Aedan followed.

"She came in about forty-five minutes ago. I just happened to be headed home and heard the call on my radio. We're waiting on the orthopedic surgeon on call to get in here. Called in a plastic surgeon, too. They need to decide which of her injuries is most pressing before they take her into the OR."

Mark spoke quietly, his voice steady as he fiddled with the toothpick in his mouth. He sounded like a man with a hundred years of cop experience, which he had. They walked down a wide hallway that was buzzing with activity. Doctors, nurses, and techs swarmed like bees, ordering labs, transporting patients in wheel chairs, and calming people who were in the ER on what was likely one of the worst days of their lives. Aedan sensed the woman Mark wanted him to see was experiencing the worst day of her life at this very moment.

"She's sedated," he said. "So we can't talk to her right now. Might be days before we can. I just needed you to see her." He stopped at a curtained cubicle near the nurse's station and glanced at Aedan.

Aedan nodded, wishing he were somewhere else, anywhere but here. His sense of dread escalated to the point that his chest felt tight and he was struggling to take even breaths.

"Teesha?" Mark called softly into the opening of the curtains. He tucked his toothpick into his pocket. "It's Detective Karr." He waited a second and then drew back the curtain and walked in, holding it back for Aedan.

Aedan didn't know what he had expected. He guessed he had expected an injured woman, but one look at Teesha's face and his knees weakened. He dropped all six-foot-five inches and two hundred and forty pounds of himself onto the hard plastic chair beside the bed. His fingers found the crucifix beneath his shirt. "It can't be."

Mark drew back the sheet from the young black woman's chest to reveal a bloody wound on her breast. "Nonetheless, I think it is."

# Chapter 2

Aedan stared at the young woman who had, no doubt, been beautiful only an hour or so ago. She wasn't any longer. She would never be beautiful again, no matter how talented her plastic surgeon. Aedan didn't recognize her face, but he recognized her attacker. His gaze fell to her bare breast again.

*Raped?* Aedan mouthed the word.

Mark made a sound of affirmation. "She was found in a parking lot off Rehoboth Avenue not far from Dogfish Head. I haven't been to the scene yet, but the local cops think it happened in an alley. She crawled out into the parking lot before she passed out, probably from blood loss. Name's Teesha Jones. Twenty-three. She managed to find her handbag after he attacked her and left her for dead, and drag it with her. That's how we were able to identify her so quickly. Can you believe she had enough wherewithal to do that?" He shook his head. "Survival instinct. You know how it is. Some humans have it. Some don't. She works at a gift shop on the main drag. Found her nametag in her bag. We're guessing she went out for drinks after work. Probably Dogfish Head; it's popular with young people. Her car was in the lot. We'll have to wait until tomorrow to ask around."

"I was just there," Aedan said, his voice sounding strange in his ears.

"Dogfish Head?" It was a local microbrewery and restaurant and popular with locals as well as tourists.

"In Rehoboth. Brew, on Wilmington Avenue. I was sitting on a barstool while this was happening to her."

"You couldn't have known." Mark sighed and drew the sheet over the woman's bare breast.

It didn't matter. Aedan could still see the cursive "J" carved in her flesh. He'd never understood why Jay felt it necessary to sign his work. Wasn't what he did to the women's faces signature enough?

"I guess she's going to live," Aedan said. She was hooked up to an IV and a heart monitor, but she was breathing on her own. And the fact that she had been left alone in the trauma room suggested she was out of immediate danger.

"She lost a lot of blood, but no vital organs were affected. You know how he is. He's good with a knife." Mark hesitated. "It's him, isn't it, Aedan? It's Jay come across the pond?"

Aedan lowered his face to his hands for a moment, then slowly looked up, his gaze settling on the woman's bloody, mutilated face. The medical personnel had been able to stop most of the bleeding, but now her face was beginning to swell. By morning, she'd be lucky if she could open her eyes. The surgeon would stitch up her cheeks, her forehead, her nostrils, the flaps Jay had created under her eyes. He would repair her mouth as best he could, and there would be lots of future surgeries, but Teesha would be forever left with the permanent smile Jay had carved into her face.

Aedan got up out of the chair and stepped through the opening in the curtain, out into the hall. No one paid any attention to him. A small child whimpered a few curtains over, and his mother soothed him with gentle words. Mark joined Aedan in the hall. They didn't make eye contact.

"He's never come to the U.S. before, to our knowledge."

Aedan shook his head. "But the timing is about right." His head was so full of thoughts and images that he couldn't think clearly. He couldn't grab any one idea and hang on to it. He'd always known Jay would be back. He'd hoped he wouldn't. He'd prayed. But he had always known Jay would be back again.

"You'll have to go to the General Council and get put on the case. I can do the investigating, but I need your input. And you deserve the kill."

"I'm on sabbatical," Aedan said. "I'm not supposed to be working." The sept insisted on a certain amount of downtime, especially for those on Kill Teams. His primary job on the team was investigating, because of his unique gift, the ability to shape-shift, not just into animals, but also humans. But he was still required to kill sometimes, and he was still required to follow the rules for kill-team members. Some people stretched the rules, people like Liam Kahill, but not Aedan. He liked sabbaticals; they helped to ground him so he could do what he had to do.

"I know you're supposed to be taking a break, but these are . . . special circumstances. There's no one else available. No one who knows him like you do. The Council will complain, but they'll go with it." Mark glanced over his shoulder at the curtain. "You need to be—"

"You think he's got it out for me?" Aedan interrupted.

Mark exhaled heavily. "I think by now he knows you've got it out *for him*."

Aedan closed his eyes and rubbed his temples. Suddenly, he was tired to the point of exhaustion. Maybe that was why he couldn't think. "I'm going to go home and get some sleep." He opened his eyes, letting his hands fall. "How about we talk in the morning. Breakfast?"

"I can meet you at the diner. Can we make it late? I've been at it over twelve hours. I need some shut-eye, too."

"Call me when you get up." Aedan walked away. He almost called out "thanks," and then realized the ridiculousness of it. Who thanked someone for hooking them up with a serial rapist?

Aedan pulled his Honda up in front of the house, hoping everyone would be asleep, *expecting* everyone to be asleep; it was going on two in the morning. But no such luck. The lights were blazing from Peigi's cottage, only a block from the beach in Clare Point, as if it were midday. He let himself in the front door. The sound of automatic gunfire blasted from the den. He walked through the living room, with its chintz curtains and Georgia O'Keefe prints on the walls, flipping out lights as he went. He stuck his head through the doorway into the den. He recognized the video game on the flat-screen TV. "Black Ops."

"Hey, Brian."

Peigi's husband didn't look away from the TV screen. He'd died and been reborn a few months ago, so Peigi, sixty-something, was now married to a pimply-faced sixteen-year-old. Usually, there wasn't such an age discrepancy between married couples, but because Brian had been older than Peigi the first time they had married, and because no one died and was reborn at exactly the same age each life cycle, sometimes couples got *out of whack*. Peigi and Brian were definitely *out of whack*.

Aedan glanced at the two teenage girls sitting on the couch, one on each side of Brian, both texting on their cell phones. He knew Katy Hill, but he didn't recognize the girl with the long, dark hair and olive skin. She wasn't a Kahill, but she was most definitely vampire. "Hey, Katy," he greeted.

"Hey," she called cheerfully, continuing to text. "You know Lia?" She motioned with her phone, but continued pushing buttons.

"Ah. I don't know Lia, but I know *of* Lia." She was vampire, all right, but her story was complicated. She hadn't originally been a Kahill, but had come from a family of vampires in Italy. Last summer, she'd taken a family holiday in Clare Point and had murdered several humans. Her life had been spared by the sept after Kaleigh, their teenage wisewoman, discovered a technical detail. Lia had been allowed to live, but had been forced to leave her family and all memory of them and be reborn a Kahill vampire. Now she was one of their own.

"That's Aedan, Lia. He's assigned to Paris right now, tracking crazies."

The dark-haired girl dropped her phone to her lap, making eye contact in a very non-teenager manner. She had a pretty smile. "It's nice to meet you."

"Nice to meet you." He nodded.

"Lia's at that stupid vampire boarding school in Massachusetts," Katy explained with an eye roll. "We're on a mission to get her back to Clare Point. She's not going to go AWOL. Where's she going to go? She doesn't even remember those Vs in Italy. There's no need to keep her a prisoner anymore."

"I'm on spring break right now," Lia said.

Aedan looked to Katy. "Which doesn't explain why *you're* awake in the middle of the night. You have school tomorrow."

Katy frowned. "I'm a teenage vampire. I can't sleep at night."

She said it as if he was dumbest guy on earth. He shook his head, but smiled all the same. It wasn't easy being a teenage Kahill. He knew that from experience. "Peigi still up, Brian?"

He didn't answer. An endless flow of zombies was coming down a dark hallway on the television. Brian frantically uttered, "Hit the button." Aedan knew Brian was talking to whoever was on the other end of his headset and not to him.

Aedan raised his eyebrows. On the screen an elevator

door closed and a virtual Fidel Castro reloaded a Kalashnikov 74.

"Kitchen, I think," Lia offered.

"Okay." Aedan turned to go.

"Hey, Aedan," Katy called after him.

He stuck his head back through the doorway.

"Could you check the mozzarella sticks in the oven? They're gonna beep in a minute." She flashed him a smile and then returned her attention to her phone.

"No problem. "

Aedan found his Aunt Peigi seated at the table in the big country kitchen. She had her coffee mug in front of her, but a bottle of Powers Irish whiskey on the table, too.

"That tea or whiskey in that cup?" he asked, going to the oven to check on the teens' late-night snack.

"A little of both." She frowned. "I couldn't sleep."

Aedan peered into the oven, grabbed a hot mitt, spun the tray of mozzarella sticks, and set the timer for another five minutes.

"I've got 'Black Ops,' screaming zombies, and a list of topics a mile long for the next General Council meeting keeping me up," she grumbled. "What's your excuse?"

He tossed the hot mitt on the counter and took a chair across from Peigi. She wore her gray hair in a short, sensible haircut. It matched her sensible personality, which was good. As the leader of the sept's General Council, sensible Peigi kept everyone in line. Tonight she was wearing an old, plaid flannel robe and wool slippers. She looked like an ad for nightwear in an L.L. Bean catalog. Her day wardrobe came from the same company.

He shrugged noncommittally. He wasn't ready to talk to her, to anyone, about Jay. Not yet. "Takes me a while to adjust, I guess. You know, being home. Being sort of . . . normal."

She slid the bottle of Powers across the table to him.

He grinned. "Thanks. I think I'll just head up to bed."

She nodded, cupping her mug in her hands, but not taking a drink. He could tell something was weighing heavily on her mind. Something more than video game zombies. A part of him just wanted to get up, say good night, and be on his way. He had his own problems. But Aunt Peigi had been too good to him all these years. Since his mother's death, she had been as good to him as any mother could be.

Aedan folded his hands on the table. "So, what's going on with you?"

"You can hear what's going on." She motioned in the direction of the machine gun fire. "Guess you've heard. No one here can keep a secret or stay out of other people's personal business. Brian's not adjusting all that well. He refuses to go to school. He doesn't want to talk about anything related to . . . his situation. He sleeps all day and plays those stupid video games all night."

He studied his folded hands. "Sometimes it takes longer to adjust. You know that. It's overwhelming. The memories. The whole coming of age thing again and again. Realizing you're a vampire is pretty heady stuff. Having to relive the truth of the matter, life cycle after life cycle. It's hard. Brian always did take it harder than most of us. He'll come around."

"I know. I know." She turned the coffee mug in her hands. "I'm trying to be patient. I've been through it before, too. But our age difference is getting to be a problem, Aedan. A serious problem. I could live another fifteen years. Longer." She didn't look at him.

Aedan didn't know what to say. He was saved by the buzz of the timer on the stove. He got up and pulled out the mozzarella sticks. He dumped them on a plate and grabbed the plastic tub of marinara sauce Katy must have set out. "Anything I can do?" he asked, turning off the oven.

She looked up and smiled. "I'm glad you're home, Aedan."

He picked up the plate. He'd take it to the kids on his way upstairs. "Me too."

She held his gaze, and her focus narrowed. Even though he'd been careful to keep her from reading his thoughts, she was obviously aware something was going on with him. Something bad. Very bad. "How about you?" she probed. "Anything I can do for you?"

He halted in the door, snack plate in hand. He exhaled. "Not tonight."

"When you're ready," she called after him.

Dallas glanced at the clock on the nightstand. The red numerals glowed 3:25. She groaned and closed her eyes, willing herself to lie still so she wouldn't disturb her daughter. The single bed was really too small for the two of them. It was childish, climbing into Kenzie's bed with her, pulling her daughter's Batman sheet over her head as if *she* were the ten-year-old.

But Dallas was scared. The ginger in the bar tonight had scared her. Who was he? What was he that he could have memories of so many people? Why had he come into her bar tonight? Had he been looking for her?

That was stupid, of course. Who would be looking for her? She was being paranoid. Being accused of being a witch in New England, even in the twenty-first century, could make you paranoid. Especially if maybe you very possibly *were* a witch. It was just coincidence, the guy wandering into her bar. Had to be.

Dallas tightened her arm around Kenzie's sleeping form and breathed in the scent of her sweet blond hair. Kenzie didn't smell the same as she had when she was first born; the baby scent was gone. But there was still something very reassuring, very primal, in the scent of one's own child. It brought out Dallas's need to protect the little girl, no matter what she had to do. It was why she'd brought her here in the first place. Dallas had taken every bit of insurance money she'd gotten and put it into the bar.

Was Kenzie in danger, here in Delaware? Was the ginger a threat to Dallas, and therefore, to Kenzie? Did Dallas need to flee Delaware the way she had fled Rhode Island?

She *was* paranoid.

She'd not gotten an impression from the ginger that he was a danger to her. At least not physically. All those people in his head had just startled her, was all. She hadn't been expecting it. She hadn't expected to feel such an immediate and strong attraction to him, either. What the hell was she thinking?

It had been a very long time since Dallas had felt that kind of sexual attraction to a man. She hadn't slept with anyone since John's death.

John. The bastard. How could he have done that to her? To Kenzie. Not that the marriage would have lasted . . . But it was such a coward's way out. Suicide by overdose.

She snuggled closer to Kenzie, closing her eyes. Her thoughts drifted back to the ginger. He was not a problem. She wouldn't let him be a problem. She was in control of her life and Kenzie's, no one else but her. She didn't know what the ginger's deal was, possessing all those people's memories. But it wasn't her problem. It was his.

Kenzie sighed in her sleep and snuggled closer to Dallas. Dallas could finally feel herself drifting off to sleep.

She'd probably never see the ginger again, she thought, her mind beginning to drift into sweet oblivion. If she did see him, she'd make it clear she didn't want anything to do with him or his crazy memories.

She couldn't get involved, no matter how curious she was.

* * *

Aedan didn't really like coffee, but he was on his second cup. He was waiting for Mark in a booth in the old-fashioned diner that was a landmark in Clare Point, to locals and tourists alike. Fortunately, it was still early in the year for the tourists who would flock to the quaint little beach town, the way they did every year. It was after Easter, but before summer break for students. This morning, there wasn't a single person in the diner who wasn't a vampire. The idea made Aedan smile. It was good to be home.

He made eye contact with a pretty, red-haired teenager at the cash register and smiled. She smiled back. After she paid for her cup and whatever was in the brown bag, she approached his booth.

"Good to have you home, Aedan." Kaleigh slid onto the bench seat across from him.

"Good to be home." He frowned. "Shouldn't you be in school?"

She grabbed a straw off the table and stabbed it into her cup. "Everyone in this town thinks they're my mother."

"Actually, everyone in this town thinks *you're* his or her mother."

Kaleigh was their wisewoman; at nearly eighteen, she was just beginning to grow into the huge responsibility she had made for herself over the centuries. But she was still a teen and had to be given certain allowances. She also had to be protected. As a full-grown vampire, her gifts would be greater, stronger than those of any other individual in the sept, but she was still growing into the role.

"I had a dental appointment, for your information." She grinned broadly, showing him shiny, polished teeth.

"So *now* you're on your way to school."

She rolled her eyes and took another sip of her drink.

"You'll be graduating high school. Will you be headed to college in the fall?" he asked, changing the subject to something she might deem more pleasant. "I know you were debating what to do. Stay here or go away." He was quiet for a moment. He knew she was thinking, but he took care not to butt into her thoughts. "I know you feel a responsibility to everyone here, but I think college would be good for you, ultimately good for the sept."

"Were you always such a nice guy?" She sat back on the bench. "Because you always seem like the nicest guy."

He looked down into his coffee mug. "I'm not always a nice guy. I've done some terrible things in my lives, Kaleigh. Things I'm not proud of."

She gave a wave as if she could dismiss them all with a minor gesture. "Haven't we all?"

"You always been so wise?" he asked.

She laughed. "Apparently." She grabbed her cup. "So what are you going to do while you're home? Dating anyone? You really need a nice girl, Aedan. Preferably not human, though." She wrinkled her cute, freckled nose. "Poor Liam, he fell for a human, and you heard what happened to him."

He *did* know what had happened to Liam. He'd been home over the winter for a few days and had gotten a little mixed up in Liam's problems. Liam was back in Paris now. They were on the same team. But Aedan didn't feel right talking about Liam's personal life, not with Kaleigh. Not with anyone. "I don't do HFs." Vampire-speak for *human females*.

She nodded like a cartoon wisewoman. "That's what everyone says." She sucked on her straw, adding thoughtfully, "If I wasn't mated for life, I might try a human. Just to see what they're like."

He chuckled and took a sip of coffee. "Trouble. That's what they're like." Out of the corner of his eye, he saw Mark enter the diner.

Kaleigh glanced in the same direction, then back at Aedan. "Something up?" She went on before he could respond. "Because from the look on Mark's face, I would guess something's up in po-po land."

"When's the next General Council meeting?"

"Monday."

He could feel her mind probing his for information. She was good. Very good. He didn't let her in. "You should probably be there. We may have a *situation.*"

"Hey, Kaleigh." Mark approached the booth. He was wearing khakis and an oxford shirt, sans tie. It was his official detective uniform when he could get away with it.

"You want me to leave?" she asked both men. She looked hopeful. "Or stay and give counsel?"

"Leave," they said in unison.

She snatched up her bag and cup as she slid off the bench. "I don't get a lot of respect from you people. You'd think I'd get some respect, me being your wisewoman and all."

"Go to school, Kaleigh," Aedan said.

She waved and walked away. "See you Monday night."

Mark slid into her seat, and Maryann, the owner of the diner, immediately appeared with a white coffee mug and filled it with coffee. She took their order and was gone a minute later. She was usually a great talker, but this morning she must have sensed that no one was looking for idle chitchat.

"You talk to the hospital this morning?" Aedan asked when Maryann was gone.

"Teesha's right femur and left forearm were operated on last night. She ended up with pins in both. What the hell does he do to them that he can shatter bones?" Mark poured a healthy dose of sugar into his coffee. "He's got to be awfully strong. Superhuman strong."

"He can't be human, Mark." Aedan was quiet for a minute. He stared into the depths of his coffee cup. "Humans don't live for hundreds of years. They don't live to kill in cycles for hundreds of years." His mind drifted back over the decades, over his encounters with Jay. He'd never met him face-to-face, at least not to his knowledge. But he had seen plenty of his work. And he knew his habits. Jay would kill for two full cycles of the moon, and then he would be gone again for fifty years. By the time he was back, somewhere in the world, Aedan would have died and been reborn. He would probably be a teenager, his gifts not yet fully developed. The sept would never give a vulnerable teenager permission to go after an enemy as formidable as Jay. So this was Aedan's opportunity to nail the bastard, nail him, or go who knew how long before he'd have the chance again.

"So what *do* you think he is?" Mark asked. "He's not vampire. That's for sure. He's not werewolf. He's not zombie." He sipped his coffee and began to add more sugar. "Maybe he is human. Not one, but different humans. You know, like one training another and then passing the task on to the next."

"I don't know," Aedan said, trying not to sound irritated, even though he was. Not that he was irritated with Mark. He was irritated with himself. Angry with himself that he couldn't catch this guy. Angry that he had let him . . . *it* get to Madeleine. And all the other victims since. "I don't think he's human. Just a feeling."

"Then what is he?" Mark demanded.

"I don't know." Aedan forced his tone to remain even. "But I'm going to find out. This time, I'm going to find out." He looked up. "So when can we talk to Teesha?"

"*We're* not going to talk to Teesha. Not yet. *I'm* going to talk to her—when I can. I'm going to see what the police have. I'm going to talk to her when her doctors give the okay. Then I get back to you. You have to stay in the background, Aedan. You know that."

Aedan pressed both hands to the gold Formica table. "I have to talk to her. I've got questions that might lead us to him before he strikes again."

"I understand that. You'll get to talk to her. But not today. I don't know if I'll get to talk to her today. The plastic surgeon wants to get her back into the OR as soon as he can. She might be facing multiple surgeries over the next few days."

Aedan tightened his fists on the table. Slowly released them. "And in the meantime, what am I supposed to do?"

"You're supposed to rest and let me do what I do. You're supposed to recuperate from the last year of work. Read a book. Rent a movie. Go for a walk on the beach."

Maryann arrived with their breakfast. Hotcakes, sausage, and hash browns for Mark, scrapple and scrambled eggs for Aedan. Aedan was excited about the scrapple. It wasn't something he could get in Paris, or anywhere else in the world but here.

"Maybe you should get laid," Mark suggested, reaching for the salt shaker.

Maryann smiled but didn't comment. "Anything else, gentlemen?"

"No. Thanks."

*Get laid?* Aedan thought as he picked up a forkful of fluffy eggs. That was the last thing on his mind.

At least for the most part.

Aedan had intended to stay in that night. He had dinner with Peigi and Brian, who was able to pry himself away from the TV, and several other Clare Point teens. Kaleigh was there, so he thoroughly enjoyed their company, but as the evening wore on, he became convinced he wanted a Guinness. He needed some time alone. Time to think about Teesha. And Jay.

Before he really realized what he was doing, Aedan had left Clare Point and was driving south toward Rehoboth Beach. He told himself his plan was to have a look around, maybe just cruise up and down Rehoboth Avenue, see what Teesha must have seen last night. But his car found its way to Wilmington Avenue, and before he could come up with several reasons why going into Brew was a bad idea, he was walking through the door. One beer, he told himself. Then he'd hit the street, see what he could find out. Cops didn't always get all the answers by asking questions; it was his experience that sometimes blending in and just watching and listening got better results. His gift allowed him to do that better than most.

Again, the crowd was decent, but his barstool from the previous night was open. It was almost as if he was meant to be there. He kept his leather jacket on as he took a seat. He spotted the bartender with all the tattoos. A green and yellow mermaid on his forearm caught Aedan's eye. He'd once known a mermaid.

He didn't see the blonde.

"What can I get you?" the bartender asked, dropping a cocktail napkin down in front of him.

George Thorogood was playing over the loudspeakers.

Aedan's gaze drifted to the swinging doors behind the bar as he murmured the lyrics to "Bad to the Bone." He wondered if she was in the kitchen. Maybe it was her night off. That had never occurred to him on the drive over—that she might not be there.

The bartender glanced in the same direction, then back at Aedan. "Hey, buddy. You lookin' for trouble?" His voice was quiet, but his tone was definitely threatening.

"No, no, I'm not looking for trouble," Aedan answered, purposely keeping his own tone light. He wasn't going to get into it with this guy. He wasn't going to show him what kind of badass he could be. It wasn't right to take advantage of humans that way, not unnecessarily. "Just looking for the woman who works here. Blonde. The one here last night. I . . . I need to ask her a question." He had always been pretty good at thinking fast on his feet. "There was a girl attacked near here last night."

"I heard." The guy leaned on the bar. "It was on the news this morning. It's a wonder she lived. What's Dallas got to do with her?"

*Dallas.* Her name was Dallas. She looked like a Dallas. All leggy and sassy. "How about a Guinness?" Aedan met the bartender's gaze. "And let me worry about what Dallas *did* or didn't see last night."

# Chapter 3

"You think he's a cop?" Dallas pulled a dish of bubbling hot crab dip out of the salamander and slid it onto a plate. Her short-order cook hadn't shown up, so his cousin Miguel was trying to run the kitchen alone; she was giving him a hand when Tat didn't need her behind the bar. They had just one waitress each evening, so there was no way the girl could help back here. Dallas was pleased the bar was busy again tonight, but if the numbers kept up, she was going to have to hire more staff right away instead of waiting until Memorial Day weekend. She'd interviewed a girl for a waitress spot and possibly to be a bartender-in-training just the evening before. The young woman had been pleasant, bright, and seemed willing to learn; maybe Dallas needed to call her before someone else recognized her potential and hired her first.

"He show you a badge?" she asked Tat, who had left his position behind the bar to duck into the kitchen. She grabbed a handful of pita chips and spread them around the plate and added a few slices of Granny Smith apple. She didn't give him a chance to answer. "He look like a cop to you? I don't like cops, Tat."

"I don't like 'em either, but I don't know if he *looks* like a cop. You saw him. You talked to him last night. He look like a cop to you last night?"

"I didn't *talk* to him. I got him a beer." She headed for the door and then stopped. "He ask for me by name?"

"I already told you. He just asked me where the blonde was. Said he needed to talk to you about that girl who was attacked last night."

She frowned. "I don't know anything about that. What would make him think I knew anything about that? I was here when it happened. So was he. You think it's about something else?" She balanced the crab dip in one hand, rested the other on the kitchen door. After John had died, there had been people looking for him. People he owed money. Bad people.

"I don't know what it's about, only what he said." Tat reached over her shoulder and pushed the door open. "You want me to send him away?"

Dallas thought for a minute. If he *was* a cop, it was better to just talk to him, right? She didn't allow herself to think about what had happened when they had touched last night. She'd just keep her hands to herself. "I'll take care of it."

"Order up, Corey," she called to the waitress. She slid the plate onto the bar top and wiped her hands on the little black apron she wore tied around her hips. She could feel the ginger watching her. He was sitting on the same barstool he'd been sitting on the previous night.

"Can you get this gentleman a Guinness?" Dallas asked Tat. She stood directly in front of the ginger and tapped the bar top with her fingertips, taking care to keep out of his reach. "I understand you're looking for me. You a cop?"

She looked him right in the eyes, which startled Aedan for a second. He usually wasn't one for hemming and hawing, particularly not with women, but there was something in her dark brown eyes that made him tongue-tied. "Um. No."

She narrowed her gaze. "Is this about the liquor license?

My understanding was that everything is in order. I've been here for four months. I just had an inspection last month."

"You own this place?" Aedan asked. He hadn't been expecting that, which made him feel like a sexist jerk. Why couldn't the pretty blonde own her own bar? He really wasn't sexist; he was just fifteen hundred years old. Women had only begun to readily hold their own properties and businesses in the last two hundred.

She gave him an exaggerated smile. "I get that a lot. Guess I don't look like a business owner. So you a cop or not?"

"I said I wasn't. Private investigator."

"Guinness stout." The bartender reached around Dallas and set the frothy beer on the napkin in front of Aedan. "Happy hour ended fifteen minutes ago, but I'll give you this one at the reduced price."

"Thanks." Aedan waited until the guy walked away before he looked at her again. "I should have introduced myself last night." *You just didn't give me the opportunity.* "I wanted to. Aedan Brigid." He offered his hand.

She glanced at his hand with a strange look on her face and sort of tucked her hands behind her. "Dallas York. What can I do for you Aedan Brigid, private investigator? Tat, the bartender, said you wanted to ask me about that girl who was attacked last night. I thought that was kind of weird, since I was here last night *with you* when it happened."

He reached for his beer, mostly so he would have something to do with his hands. Here was where his good idea kind of fell apart. And now he was beginning to feel like a *complete* jerk. He'd used some bad pick-up lines over the years, but using a woman's brutal attack to meet someone, even someone as intriguing as Dallas, was just plain wrong. "I'm sorry," he said, swallowing his mouthful of beer. "I am a PI, and I am investigating that attack, but I didn't walk in here intending to ask you about Teesha Jones." He looked up at her sheepishly. "I was just trying to come up with a way to get you to talk to me."

Dallas rolled her eyes and picked up a bar mop off the lower bar. "You've got to be kidding me. You're an asshole. If you think—" She started to turn away, then suddenly turned back. "Wait—what did you say her name was?"

"Teesha Jones."

Her name probably hadn't been published in the paper for privacy reasons. He knew enough not to go blabbing a victim's name around; he also knew it was sometimes necessary in an investigation, particularly one like this that was definitely time-sensitive. Besides, he had the feeling Dallas York was a woman he could trust.

"Teesha Jones?" she asked, looking startled.

"You know her?"

Dallas folded her arms over her chest, looking straight into his eyes. Obviously, she knew something. "I'm not talking to you unless I see a badge or something."

"Is she a friend? She worked nearby on the avenue at a gift shop."

"She isn't a friend," Dallas said softly. She looked up at him. "Have you got some kind of identification? Otherwise, I'm going to call the police."

"I've got identification that says who I am." He stood and pulled his wallet out of the inside pocket of his jacket. "If you don't want to talk to me, I understand. I was a jerk." He pushed his Delaware driver's license across the bar. "But there's a state police detective you definitely need to talk to." He dug around in his wallet, pretty certain he had one of Mark's cards in there somewhere.

Dallas picked up his license and studied it carefully. "You're from Clare Point?"

"It's north of here. Just off Route 1."

"I know. I checked out the town this winter when I was

looking for property. Nice little town. Nothing for sale in the whole place, though. Struck me as odd."

He gave her a quick smile. Nothing ever went up for sale in Clare Point. The owners lived forever; that, and the Kahills liked their privacy in the off-season months. They didn't really want humans owning property in their town. "I've got extended family there. We've been there a long time. Properties usually get handed down generation to generation," he responded casually.

She was watching him, his license still in her hand.

"Here it is," he said, finding a dog-eared business card. "Detective Lieutenant Mark Karr with the Delaware State Police." He offered it to her.

"Put it on the bar," she said.

It wasn't until she carefully laid his driver's license on the bar and picked up the business card that he realized she was purposely not taking the chance of touching him. She'd felt it, too. Last night. She knew something had happened between them.

"You don't have to give me any particulars." He retrieved his license. "But you know her? Teesha?"

Dallas fingered the business card, looking genuinely upset. "Not really. I just met her last night. She came in for an interview. I liked her. I was thinking today that I should give her a call and offer her a job." She looked at him. "Maybe it was a different Teesha?" she asked hopefully.

He sat down on the barstool again. "Young black woman. Pretty. Hair down to here." He motioned to his shoulder.

She hung her head. "Same girl. It's an unusual name, Teesha. I have a daughter named Kenzie so I tend to remember—" She met his gaze and halted mid-sentence. "I gotta get back to work," she said suddenly. She shook the business card at him. "I'm calling the state police tomorrow. If they don't have a Detective Mark Karr on staff, you're in trouble, buddy. I've got your name, your address, and your license number. I can have you arrested for impersonating a police officer."

"You've got a pretty wild imagination, Dallas. I never told you I was a police officer."

"So?"

He lifted a brow, impressed. This was a pretty tough woman, this Dallas. He sensed she had needed to be in the past.

She hooked her thumb and motioned toward the door. "Finish your beer and get out of here."

He watched her walk away. She tossed the bar mop in a sink, tucked the business card into the back pocket of her faded blue jeans, and disappeared into the kitchen.

Aedan drank his beer, left enough money for a generous tip, and walked out of the bar. He knew he'd be back. He had a feeling he might even get Dallas to speak with him again, once Mark verified he wasn't a crazy.

He gazed up one side of the street and then down the other. Now it was time to tuck away thoughts of pretty, strange Dallas and get to work.

As Aedan walked west on Rehoboth Avenue, his back to the cool breeze coming off the ocean, he tried to wrap his head around the logic of the case, rather than the emotional side. This couldn't be about him. He took this case personally, even though he'd been trained not to. It wasn't about Madeleine. It wasn't even about poor Teesha Jones, lying in a hospital bed, facing months, perhaps years, of surgeries and recuperation. It wasn't about the scars Jay left behind, physical or emotional. It was about protecting the next would-be victim.

As he walked, his gaze traveled over the faces of the women he passed: the cute brunette with the sultry laugh, hanging on her boyfriend's arm; the blonde dressed in black, wearing an apron, hurrying, probably so she wouldn't be late getting back from her fifteen-minute break at the caramel popcorn place; the forty-something-year-old woman carrying a pizza box. She had probably stopped at Grottos to pick up a large extra cheese for a late evening dinner. Jay tended to choose younger women, pretty women, but no one was immune when he went on one of his sprees. Fifty years ago, he had raped a grandmother.

The thought made Aedan sick to his stomach. He stepped out of the light cast from the lampposts, into the shadows of a store that was closed. As he began to morph his eye caught one of the banners trembling in the wind. They lined the east end of the avenue, a tribute to the state's fallen soldiers. He stared at the picture of the young army specialist who had given his life in Iraq, and for a moment Aedan felt as if they made a connection. He sometimes wondered why God could ever have allowed evils like war or creatures like Jay to exist. But then he got into the whole religious thing of God and Satan. Aedan had accepted a long time ago that the world was too complicated for his vampire brain.

He touched the crucifix around his neck, said a silent prayer for the young man, and for his family . . . and morphed.

Aedan had entered the shadows of the beachwear store as a six-foot-five, red-haired, thirty-something male wearing a leather jacket. He left a five-foot-five, twenty-one-year-old woman with short, sandy brown hair, a hoodie sweatshirt, and peace signs dangling from her earlobes. He had to admit as he fell into the walking rhythm of the temporary form that the earrings had been a nice touch. Very authentic.

His intention this evening was to get the lay of the land and to see what Teesha might have seen on the street the previous night. Mark had promised Aedan that he would get a chance to talk to her, and details she could relate might be helpful, but his years of training had taught him to make observations other people didn't make. Maybe one of those details might lead him to Jay.

As Aedan walked, he took notice of what places were open at ten o'clock. The attack had taken place sometime between ten and eleven-thirty. According to Mark, after the attack, Teesha had crawled to a parking lot and laid there for a short time before being discovered.

Of course Aedan didn't know what she had been doing or where she had been going when she was attacked, but this stroll tonight was just about seeing the place after dark. He knew from Jay's past that his attacks were rarely random or impulsive. He chose a victim and sometimes stalked her for days before attacking her. Jay would have walked these streets the way Aedan was walking them now . . . probably without the peace sign earrings.

Aedan spotted the souvenir shop where Teesha worked. The OPEN sign had been turned off, but the lights were still on inside; he could see two young women unpacking boxes. He stopped in front of the door, thought for a moment, then knocked.

"We're closed!" one of the young women shouted. "Open at ten tomorrow."

"I was looking for Teesha. Wasn't she working tonight?" He flashed a smile as close to Kaleigh's as he could muster. She had a pretty smile, one that made a person immediately comfortable.

"You a friend of Teesha's?" a girl wearing a tie-dyed T-shirt asked, approaching the door cautiously.

"Is she here?" Aedan called through the glass door. His voice wasn't his own, of course. He sounded like a twenty-one-year-old with a slightly squeaky voice.

The girl in the tie-dye hesitated and then turned the deadbolt.

"Friend of a friend," Aedan said, casually sticking his foot in the doorway when she opened the door. He wore pink flip-flops.

"Didn't you hear?"

He pulled a ChapStick from his jeans pocket and applied it the way he saw young women do. Another nice detail. He hoped it covered for the way he didn't feel quite right inside the body, making him seem awkward. "Hear what?"

"She was attacked last night. It was bad," the young woman related, resting her hand on the doorjamb. The other girl continued to unpack tacky plastic statues of seagulls on a piling. A little sign under each one read REHOBOTH BEACH, DELAWARE.

"Oh my God!" Aedan exclaimed. He could feel his earrings swinging in his ears. It was weird morphing into a female. He felt like he never quite pulled it off, but it was a good disguise in this situation. A young, slight woman wasn't a threat to others; at least humans never perceived her as one. He had killed in this morph. "Is she going to be all right?" he asked.

"It's really bad," the girl repeated, fretting now.

"Where was she? When did it happen?"

"Marylou, we're not supposed to open the door after closing," the girl with a plastic seagull in each hand said. "You're going to get written up again."

Marylou glanced over her shoulder, then back at Aedan. "Last night. She left here early because she had an interview somewhere. About another job. I covered for her." She lowered her voice, so her coworker couldn't hear. "This job is for shit. I'm only keeping it until I find another one."

"So she left early last night? Before you closed?" Aedan said.

The girl nodded. "She went to her interview, and then we met at the pub. Across the street." She pointed to a bar with green neon shamrocks in the windows. "We were supposed to separate, you know, check out the guys and then meet up later at Dogfish Head. Only Teesha never showed. She was talking to this cute guy at the pub." She shrugged. "We thought maybe she, you know, hooked up with him or whatever."

Would Jay have been so bold as to have chatted with Teesha in a bar? It wasn't his typical MO, but he'd done it before. "What happened? After she didn't show up?"

Another shrug, this time with hand gestures. "We don't know. It was on the radio this morning. Teesha's almost being killed and all. My mom always listens to it when she gets ready for work."

"They gave her name on the radio?" he asked, suspiciously.

"Oh, no." She shook her head. "Only that a young woman had been attacked and, you know, raped and cut up. We found out it was Teesha when we came to work. Our boss has a sister who works in the ER or something." She wrapped her arms around her slender waist. "I feel so bad for her. We were thinking about going to see her, you know, at the hospital. Putting some money together on payday and buying her a fruit basket or some flowers. All of us here. But we thought we better wait a few days. I don't even know if I want to go." She hesitated. "You know, what do you say?"

"You need to lock the door, Marylou," called the seagull girl. "Your friend can't come in here."

"I should go." Aedan took a step back. He'd gotten the information he needed, and probably as much as the girl knew, anyway. "Thanks for letting me know about Teesha." He started to turn away, then looked back. "You just say you're sorry."

"What?" the young clerk asked through the narrow crack in the door.

"When you see Teesha," he said softly. How many victims had he spoken to over the years, not just on Jay's case, but others? Far more than he cared to count. He made eye contact with the young woman. "There isn't any right or wrong thing to say. You just tell her you're sorry it happened to her."

Peigi stood in the doorway of the den, listening to the sound of rapid machine gun fire. She didn't like video games. She particularly didn't like violent ones, and she sure as heck didn't like Brian playing them. But it was what all the teen boys did; it was part of American culture, and the Kahills tried hard to allow their teens to assimilate with typical human culture.

Dinner had been nice. It was good to have Aedan home. She had missed him. He reminded her in so many ways of her sister, Brigid. In the life cycle after her death, Aedan had taken her first name as his last to honor her. The small gesture had made her proud of him. Not that he could replace his mother, or Peigi's son and daughter, long gone and dead, but he was like a son to her. To Brian, too, when he was himself.

She scowled. This shooting, cursing, sour young man was not her Brian. He wasn't the man she had loved for fifteen centuries. He would become that man. She knew he would, because it happened every life cycle. But she felt so far apart from him now that she wasn't absolutely sure it would work this time. And how many years would it take? By the time he reached his mid-twenties, she'd be an old, wrinkled lady, more wrinkled than she was now. Would he desire her, then? Even if he did, how much time would they have together? She'd be old; she would die and be reborn, and *he'd* have a teenager on his hands. From her experience, the only thing worse than a teenage male vampire was a teenage *female* one.

This was the way it worked. It was God's way for His Kahill family. That didn't make it seem fair . . . or any easier.

"Hey, Brian?"

He didn't answer. A window broke on the TV screen as

the avatar soldier "Brian" opened fire on someone crossing the street. He had the TV turned up so loud that it felt as if the gunfire was exploding in her head.

"Brian!"

Just when she was certain he still hadn't heard her—possibly because he'd gone completely deaf—he twitched. He didn't look at her, but he responded. "Yeah?"

"Could we talk?"

"I'm in the middle of a game here."

She stepped into the den. She'd changed into a pair of flowered flannel pajamas and her slippers. She had some more work to do for the sept's General Council meeting, but she was headed to bed soon. Alone. There were no conjugal rights at this point in their relationship. Sept members, even spouses, were forbidden to have physical relations with teenagers. Not that either of them found the idea, at the moment, even slightly appealing.

"Could you pause it?" she asked.

"I told you." Brian stared at the screen. Nothing moved but his thumbs. "It's 'Black Ops'; I'm online. I can't just tell the other team to wait a minute."

She frowned, leaning against the doorjamb, crossing her arms over her chest. She was planning on having a cup of tea before she turned in; she might have to throw in a shot of whiskey. "I'd really like to talk with you."

He exhaled. He still didn't look at her, but his body language made it pretty plain he'd rather turn his virtual M16 on himself than have a conversation with her.

"We need to talk, Brian." She tried to keep the impatience out of her tone, knowing it wouldn't serve either of them well.

"About what?" He yanked the cordless game controller, dropped an F bomb under his breath, and waited for the game to drop him back in. Peigi had seen enough of "Black Ops" in the last few months that she knew that much. She liked the mode with the zombies. She sure didn't like zombies, but at least she understood them. She knew what made them tick, which was blood and gore. This teenage vampire boy who had been her beloved Brian six months ago, she didn't understand him at all.

Peigi shifted her gaze from the TV to the young man who had just started sprouting facial hair in the last two months. Tonight his razor stubble didn't make him look older. It made Peigi *feel* older.

"Look, Brian." She took a breath and started again. "I know you and I don't have a lot in common right now. I know your friends mean a lot to you, but I have certain obligations. There are things we need to talk about that I think would ease your transition."

He didn't say anything. Soldiers on the screen, planted in an urban setting, crept around crumbling buildings and burned cars. She wondered if it was meant to look like Beirut. It looked like Beirut.

"Brian?" she said after a rather long pause.

"I told you before. I don't want to talk. I'm not ready to talk, and if I am, I'll talk to Kaleigh or one of the guys."

She brushed her hair off her forehead. It felt long. It was getting in her eyes. She needed a haircut. "I don't understand why you don't want to talk to me. I . . . know you don't exactly remember the details, but I'm your wife, Brian."

"I don't care." He snapped his head around, looking at her for just a second before returning his attention to the game. "Don't you get it? I don't give a shit about who you are or who I'm *supposed* to be. I don't want to be an *effin'* vampire!"

"Neither do I," Aedan said from behind, startling Peigi.

She'd been so intent on her conversation with Brian that she hadn't heard Aedan come in the front door or felt his presence. She chuckled at his comment. This was one of the things she wanted to talk to Brian about. About how none of them wanted to be vampires, but God hadn't given them a choice. It wasn't optional. That was the whole point of a curse.

"You want me to work him over?" Aedan asked Peigi, acting as if Brian wasn't in the room. "Because I can jack up his punk ass." He made a fist and punched it into his palm.

Brian actually looked in their direction long enough to allow himself to get shot, and the word DEFEAT appeared up on the screen in bold red letters.

"You need to pay attention, *duuude*." Aedan pointed to the TV screen. "Man, you *suck* at this game." He sounded just like Brian and his friends when they talked to each other.

Peigi laughed out loud, grabbed Aedan's arm, and led him out of the den. Leave it to Aedan to alter her perspective. "Come on, have a whiskey with me."

"I don't want anything to drink," he told her.

"Fine. You can watch me drink."

# Chapter 4

Interviews with victims and their families were always hard. No matter how many times Aedan did it, he always felt awkward, and he found it difficult to keep his own emotions in check while others poured out theirs. Peigi said the fact that he could still feel for the humans after all these years of doing what he did was what made him so good at his job as a key investigator. Some days he wished he wasn't so good at his job. Days like today.

"Thanks for seeing me, Miss Jones," he said, making a point to look directly at her. In order to make Teesha more comfortable, he had shifted into a woman: mid-thirties, long, brown hair pulled into a ponytail, a nondescript blue suit a female detective might wear. And kind, blue eyes. "Mind if I sit down?" He indicated the chair beside the hospital bed.

"I'll be out in the hall making some phone calls, if you need me," Mark said to her. He looked to Aedan. *You look cute in blue*, he telepathed. *Matches those pretty eyes. Make it snappy. I've got a rookie shadowing me today. I sent him for coffee, but eventually he'll find his way back up here. Obviously, I'm not supposed to be letting civilians interview the victim. And the sept hasn't put you on the case yet, either. I don't want to get my ass in a jam with Peigi again.*

*Just a friend stopping by to say hello,* Aedan telepathed back. He returned his attention to Teesha Jones.

"Sure. Sit down," she said in a tiny voice.

She was a tall, slender girl, but she looked small in the bed, lost in the sheet, in the tubes and the wires and the bandages that covered much of her face and both arms. Her speech was slightly slurred, perhaps from the painkiller being administered through her IV, but most likely due to the severe damage done to her face by Jay's razor.

"I know Detective Karr has asked you a million questions. I got a lot of the details from him this morning." Aedan already had the basics: She'd left work early, interviewed at Brew, met her friends at the Irish pub, lost track of them, and left the bar alone. Her intention had been to just go home, but when she couldn't get any of her friends on their cells, she'd decided to run into Dogfish Head, just to tell them good night. She'd taken a shortcut through an alley, between two buildings. Jay had attacked her in the alley. What Aedan was hoping was that she could tell him something about Jay that he didn't already know.

"I'm going to try not to repeat all those questions. I know this is hard for you. I just need some details about your attacker. If you can answer, great. If you can't, don't worry about it." He kept his tone light, but businesslike, as if they were discussing the details of a fender-bender, rather than a brutal crime.

Teesha had been looking at him. She had big, beautiful cinnamon-brown eyes. When he mentioned Jay, she glanced away; a tear drifted down to be absorbed by a gauze bandage.

Aedan waited a moment, then went on, using the female detective's voice. "Had you seen your attacker earlier that evening? In the bar? On the street maybe?"

She shook her head "no" slowly, as if truly considering the question. That was good. She was thinking. And she obviously had at least some memory of the events leading up to the attack. Often, victims not only could not remember the violence, they lost hours or even days leading up to the attack.

"Think back on the customers you had that day in your shop. Do you remember seeing him there?"

Again she responded with a slight shake of her head. Her face was so swollen from the attack and subsequent surgeries that she barely looked human. Her beautiful face, so disfigured, made Aedan ache for all she had suffered. For all the suffering yet to come.

"One of your friends said you were talking with a guy at the Irish pub across the street from where you work. It wasn't him?"

"No." Her voice was raspy.

Jay liked to strangle victims—not enough to kill them, just enough to cut the oxygen off to their brain long enough to subdue them. Aedan suspected there would be strangulation bruises on her neck if he looked. He'd check with Mark later.

"His name was Alex," she continued. "The guy I was talking to. He seemed really sweet. He works at Blue Moon. You know, the restaurant. He's a barback. He . . . he asked for my number, and I gave it to him." She was obviously trying to be strong, but a little sob escaped her throat. "He asked me out. We talked about going kayaking because we both like outdoor sports." She bit down on her swollen lip. "I guess that won't be happening, will it?"

Aedan knew that, at this stage, there was no sense in arguing with the victim. Right now, her wounds were so raw, emotionally and physically, that there was no way for her to see through to the other side. From where she lay, there was no future, no hope. This close to the assault, the best thing he could do was just listen.

Teesha sniffed and looked up at the harsh fluorescent light over her head. "It wasn't Alex."

"Did you see the man who attacked you?"

"He came from behind me. He must have followed me into the alley. Maybe from the bar?"

He could tell by her tone of voice that she was just guessing. "But you don't remember being followed?"

"No."

"Could you identify your attacker's race?"

She thought for a second, then turned her head. Even the slightest movement caused her pain. "He was Caucasian. Brown hair. Average height. Five-nine, five-ten, maybe. That's how tall I am. Five-ten. Average looking. He was wearing a black hoodie, so I didn't really see much of his face."

That was part of the problem. Jay was good at blending in. Women who could remember anything about him gave slightly different descriptions of him, but never so different that all the descriptions couldn't have been of the same man. Jay was, according to his victims, Mr. Average: average height, average weight, brown hair, brown eyes. And he always wore common clothing; when Aedan had morphed the previous night into the young woman, he'd worn a black hoodie. So had twenty-five percent of the people on Rehoboth Avenue on a cold April night.

"Was there anything that stood out about him, *anything at all* you remember?"

She thought for a moment. "He was wearing gloves. Not like cotton ones or wool. Medical gloves. Like they use here in the hospital."

That wasn't unusual; many rapists did. It prevented them from leaving fingerprints. But it was a new detail for Jay. Of course, fifty years ago, when he'd last reared his ugly head, gloves hadn't been as readily available as they were today. Now, anyone could walk into a drugstore and buy a box of a hundred.

"And a condom." Her voice cracked.

"Did he say anything?"

"No. I remember thinking that was weird. That he didn't

speak. He didn't have to. I was sure he was going to kill me. I tried everything, you know, what they say you should do if it happens. I begged; I cried; I told him my name. He cut me when I screamed. Then he stuffed a handkerchief in my mouth."

Mark said the police had found a plain, new, men's white handkerchief in the alley. Teesha had already identified it as what she had pulled out of her mouth when he left her to die.

"He didn't act like he was in a hurry. He didn't seem to be afraid anyone would see us. He took his time." She met Aedan's gaze, then looked away, embarrassed. "He took his time with the condom, too."

Aedan would double-check with Mark, but he would bet no used condom had been found at the scene. In fact, Jay was so clean, so careful that the police had had a hard time finding exactly where the attack had begun. They'd had to follow the blood trail from the parking lot where Teesha was found, backwards to the scene of the crime.

"You said you knew he wanted to kill you?" Aedan said thoughtfully. "Do you think he meant to? Was that his intention when he attacked you?"

She thought for a moment, then shifted in the bed ever so slightly. What he could see of her face grimaced in pain. "I thought at the time that he was going to kill me, but I know now he never meant to." She clasped her bandaged fingers. "Otherwise, I'd be dead."

They were quiet for a minute. Aedan sometimes wished he had Kaleigh's power to read humans' minds—it would have made investigations so much easier, for him and the victims—but he didn't. "You've been a lot of help, Teesha. I appreciate your willingness to talk with me. I'll be back in a few days to check on you, and probably ask some more questions." He paused. "Can you think of anything about your attacker that might help us find him? Any details? Even the smallest, most insignificant detail? The kind of shoes he was wearing? Any tattoos? Body piercings? Cologne?"

"I can't think of anything distinguishing about him. Which is weird, because it seemed like I laid on the ground under him for hours." She was quiet long enough that Aedan thought she was done, then she spoke again. "He was cold."

He met her gaze. "The ground was cold?"

"It was, but that's not what I meant. *He* was cold. His body. You know"—again she teared up—"where he touched me."

There was a knock on the door, and it swung open. *Incoming,* Mark telepathed.

"I've stayed too long, Miss Jones." Aedan stood. "I'm going to go, but would it be all right if I came back?"

"Sure. Whatever it takes." She stared at the ceiling and pushed a button on a handheld device that he knew administered more painkiller. The machine beeped. "I'll do anything to help you catch him." She was getting teary again. "To keep this from happening to someone else."

"You take care, Miss Jones."

"Call me Teesha. I don't mind." Her eyes drifted shut.

Aedan walked out into the hall, leaned against the wall, and closed his own eyes.

All evening, Dallas glanced in the direction of the door every time it opened. She'd pretty much kicked Aedan Brigid out of her bar; she doubted he'd be back. So why did she keep looking for him? Why was she disappointed he hadn't returned?

She swept up several empty pilsners off the bar top, hitting them together a little harder than she should have. She carried them to a dishpan under the bar.

She'd checked up on him just as she had said she would. She'd called the state police first thing this morning after she dropped Kenzie off at a friend's. That really was his name—Aedan Brigid. The detective she had spoken to had confirmed that he really was a private investigator and sort of talked him up, though not in an obvious way. Detective Karr had stopped by midday and asked her a few questions about her job interview with Teesha Jones. Dallas wasn't entirely sure why the detective had come downtown to question her personally. The interview had taken less than ten minutes. Dallas knew nothing about where the girl had been before she had come to the interview or where she had gone afterward. The detective could have asked his questions over the phone . . . unless of course he was scoping her out for his ginger friend, which would be totally weird. But she wouldn't put it past a bunch of cops.

It was getting late. Things were beginning to wind down in the bar, though last call wasn't for another hour. As Dallas scooped up a tip and dropped it into a mug, she seriously considered letting Tat close and going upstairs to bed early. She'd hired two college students, twin sisters, to watch Kenzie. That way she always had coverage. Ashley was here tonight. Dallas was sure she'd appreciate an early night. There was no reason why Tat couldn't close. He knew the routine. He offered to do it all the time, but she rarely let him.

Dallas was a bona fide workaholic. She was either with her daughter or working. She worked days from midmorning 'til three, when she left to pick Kenzie up from school, then she spent time with her daughter until bedtime at nine when one of the sisters took over for her. Dallas didn't usually mind working those evening hours. It was better than sitting in front of the TV thinking about all the ways she'd screwed up her life. All the ways things could have been different if she hadn't inherited her mother's gift. But those thoughts just led to making friends with a bottle of Grey Goose. Being a bona fide workaholic, she had decided, was better than being a bona fide alcoholic.

It might be nice to go to bed early, for once. Tomorrow she and Kenzie had a big day planned: Kenzie's horseback riding lesson, a birthday party for a classmate, a trip to the grocery store, and they were going to make chicken enchiladas. Dallas didn't intend to step back into the bar until tomorrow night at nine . . . unless she and Kenzie stopped by for a few minutes in the afternoon to check the produce delivery. Kids didn't belong in bars, but Kenzie loved to sit in the kitchen with Miguel or his cousin Carlos, and "help" with prep work. And they'd help her with her Spanish. Miguel and Carlos were beyond patient with Kenzie; for that reason, Dallas would never fire either of them.

The bar door opened behind her. She heard a couple of guys leaving; they were horsing around, shoving each other and laughing loudly. Typical bar behavior at midnight on a Saturday night. She didn't turn around. She popped the pour-top off an empty bourbon bottle and dropped the bottle into the recycling bin. From under the bar, she produced a new bottle of Jack.

"How about if we start all over?"

It was a male voice. It was *his* voice. Aedan Brigid's.

Dallas spun around, gripping the bourbon bottle in one hand, the pour-top in the other. He must have come in the door at the same time the rowdy guys were leaving.

"I didn't mean to startle you," he said, sliding onto the barstool.

She swung her hair over her shoulder. She usually wore it pulled back in a knot or a ponytail. Often a little dirty. She'd showered before she came down to work tonight, had had wet hair, and had left it down. She hoped to God not, in some subconscious way, for his sake. "You didn't startle me," she said defensively, sounding totally unconvincing. She set the bottle and the pour-top on the bar, looked at him and then back at the bottle, like a complete idiot.

"I wanted to apologize for my behavior," he said. "Coming in here under the pretense of something like that."

She couldn't help herself. She felt a smile tug at the corners of her mouth. She tried to twist the top off the Jack Daniels. It didn't budge. "It's all right. Pretty creative pickup line. I'll give you that." She twisted again. Still nothing.

"Want me to do that?" He put out his hand.

"You know how many of these I open a week?"

He drew back his hand, but he was watching her intently. He was quiet long enough for her to give the cap two more tries before she finally gave up and slid the bottle across the polished wood to him, quickly withdrawing her hand. She had to make sure they wouldn't accidently touch.

Still watching her, he twisted the cap and broke the seal. He slid the bottle back to her, making a show of pulling his own hands back, so they didn't touch.

*He knew*. She didn't know what he knew, but he knew *something*. About her. About what she could do.

The metal cap was still warm from his touch, and the warmth radiated through her. She missed the warmth of a man's touch. With John, after a while, she had known all his memories. Eventually they sort of faded until they were barely present when they touched. That, and apparently his brain had been so hazy with the drugs she hadn't known he was doing, that he hadn't been retaining much. It had made their relationship possible. Before that, Dallas had rarely had sex, and when she did, she had mixed in plenty of alcohol. Alcohol dulled the *gift*.

Dallas concentrated on removing the cap and placing the pour-top in it just so. When Aedan spoke again, his voice was very low, its timbre reverberating in her head. In her entire body.

"I had to come back, Dallas. I had to know what that was."

He paused, and she found herself hanging on his every

word. Her hands were actually shaking, he had her so keyed up. A single shot of JD and he probably could have had her panties around her ankles.

Never in her life had a man affected her this way. She'd built up too strong a wall to let anyone touch her. In any way.

"What happened the other night when we touched?" he asked.

As if there was any confusion whatsoever in what he was talking about.

Her first inclination was to deny the whole thing. Play stupid blonde. But she made the mistake of meeting his gaze. "You don't want to do this," she whispered. She found herself leaning over the bar to get closer to him. "You don't want me. At the risk of sounding like a bad movie, Aedan Brigid, I'm bad news."

She was surprised by the faint smile he offered. "Probably not any worse news than me. In fact, I can pretty much guarantee it."

He was teasing, but it was still sexy as hell. And there was something dangerous-sounding in his voice. This was no badass wannabe. He was the real thing. A serious badass.

She wanted to groan. She had always fallen for the dangerous guys. "No. I don't think so." She tried to make light of his words and the feelings rippling through her. She had to be totally hormonal. Pheromones and all that crap. "You couldn't be trouble. Not a clean-cut guy like you, a private investigator who's got cops singing his praises."

He sat back on the barstool. "People are never what they seem to be, Dallas." His gaze searched hers, his blue eyes seeming to penetrate to the very soul of the matter. And of her.

She liked the way he said her name. *Dallas,* with a strange lilt to his voice. She liked the fact that there were no Texas jokes to go with it. Dallas had been her mother's last name, and since her father didn't think his little baby daughter

Ruth Dallas York looked like a Ruth, he had called her Dallas, and the name stuck.

"Isn't that the truth?" she mused. John had certainly fooled her: wealthy, handsome, just a little dangerous, successful. It had all been right on his business card . . . except for the heroin addict part. She looked up at Aedan. "The girl who was attacked. Teesha. Is she going to be okay?"

He took his time in answering. "She's going to live. Is she going to be okay?" He rested his hands on the bar and looked down at them. "I don't know. Is anyone ever okay after something like that?"

The way he said it made her think he knew what he was talking about, in some very personal way. Again, she felt his pain, only this time she hadn't had to touch him to feel it. And a part of her felt as if he wasn't just talking about his own experiences, but hers as well. Except that he didn't know her. Couldn't possibly have known what she'd been through in her short life.

What the hell was going on here? A part of her wanted to just ask him to leave and never come back. She half thought he'd respect her request. But a part of her wanted to take the barstool beside him and rest her weary head on his broad shoulder.

So much for being the strong, independent woman.

"I read in the paper what happened," she said, finally setting the bottle aside. "Can I get you a beer?"

He smiled again, and she was smiling when she turned away.

"You good?" Tat called to her from the other end of the bar. He was talking to two cute girls wearing way too little clothing for an evening at the beach in April.

She gave her bartender a thumbs up. When she brought the Guinness to Aedan, she set the cocktail napkin on the bar out of his immediate reach and put the glass on top.

"You don't have to be afraid of me," he said. Again, the quiet, reverberating, sexy voice.

She gave a little laugh, pulling her hands back, leaving it up to him to bring his beer closer. "Oh, no? That's funny, because I get the feeling I *should* be. I should be *very afraid*."

"You don't want to talk about what happened between us?" he asked, reaching for his beer.

"Nope."

"Okay."

The man was full of surprises. She hadn't been expecting that.

"So what *do* you want to talk about?"

His question was so *not* what she expected that she had to think for a minute. "How about the Middle East?"

He groaned and took a sip of beer. "Too depressing for a Saturday night."

"The economy?"

He shook his head, taking a sip of his beer. "Depressing."

"Well, I certainly don't want to talk about that girl." Dallas tucked a lock of hair behind her ear. "I can't believe someone would do something like that here. That was part of the reason why my daughter and I came here, because it was such a safe place to raise a kid."

"How old is your daughter?"

Dallas put the heels of her hands on the bar and straightened up. "I don't talk about her with my customers. I don't talk about personal stuff."

"Join me in a beer?" he asked, leaning toward her.

He said it so casually, changing the subject so quickly, that she laughed again. How long had it been since someone had made her laugh like this? "I don't think so."

"Ever had Murphy's Irish Stout?"

She smiled. "Actually I have. In Boston."

"Ah. A New Englander." He sat back as if she might be tainted or something. "I suspected as much."

She leaned on the bar again. "What's that supposed to

mean? Do I have an accent? I don't have a New England accent."

"No." He waggled his finger. "But you have a New England, Puritan way about you."

"Puritan? Me?" This time her laugh was sarcastic. "Not hardly." She almost said *you don't know me too well,* but of course that was true, and if she had any sense, she'd keep it that way.

"So, you said you just moved here?" He was smooth with his transitions.

"I did?" She raised a brow, then realized she was sort of flirting with him. She knew all the body language from working in bars and restaurants all these years: the leaning on the bar, then standing upright, then leaning in toward him again, tossing her hair out of her face, laughing at everything he said. It was embarrassing.

And for some reason, fun.

"You just took over the bar and you mentioned looking in Clare Point for property," he pointed out. "So I assume you just moved here. And you mentioned Boston." He shrugged as if his conclusion was obvious.

She scowled. "I could have been from Atlanta—visiting Boston when I had that stout."

"You're not from Atlanta." Again the waggling finger. "You're a New Englander all right. A little standoffish. Guarded."

She folded her arms over her chest. "What if I have a reason for being those things, beyond being a New Englander?"

"Where did you go to school?" Again, switching subjects smoothly. "Let me guess." He paused. "Dartmouth."

"Dartmouth? No way. Brown," she said proudly.

"So you *are* a New England girl?"

She started to make a snappy rebuttal, then leaned on the bar again. "You going to tell me where *you're* from? Because you're not from around here. I have powers of observation, too. You don't *sound* like you're from around here. You don't *act* like it. You certainly don't drink like it." She glanced at his Guinness. "Guinness? Murphy's? I'm not even sure you're from the U.S."

"And what makes you say that?" He was enjoying their conversation as much as she was. "I don't have an accent."

"No, you don't." She tried not to think about the memories she had seen in his head, most of which were definitely *not* in the U.S. Of course they weren't mostly from the present century either, so she had no real frame of reference for him. They couldn't be memories. "But there's something about the cadence of your speech." She studied his handsome face. "Are you *really* a private investigator?"

"A state police detective told you I was."

She looked at him for a minute and then smiled. She needed to go before she got herself into trouble with this guy. Because this guy was definitely trouble. "I'm out of here." She pulled off her apron. "You have a good evening. Be safe."

"Is it okay if I come back? Just to talk."

"Bad idea." She shook her head as she walked away. What she didn't say was no.

*"She's pretty," he heard her say.*

*He was seated at the little table, naked. The stew she had brought him was excellent: root vegetables, bits of lamb, and herbs.*

*Madeleine lay naked on the bed, her youthful body slender, but ripe. Her blond hair tumbled all around her, tempting him. But first, sustenance.*

*"Did you hear me? I said, she's pretty."*

*He washed down a mouthful of stew with a gulp of ale. "Who?" he asked. It was only then that he realized they were speaking French, not English. "The new maid? I've no interest in her,* ma beauté. *I love you. Only you, always."*

*"Not her."*

*He tore off a bit of bread and dipped it into the bowl. "Whom do you speak of?"*

*"The girl in the bar. Dallas."*

Aedan woke from the dream startled. Shaky.

The dream had made no sense. Madeleine could not possibly have known Dallas.

# Chapter 5

Aedan's petition to be assigned to Jay's case, despite his sept-imposed hiatus, was on the agenda for the General Council meeting on Monday night. Peigi had left early for the meeting, before midnight, so he walked alone through town from her cottage to the museum downtown. It was a quiet night, too early in the season for insect song. He'd worn his leather jacket; there was a chill in the air, but there was the promise of the warmth of spring to come.

He breathed deeply as he crossed an empty street. Somewhere a dog barked. The tangy bay breeze was cleansing. Healing. This was why the sept required its members to return home. Because they needed it, as much as they hated to admit it. Aedan always dragged his heels about taking a holiday from the business of pursuing bad guys. It was so much easier to just forget how good it felt to come home.

Half a block ahead, he spotted a figure. A woman. Vampire. *Mary Kay,* he telepathed.

She turned. *Sorry, lost in my thoughts. I didn't know you were there.* She waited for him. She was a Council member and headed toward the museum for the meeting, as well.

"Good to see you, Aedan." She shifted a plate of some

sort of cinnamon-baked deliciousness from one hand to the other and rubbed his arm.

Mary Kahill, called Mary Kay to distinguish her from all the other Marys in town, was a pretty woman for her age. She looked like her daughter, the hotshot FBI agent; Aedan had had a crush on Fia once upon a time. Both women had inky dark hair and amazing cheekbones. There was no way Mary Kay looked her fifty-some years, well, fifty-some human years in this life cycle. Mary Kay, during the summer months, ran a B & B for tourists in her old Victorian mansion in town. Some Kahills didn't like humans under their roofs, but Mary Kay always said she liked it; it allowed her to keep tabs on them, and it was a good way to get rid of all the baked goods she made.

"Good to see you." Aedan leaned down and kissed her cheek. "Let me carry that." He took the foil-covered plate.

"Pecan sticky buns. I'm running late. I got caught up cleaning my pantry and didn't get the dough rising soon enough." They walked side by side toward the museum.

"They smell amazing." He tugged at the corner of the foil.

"Leave them alone." She slapped his hand none too gently.

Aedan laughed. "How are your boys?"

"Fin is fine, as always. You know, Regan's been clean a while now. He's running the arcade again this summer for Mary McCathal. Who *still* hasn't returned to her senses, by the way." She shook her head disapprovingly. "I can't believe she and Victor ran off like that just because the Council wouldn't let them tie the knot. Why couldn't they just live in sin the way a lot of us do?"

Aedan, guessing it was a rhetorical question, didn't answer. Victor and Mary's romance had been the scandal of the previous summer, or would have been if the Italian girl, Lia, hadn't been killing humans. Mary's husband Bobby had been murdered two years ago by teenage vampire-slayers, releasing her from the eternal bonds of marriage with her husband. *Murdered and destroyed; he could never be reborn again.* After Bobby's death, Mary and Victor had fallen in love, or so Aedan had heard. For some reason, the senior citizen Victor had gotten it in his head that he wanted to wed Mary. The General Council had denied their request; sept rules required members to keep the partner they had when they were cursed. Instead of just having an affair like many couples did, Mary and Victor had surprised everyone by running away from home and eloping. They were still MIA, a concern of many sept members. With no support system, there was no telling what kind of trouble two old vampires could get into.

Aedan and Mary Kay cut across the parking lot toward the rear door of the darkened museum. "I have to admit, it is kind of romantic, Mary and Victor eloping," Mary Kay said. "In love . . . running away together. Even at their age. I heard they were in Papeete."

"I heard they were in Fort Lauderdale."

"Tahiti makes a better story."

He chuckled. "Fair enough."

They reached the back door, and Aedan keyed in the necessary numbers to gain admittance. The building served as a museum for tourists, featuring the history of the old town. In truth, it featured the story the sept had concocted to protect themselves. The tall tale, conceived by certain creative sept members, had been woven with just enough threads of truth to sound believable. It portrayed Clare Point as having been a pirates' den of sorts in the early days, back in the seventeenth century. The artifacts displayed, for the most part, were authentic.

When the vessel the Kahills had traveled in from the shores of Ireland had wrecked on a reef in a storm, they had been washed ashore. Sept members had collected the objects now displayed in the museum, as well as scrap wood from the ship's decks and splintered hull. They had built their first homes on the sandy beaches with those warped planks; portholes had become windows, and the simple bone china, now displayed in the museum, had been used on their kitchen tables.

The *pirates* on the shores of Clare Point when the Kahills had arrived had actually been wreckers who made their living luring ships into shallow water. When the ships sank or washed ashore, the vultures profited heavily from the bounty of the shipwreck. Any survivors, they killed. What the story told in the museum did not relay was that the Kahills, close to starvation for lack of blood by the time they reached the New World, had fed on the wreckers. Those wreckers who had survived had made the decision not to fight vampires for their little Eden and had fled south to safer waters. It wasn't until after the Kahills were settled on the shores of Clare Point and had breathing room that the sept's chieftain, Gair, had had his epiphany and the members had agreed to stop hunting God's humans and begin helping them.

The museum, built in the sixties to encourage the town's burgeoning tourist trade, sported glass cases filled with artifacts from the pirate age, identified with printed signs and sometimes sketches. There were pieces of china marked with the sunken ship's name, brass candlesticks, and other assorted stuff. Most came from the ship the Kahills had arrived on, although some of it was bounty left behind by the wreckers in their eagerness to escape their would-be victims. There was also a small exhibit of arrowheads and spear points from the area's early history when the Lenni-Lenape had fished the waters and hunted in the forest.

During the museum's operating hours, during the tourist season, a twelve-minute film was shown and there was a small gift shop near the restrooms. There, plastic swords, eye patches and fake coins, tomahawks, and other junk were sold.

The museum was a crazy mixture of the Kahills' past and present, all jumbled up until it was hard to separate fact from fiction. Some of the items were displayed on the round table that had come from the ship's captain's cabin; it was the same table the High Council convened around when voting as to who would be the next human to die. It was those High Council members who ultimately gave Aedan his orders.

Aedan held the door open for Mary Kay. She plucked the baked goods from his hand and marched up the dark hallway toward the bright lights of the community room, where the General Council met. As he followed her down the hall, he wondered why they turned on the lights at all. As vampires, they saw just as well in the dark.

When he entered the museum-turned-community room, it looked more like a gathering of PTA parents than vampires. There were tables with coffee and assorted baked goods, and everyone was standing in small groups laughing and chatting while having a snack. At the door, Mary Kay marched off to set out her contribution.

"Aedan."

Aedan turned to see Gair, who appeared more like a senior citizen bound for a day-trip to the zoo than the leader of a clan of vampires. Despite the fact that it was April and still cool, and the fact that he was an eight-hundred-year-old sept chieftain, somewhere in his late seventies, he wore shorts, flip-flops and a Corona T-shirt featuring a busty girl in a bikini riding a bottle of beer. He brushed a crumb from his snowy beard and took another bite of a chocolate chip cookie. "I've been expecting you at the house."

"Sorry," Aedan said. "I've been meaning to come by. Things have been a little crazy since I got home."

"Brian?" he asked. He didn't wait for Aedan to answer. "Peigi's been trying to keep it all hush-hush, but I know Brian's gone a little cuckoo since he was reborn." He shook his head, stuffing the rest of the cookie into his mouth.

"Happens to the best of us. I just hope she can keep him under control until he comes to his senses. We don't need any Kahills running around sucking the blood from our summer visitors, do we?"

Aedan grinned. "No, we don't. But I don't think that will be an issue. She can barely get him off the couch. Video games," he explained.

"Work of the devil, some say." He gave a wave. "I think it's bullshit. They say the same about the casino over in Harrington. I like to play the slot machines once in a while." He gestured as if pulling the arm of an old-fashioned slot machine. "Never seen the devil there. Not any more often than I see him anywhere else, anyway." He winked.

"It's good to see you, Gair. To see you so healthy." Aedan offered his hand.

Gair switched his napkin full of cookies from one hand to the other and shook Aedan's hand. "This shouldn't take long, you getting approval to work this case. Just be ready to answer questions regarding the incident at Château Dumont."

Aedan groaned as the old man shuffled away, headed back to the snack table. He had thought tonight was just a formality. He hadn't anticipated having to hash over an incident that had been unfortunate but not his fault. He already felt bad enough about it; he didn't need a bunch of old ladies who didn't know what it was like to be in the field accusing him of getting sloppy.

"Hey, sexy."

Aedan turned. "Fia." He put out his arms to her and hugged her tightly when she came to him. She was a gorgeous woman, full of what could only be defined as *sass.* "Arlan kick you to the curb yet?"

She kissed his cheek and took a step back. She was dressed in full FBI agent attire à la *Men in Black:* dark pants suit, white shirt, and black boots. All that was missing was the dark sunglasses and Will Smith for a sidekick.

"Not yet. But I'm sure he's been tempted." She chuckled. "So how are you?"

Council members were beginning to take their seats in the large circle of folding chairs.

"I'm good. Great," he said.

She scowled. "I'm serious. This whole Jay thing has got to have you spooked." She knitted her brow. "And what's with the blonde in the bar?"

Aedan always tried to put up a barrier to block his family and friends from his head unless he wanted them in it.

"Don't tell me you're hooking up with a human. I thought both of us learned from our mistakes." She looked at him hard.

"If we'll all take our seats," Peigi announced from the far side of the room, "we can get this ball rolling. We've got a lot of ground to cover tonight, folks."

Aedan glanced at his aunt, then back at Fia. "Stay out of my head."

"Stay out of human bars," she warned with a chuckle, walking away. "Nothing but trouble."

Although Gair was the chieftain of the sept and would be until the end of time, it was Peigi who ran the day-to-day operations of the family. Meetings didn't interest Gair all that much; he came mostly for the snacks. It was Peigi who had been running them for the last fifteen years or so. Peigi opened the meeting without any fanfare and, thankfully, Aedan was first on the agenda. Once his business was complete, he wouldn't be required to remain at the meeting, which could possibly last until dawn. He hated Council meetings. He hated red tape. Everyone in the sept was required to serve on the Council occasionally, but he avoided it as often as he could. He didn't like making decisions. He liked being handed a task and fulfilling it.

Peigi gave a brief reminder of who Jay was and his peculiar circumstances and why it was important that Aedan be permitted to *work* despite his current status as inactive.

She explained that Mark Karr and the state police would be the ones to do the detective work, and that, basically, Aedan's job would be to follow through on the High Council's judgment of execution, once the criminal was located. She then opened the floor to any questions or concerns.

"We've got to stop making rules and then breaking them." Mary Hall was the first to speak. She usually was, if she could manage to get Peigi to recognize her. She was what Peigi referred to as a *squeaky cog in the wheel*. She believed Mary Hall and members like her were necessary to the workings of the sept, but that didn't mean she enjoyed the process. Mary had an issue with *everything*.

There were several muffled utterances. A lot of people didn't like Mary's comment. And more than one chuckled or whispered a sarcastic remark, not out loud, but they were thinking it, and in such close quarters, they might as well have been shouting. Everyone heard, including Mary, whose cheeks flushed red.

Mary Hall rose from her folding chair, mouth tight. "This is serious."

She might be an old fuddy-duddy at times, but she was still vampire and still very much lethal.

"You can mutter under your breath as much as you want, Tavia," she accused, cutting her eyes at one of the town's bar owners. "A hiatus is a hiatus." She folded her arms over her ample bosom. "We impose these rules to keep ourselves safe and to protect the humans we've vowed to protect. We know from experience that leaving someone in the field too long can be dangerous. They crack, and then we have to clean up the mess."

"He's going to let Mark do the legwork. All he has to do is the kill," Tavia argued.

Mary looked at Aedan. "He isn't the only competent member of the sept. Let someone else take the case."

Again, there were murmurings.

Peigi glanced at Aedan.

He had been hoping he wouldn't have to speak. He cleared his throat, but did not stand. "I know our suspect better than anyone."

"But you don't know him at all; otherwise, you'd have caught him," Mary challenged.

"Anyone for another pecan sticky bun?" Mary Kay asked cheerfully, rising from her chair.

"I'll take one." Gair raised his hand.

It fascinated Aedan that they could be gathered in a room talking about serial killers and baked goods in the same breath. "I almost had him last time," he said. "He escaped only minutes before my arrival."

"*Escaped* being the key word," Mary said tartly. She looked at Peigi, who sat in a folding chair balancing a clipboard on her knees. "I thought part of the reason Aedan was called in for a cooling-off period was because of the incident at the Château Dumont. Is anyone going to bring up that matter?"

"Apparently, you are," Tavia quipped.

A couple of Council members chuckled.

"I was cleared in that investigation," Aedan said testily. "Everyone's heard the story."

Mary rested her hand on a hip that could have held up a dictionary. "I'd like to hear it from *you*."

Aedan looked to Peigi for a life ring. She tossed him a piece of Styrofoam. "A quick recap," she suggested. "Mary has a point. You never actually appeared before the Council."

"I was busy. Chasing bad guys," Aedan argued.

"And turning into a gorilla in a park in Paris," Mary accused smugly. "You boys don't think these things get back to us."

He groaned. "*That* was a joke. *That* had nothing to do with what happened at Dumont. No one was hurt."

"Please, Aedan. A brief recap of the incident at Dumont." Peigi offered a quick smile.

She was obviously taking care not to let anyone think she was playing favorites. It still pissed him off. He took a deep breath, promising himself he wouldn't let himself get dragged down emotionally, but it became an empty promise as he began to talk. It was like that when innocent people were murdered.

Dallas rolled onto her side and glanced at the bedside clock. She had left Tat to close the bar. She was beat, and she wanted to turn in at a decent time. It was one-twenty. And still she couldn't sleep. She closed her eyes, groaned, and rolled onto her back again. The minute her eyes closed, though, she saw Aedan. He was in a mansion of white stone. People around him were speaking French. One moment he was standing there, serving champagne on a silver tray, and the next moment the white floor was covered in blood.

Dallas's eyes flew open as she sat upright in her bed. "What the hell?" she panted, her heart pounding. "Who is this guy?"

Aedan had been working undercover that evening at Château Dumont. Because he could hold a morph for only a short length of time, no more than half an hour, he had chosen to stake out a party in Bordeaux in his own form. It was hard to be inconspicuous when you were a six-foot-five redhead, but it was amazing to him that, particularly among the vastly wealthy, if you put on a waiter's uniform and carried a tray of drinks or hors d'oeuvres, you practically became invisible. It was a truth that applied everywhere in every culture.

Aedan had been there with another team member; they had ramped up their investigation on a man who was a known sex offender and bought and sold children in the sex slave market. So far, the French government had been unable to make a conviction. He was a sly, handsome man, this Alphonse Michel. A man as evil as any human Aedan had ever known.

Aedan and his companion, Eilin, thought Michel was aware he was under surveillance, but not by them. In fact, he probably wasn't aware that the Kahills even existed. He was a suspect in several international cases and was probably under surveillance not only by the French government but the Spanish and Greek, as well. Aidan and Eilin were there to see whom he spoke to; they were working on his connections and possible additional suspects. Aedan had had no idea the stakeout was going to go bad until it did; it was usually that way. The whole premonition thing, that wasn't one of Aedan's gifts.

It had been a beautiful evening on a terrace in the French countryside at a château that had once been a castle. One minute Aedan was offering a champagne flute to a pretty young French guest who liked to flirt with the servers; the next minute someone opened fire with a semiautomatic weapon. Aedan quickly assessed that he was not the assasin's target; a French undercover investigator was. The Frenchman was dead before he hit the ground. Michel's bodyguards drew and fired at the man with the gun, spraying bullets, not taking into consideration their boss's party guests, or family for that matter. Another stranger with a gun appeared, apparently a partner to the first assassin who killed the Frenchman.

Aedan's first thought as the gunfire sounded was to protect his partner, then the civilians. A stray bullet hit the host's daughter in the first burst of gunfire. Eilin took cover behind the bar. Aedan sent the tray of champagne flutes flying and reached out to drag the daughter out of harm's way. She was covered in blood, her own and the man's who had been the original target. Blood spattered, then pooled on the white marble floor of the balcony where the host had been serving cocktails to his guests. Pandemonium broke out as the air cracked and popped with the gunfire. Guests ran screaming. Two guard dogs were released from somewhere in the house and tore across the terrace, barking ferociously. A waiter was hit with a spray of gunfire as two more gunmen returned fire on an unknown party guest carrying his own weapon.

Aedan never ceased to be amazed at just how far a few drops of human blood could go; and when it was more, like the amount a man loses while bleeding to death on the floor, it seemed as if it ran in rivers. Aedan had become so accustomed to human blood that it rarely tempted him; he didn't want it. Not in these circumstances. It actually horrified him, the way humans spilled each other's blood so easily.

Aedan's job, in circumstances such as what had occurred at Château Dumont, required that he leave the premises at once; he could not get caught up in police investigations. He wasn't even supposed to help defend the humans. His orders were to get himself and his partner safely out of the environment. But he couldn't just leave the injured young woman bleeding on the floor.

*Aedan!* Eilin telepathed as she raced across the balcony, headed for the doorway that would lead them to safety. *We have to go! Leave her!*

But the HF in his arms was breathing heavily; she'd been hit in the chest. He fell in behind Eilin, but he carried the girl, thinking he could at least remove her safely from the fray.

They came around the corner of the doorway, meeting two men carrying automatic weapons. Eilin and Aedan both wore concealed pistols, but this was not an assignment that should have required serious weapons. Eilin was the first to bare her fangs. She flew into the nearest man, giving Aedan time to set the bleeding girl down on a settee. As he spun around, he set his fangs, hurling himself into the body of the second man, who was so shocked by the attack on his companion that he couldn't get his weapon up fast enough.

There was always a moment when Aedan released his fangs when he felt out of control. Adrenalin pumped through his veins, and he felt the ancient need to consume human blood. He hit the man with the gun full force with his body, sinking his fangs into his neck. The man screamed and fell back, losing his weapon in the fall. A part of Aedan wanted to finish him off, to drain him of every drop of blood in his body; this was no innocent bystander. Who carried automatic weapons into a cocktail party?

*Aedan! Let's go,* Eilin telepathed, grabbing him by the collar of his white jacket.

As they took off, Aedan remembered looking back at the young woman lying on the settee, blood blossoming on her white strapless dress.

He blinked. "I'm sorry?" he said aloud. One moment he had been on the marble terrace halfway around the world; the next moment he was standing in front of a folding chair, looking at Mary Hall's pudgy face.

"Was there nothing you could have done to prevent the bloodshed?"

Aedan took a moment to gather his wits. "There was nothing I could have done, Mary," he said evenly. "We were in the wrong place at the wrong time. And the review panel agreed. We got caught up in an event we couldn't have foreseen." He paused. "Four died, but the girl lived. Michel's gone into hiding, but he'll climb out of his hole soon enough; they always do. The investigation remains open."

Mary Hall crossed her arms, not satisfied, but appeased, and sat down.

"Anyone else?" Peigi questioned. "No?" She went on without waiting for a response. "A show of hands as to who's in favor of allowing Aedan to work this case, but no other cases, over the next few months while he's here with us?"

Five minutes later, after a majority of hands were raised, Aedan was back outside, in the cool night air, headed for home. With the matter of the Council taken care of, his thoughts drifted elsewhere. He hadn't gone to Brew tonight. He thought about Dallas. He wondered if she was relieved he hadn't showed up.

He'd just have to go by tomorrow and find out.

# Chapter 6

*The best laid schemes of mice and vampires . . .* Aedan had actually once met Robert Burns, while on assignment in Edinburgh sometime in the mid-eighteenth century. Pleasant enough fellow, but not someone he would have thought humans would be quoting hundreds of years later.

Aedan's *scheme* for the day had been to stop by and say hello to Teesha, who was still hospitalized, touch base with Mark and see how the investigation was going, and then go over some files the sept kept on serial criminals like Jay. Then he was going to change the filters on Peigi's heating and air unit, and have dinner with her and Brian and whatever teenagers had parked their butts on Peigi's couch. Then he planned to head to Brew, have a beer, and hopefully share in a little clever repartee with the gorgeous blonde he couldn't get out of his head. He wondered if he was attracted to her because she reminded him so much of Madeleine. Or maybe after a couple of hundred years he was lonely.

They were halfway through a dinner of pork chops, macaroni and cheese, and stewed tomatoes, one of Aedan's favorite home-cooked meals, when Peigi's house phone rang. Peigi had made enough food for an army, but none of the teens had stopped by, and Brian was in the middle of some sort of to-the-death fight with Nazi zombies; he hadn't come to the table. Aedan felt bad for Peigi, but he didn't say anything. He was on his second helping of mac and cheese when Peigi picked up the phone.

"Gair?" she said with surprise. "Sky falling? You never call." She carried the phone back to the kitchen table. Gair was one of those vampires who preferred good old face-to-face conversations or telepathic exchanges. He actually walked to people's houses and rang their doorbells to speak to them. Gair also had the rare gift of being able to telepath across town; most of them had to practically be in the same room to get a message through. The only problem with Gair's ability was that the message was then out there for any vampire to pick up on. There were no private long-distance telepathic conversations with Gair.

Which meant something was wrong.

Aedan set down his fork.

"Yup. He's here. Hold on." She offered the phone. It was obvious from the look on her face that she knew something was wrong, too. "He wants to speak with you." She shrugged as she handed him the phone.

"Gair, what's up?" Aedan said.

"Damn if he didn't die," Gair grumbled on the other end of the phone.

"Who?"

Gair sipped loudly on a beverage. "Victor. You'd think he'd know better, taking off like that at his age. He knows what a pain in the ass it is when one of us dies off the reservation."

Aedan heard something beep—it must have been Gair's microwave. He was making dinner.

"I'm sorry to hear that," Aedan said. "Mary okay?"

"Just got off the phone with her. She was all teary. Like she didn't know this was going to happen. He still has his head on, for heaven's sake; he'll be alive in three days.

They were playing bocce. Some kind of seniors' tournament."

"Did he die in public?"

"No. If there's one good thing in this, it's that. Mary had the sense to get him back to their place before he kicked. Ouch! That's hot."

Aedan pushed his plate forward, suddenly feeling full. "You okay?"

"I want the spaghetti hot, not the plate. You would think in this modern age you could get a microwave dinner that didn't burn your fingers and freeze your tongue. I need you to get on a plane, fly to Boca Raton, Florida, rent a van, and bring his body home."

"Tonight?" Aedan had been looking forward to seeing Dallas. All day, while he was sitting with Teesha, waiting for Mark, changing the filters, he'd thought about Dallas, about the sound of her voice, about the smell of her. He was definitely smitten, and today he hadn't even tried to deny it. By tomorrow he'd be dead set against any kind of relationship with her, but today he was enjoying the thought of the possibility. He'd decided that tonight, if she was receptive to his arrival, if she didn't kick him out of her bar, he was going to broach the subject of the exchange that had taken place between them the night they met. He was intrigued. Wasn't she?

"Three days," Gair said. "We've got three days to get Victor's body to the churchyard. You want to scramble on this end of a seventy-two-hour window, four of which are already up, or you want to scramble on the end when you've got a body ready to rise from the dead and you're sitting in traffic on 95?"

"Right. Sorry, I wasn't thinking." Aedan rubbed his forehead, glancing at Peigi. "I'll get a flight out tonight. I'll have Victor's body home safely within forty-eight hours."

"Excellent." Gair gave him Mary's address and hung up without so much as a good-bye.

"Victor died?" Peigi asked.

Aedan set the phone on the table between them. " 'Fraid so."

"Poor Mary. I know she's partially responsible for this mess, but that doesn't make this any easier for her." She rose and began to clear their plates. "To be sitting there all alone without friends or family and Victor dead." She shook her head. "Thank God she was there. I hate it when we have to steal our bodies back from a morgue."

Aedan touched the crucifix under his shirt. "Thank God." He got up from the table and grabbed their water glasses. "I'm going to get online and see if I can find a seat on a plane tonight. Apparently they've been living in Boca Raton. On a houseboat."

She turned and looked at him and smiled sadly. "Victor missed his boat."

Victor was one of the few of them who had been turned vampire by a Kahill, rather than by God. It was strictly forbidden, of course, but it had happened a couple of times over the centuries. Mary Kay's son Regan, who'd been a troubled soul most of his lives, had held Victor, a sailing ship's captain, prisoner, sucked him dry, then had a change of heart and made him vampire to save his life. More than two hundred years later, Victor was still pissed at Regan and at the world in general.

Aedan reached around Peigi to set the glasses in the sink. "I'll be gone two days. You'll be okay?"

She gave a sigh and then a wave. "Of course."

"Yes!" Brian hollered from the den. "Fuckin', yes! Take that, you Nazi bastard."

Peigi cut her eyes at Aedan. "I don't envy Mary, going through this. I'm beginning to think everyone was right. Maybe Brian would have been better off in another household for a while." She shrugged and flipped the faucet on. "But now he's here, and he says he doesn't want to live anywhere else. Says he won't. I just think if he got out of the house more, if he'd walk away from that damn TV once in a while . . ." She sighed and didn't finish her sentence.

Aedan thought for a second, then lowered his voice on the outside chance Brian was listening. Vampires had very good hearing. "How about if I take him with me? It might be good for him to do some sept business. It might bring back some of his memories. You mind?"

"Mind?" She gave a humorless laugh. "Not at all. I need to go to D.C. and see O'Malley about some sept business. But I've been afraid to leave Brian here alone. What if he starts bringing real zombies into the house?"

Aedan laughed and rubbed her shoulder. "There are no zombies around here. You go see Senator O'Malley; Brian and I will fetch Victor." He walked away.

"What if he doesn't want to go?"

Aedan smiled, doing his best Don Corleone imitation. "I'll make him an offer he can't refuse. If he comes along, I won't break his thumbs." He slapped the doorjamb as he left the kitchen. "I'll let you know what time our flight is."

Aedan left Brian to his shoot-'em-up game, went up to his bedroom, and powered up his laptop. He found two tickets leaving BWI at eleven forty-five and purchased them. He threw a change of clothes and his cell phone charger into a backpack, stepped into the bathroom and grabbed his and Brian's toothbrushes and a hairbrush, and headed down the stairs. He left his bag near the front door and went to the den. Brian was busy shooting up soldiers in camo. Kaleigh and Katy sat on the couch on either side of him, both texting on their cell phones. They must have come in while Aedan had been upstairs.

Aedan halted in the doorway.

"Hey, Aedan," Katy called.

"Hey," Kaleigh said, still texting.

"Hey." Aedan crossed his arms over his chest thoughtfully. "So, could you ladies explain this to me?" He motioned to Brian sitting between them with the game controller in his hands, then to the TV. Tonight Brian was wearing a headset, which Aedan had learned allowed him to talk to "team members" he was playing with on the Internet.

"What? The game?" Kaleigh wrinkled her pretty little freckled nose. "No way. We don't play stupid things like that."

"Not the game. Why do you girls all come here?" He gestured to the TV again. "To watch him play? He doesn't talk to you. He barely acknowledges your presence. You could sit at home on your own couches."

"I can hear you, you know," Brian grumbled. "Behind you!" He fired rapidly, and the screen exploded with blood and guts of an enemy soldier. "Sure, no problem, man."

Kaleigh smiled, obviously not in the least bit perturbed with Brian. "He'll come around eventually, and when he does"—she shrugged—"we'll be here."

Aedan put his hands together. "Well, there's no sense staying tonight because Brian and I are taking a little road trip." He walked in front of the TV.

"What are you doing?" Brian shouted, leaning one way and then the other. "Man! You made me get killed!"

Aedan unplugged the wire that brought the Internet connection to the house, and the screen went black.

"What the fu—"

"Not in this house," Aedan barked. "Say good-bye to your guests. You and I are flying to Florida."

"Florida?" Brian ripped off his headset and threw it on the floor. "No *fuckin'* way!"

"Florida?" Katy said excitedly. "Can I go, too?"

"I'll go," Kaleigh chimed in. "I bet it's warm there."

"Sorry, ladies." Aedan smiled. "Brian and I have sept business. And you two have school."

"I am *not* going to Florida," Brian insisted, his teenage voice cracking.

Kaleigh tucked her phone into her jeans pocket. "Why are you going to Florida?"

Aedan knew there was no sense in trying to keep the information from Kaleigh. She was the town's wisewoman. She always knew what was going on. "I don't think Gair has told anyone else yet, so you have to keep it to yourself. Both of you." He indicated Katy.

"Pinky swear," Katy said, crooking her pinkie finger.

"Sure. Whatever. You know I'll find out anyway," Kaleigh reminded him.

"I know. I just think Gair would prefer he make the announcement rather than having the information leaked and the town ending up in a big gossip fest."

"I get it. Vampires do love some good gossip." Kaleigh drew her knees up to her chin and wrapped her arms around her legs, giving Aedan her full attention.

"Victor died in Florida."

"I thought he was in the Bahamas," Katy said to Kaleigh.

Kaleigh shrugged and looked at Aedan. "So why are you going to Florida? Mary can't just rent a car and tote him home?"

Aedan opened his arms. "I don't ask questions. Our chieftain asked Brian and me to fly down and drive Victor's body back. Gair says go to Florida, we go to Florida."

"I am not going to Florida! I am not touching any dead bodies, and I'm certainly not riding in a van for twenty hours with one!" Brian turned to Aedan. "Or with you!" He stomped past Aedan, out of the room, and down the hall.

"Well, that went over well," Katy quipped.

Aedan watched him go and then looked back at the girls. "You should probably go home. This might get a little ugly. No need to make it worse by embarrassing him in front of you."

Katy jumped up off the couch, full of enthusiasm. "You're really going to make him go? Are you sure we can't go? A road trip to retrieve a dead body? It would be sooo much fun. Did Victor die near Disney World? Maybe we could stop there on our way back. Just for a few hours?"

"Out." Aedan pointed toward the door.

Katy sighed as she walked past him. "I always miss out on all the fun."

Kaleigh brushed her fingers across Aedan's shoulder as she followed Katy out of the room. "If you need me, give me a holler. Sometimes he'll listen to me."

"Thanks." Aedan followed them to the door.

The girls went out the front door, and Peigi appeared in the hallway. "Where is he?"

"In the bathroom!" Brian hollered from down the hall. "Do I need to get your permission to take a piss, too, Peigi?"

"Go back in the kitchen," Aedan instructed his aunt. "I'll handle this. We're on an eleven forty-five to West Palm with a plane change in Atlanta. I reserved a van at the airport. I'll let you know when we arrive in Boca Raton."

"You really think you can make him go?" she whispered.

"I told you. I'll take care of it."

She hesitated. "You sure this is a good idea? He hasn't been out much with humans. He—"

"He'll be fine, Peigi. Go in the kitchen. Give Mary McCathal a call and tell her we're on our way. I know she'll be glad to hear from you."

Aedan was waiting for Brian when the teen finally came out of the bathroom. "Get in my car. You're going to Florida with me to pick up Victor's body."

"So he can rise from the dead?" Brian's tone was angry

and accusing. "No way. I say we let him rot. He'd be better off. I'd have been better off."

"In my car," Aedan repeated firmly. "Peigi needs a break. You're driving her crazy."

"Yeah? Well, she's driving me crazy. 'Brian this, and Brian that,' " he whined, apparently imitating her.

"That's enough. Get in the car. We'll talk about it on the way."

"And if I don't get in the car?" The teen's tone held a challenge.

"You ever see one vampire get into a fight with another?" Aedan asked icily. He lifted his upper lip and slowly dropped down his fangs.

The teen flinched. "You'd bite me?" He was scared but trying hard not to show it.

"I'll kick your ass," Aedan warned.

Brian took one more look at him and then went down the hallway. At the front door, he picked up Aedan's backpack and then went out, slamming the door hard behind him.

Peigi came out of the kitchen, wiping her hands on a towel. "That was easy enough. If I'd known he needed a little intimidation to get up off his duff, I'd have just lit a fire under him on the couch or thrown a few fireballs around the den."

Aedan chuckled. Peigi's gift was pyrokinesis. She could make an object spontaneously combust through sheer willpower. It was kinda cool to watch and still fascinated Aedan after all these years. "See you in two days. We'll call." He leaned over and gave her a kiss on the cheek. "And don't worry."

Aedan went around the circle on Rehoboth Avenue before Brian finally spoke up. "Is this the way to Baltimore?"

"Good knowledge of geography." Aedan glanced in the

rearview mirror and pulled his fingers through his hair. "That's the Atlantic Ocean you can almost see in front of us. Baltimore is west of here." He hitched his thumb over his shoulder.

"So why are we going east, if the airport is west?"

"I have to see someone. It'll take five minutes."

Brian didn't say anything until Aedan parked in front of Brew. "A bar? You have to see someone *in a bar?* I bet Peigi wouldn't like that too much, you taking me to a bar."

"You're not going in. I am." Aedan shut off the engine.

Brian stared at the neon sign: a witch's cauldron bubbling with . . . brew. "I can't go with you? I don't want a beer; I just want to see what it's like." For once he didn't sound angry. He actually sounded curious.

"You're not going inside. Lock the doors when I get out. You just hit that little rocker button next to the door handle."

"I know how to lock a car door." The anger was back in a split second.

"How? You haven't been in a car since you were reborn, have you? If you didn't spend all your time in front of a TV playing video games, you'd have more freedom."

"What if I decide to make a run for it?" Brian asked as Aedan got out of the car.

"I don't think that's a concern. You won't get out because, right now, I doubt you could find your way home." Aedan closed the car door, waited for the sound of the lock engaging, and then headed into the bar.

"Hey, that what you've been looking for?" Tat elbowed Dallas.

She was running a credit card at the register. "What?" She glanced over her shoulder and saw Aedan taking a seat on the same barstool he'd occupied every time he'd come in.

"No," she said, whipping around, her heart beating a little faster than it had a moment ago. She glanced at Aedan again, over her shoulder. He tilted his head, beckoning her.

All she had to do was walk away. That nightmare she'd had last night, the waking dream, whatever the hell it was. It had been a warning. What was the sense in being a witch and getting these messages if you didn't pay attention to them?

"Can you take care of this?" she heard herself ask Tat. "Table four."

He looked at her, then at the credit card leaning against the cash register. "Sure."

Dallas walked over to where Aedan was sitting and leaned casually on the bar. "You buy that stool or something?"

He opened his arms. "Seems like it, doesn't it?" He leaned forward, lowering his voice. "Seems like I belong here."

She didn't know what to say, so she didn't say anything. After a second, she asked, "Guinness?"

"Actually, no. I have to go. I just stopped by because . . ." He was looking right at her, into her eyes. "I just wanted to tell you that I had planned to come by tonight, but I can't now. I wanted to talk to you."

"You're a weird guy," she said. "You came by to tell me you can't come by?"

Both of her hands rested on the bar, but she was out of his immediate reach. He smiled and glanced away. Without warning, he grabbed her hand.

Dallas prepared herself for the flood of pictures: the places, the people in costume . . . the blood on the white floor. What happened shocked her as much as the blood she had seen in her vision.

She saw *nothing*. She felt *nothing*.

Dallas pulled her hand away. "How did you do that?" she whispered excitedly under her breath.

"How did I do what?" He sounded sort of smug.

She glanced over her shoulder at Tat, who was busy trying to get the credit card to run. He was using the piece-of-plastic-wrap-on-the-magnetic-strip trick to get it to work. She looked back at Aedan, now completely entranced. "Tell me what's going on here." She pointed at him, then herself.

"I'm trying to flirt with you. I think," he added, sounding not quite as confident. Which she found sort of heartwarming.

"I *know* you're flirting with me. That's what people do in bars. That's not what I'm talking about. I'm talking about . . . you know . . . what happened when you touched me the first time. What just *didn't* happen."

He shook his head. "You go first. Tell me what happened that first night when I touched you."

She put her hand on the bar again, wanting to touch him again to see what would happen, afraid to. It was hard living without human contact. It made her feel lonely. Isolated. Her gaze met his. "Can you do it again?" she murmured.

"I don't know. What am I doing?" As he spoke, he slid his hand across the bar and covered hers with his.

His hand was big and warm and gave her the strangest sensation. He made her feel . . . *safe*. Dallas didn't know what to say. The tears that suddenly gathered in the corners of her eyes embarrassed her.

"I'm sorry. I have to go," he said after a long moment of silence that didn't feel awkward to her, though it should have.

"But you'll be back?" she asked. She knew she should pull her hand away, but she couldn't. Not yet.

"Business trip. Two days. Three, tops." He waited. "You want me to come back?" He then took his other hand and cradled her hand between his larger ones.

And she *still* didn't feel anything. She didn't see a single thing. Her mind was utterly and sweetly blank.

He had a smile that made her want to smile.

"I'll take that as a *yes,*" he said. Then he let go of her hand and walked out of the bar.

Feeling as if she was in a little bit of a daze, Dallas walked back to the register.

"I got it," Tat said. "Damned credit card machine." He glanced at Dallas. "What was going on there? The two of you playing patty-cake or something?"

Dallas grabbed the credit card and slip from his hand. "Mind your own business, nosy."

"You just watch *yours,*" he said under his breath as she walked away.

The flight to West Palm went surprisingly smoothly. Once Brian got past the fact that Aedan had basically kidnapped him, he actually began to enjoy the road trip. Not that he would have actually admitted it, not in a hundred years. By 7 a.m. they were in Florida. They stopped for breakfast and then were on the road and headed for the marina where Victor's boat was docked.

"This is all so crazy, the whole being reborn thing," Brian mused as he looked out the window.

"It is, but you get used to the idea and it's easier to accept once your memories begin to come back." Aedan glanced at the teenager. "Any of your memories coming back? Of past lives? People?"

He shrugged. "A little."

He was quiet for a minute, and Aedan waited. This was the first time Brian had initiated a conversation since they had left. Any kind of serious conversation. Mostly they had talked about food and cute girls they saw in the airport.

"So we're going to pick him up, take him back to Clare Point, put him in a coffin, and he's going to wake up in the cemetery?"

"That's pretty much how it goes. There's a ceremony that takes place. Prayers offered. You're welcome to come if you like. All sept members are encouraged to attend."

"Maybe I will come." Brian stared at a row of palm trees that ran along the roadside. "Where will Victor live after he's reborn? You said he doesn't have parents. Will he have to live with an old lady who's supposed to be his wife?"

"I don't know where he'll go. Probably not with Mary, though."

Brian worked his jaw. "But they're not married, right? Victor and Mary?"

"Yes, and no." Aedan signaled, following the onboard GPS. They were less than a mile from the marina. "According to the sept, they're not married."

"So they can be with whomever they want?"

"Any *vampire* they want. Once they're of age—which is twenty-one for us. There's a cool ceremony for that, too," Aedan explained. "You'll go through it in a couple of years."

Brian hit a button on the van door and let the window go down a little, then raised it. Then he put it down again. "I've been thinking about this whole marriage thing."

"Uh huh."

Brian thought for a minute. "And I decided I'm going to marry Katy instead of Peigi. Katy's way cuter." He looked at Aedan. "That going to be a problem?"

# Chapter 7

"You can't marry Katy, Brian." Aedan pulled into the marina parking lot and put down his window to speak to the security guard. "Keri's Carpets, slip seventeen."

The guy in the guard shack never looked up from his blackjack game on his iPad. He just waved, and the gate went up.

They had stopped at Walmart and bought a six by eight rug, some paper, markers, and tape. In the side and rear windows of the paneled rental van, they'd taped handmade signs that said KERI'S CARPETS. They'd carry the carpet wrapped in plastic onto the boat. They'd carry the same carpet back out a few minutes later, minus its plastic wrap, with Victor rolled inside. Aedan had done it before. Humans weren't all that observant. If anyone happened to be watching, he or she would assume a new carpet had been carried in and an old one carried out.

"Why can't I marry Katy? I don't mean now. Like, in a few years."

Aedan eyed him. "Katy, huh?"

"Yeah, I like Kaleigh, but she scares me."

Aedan laughed. "Not to worry. She scares me, too. She scares all of us. As a full-grown woman, each of Kaleigh's gifts will be greater than any of ours. And she has them all."

"So that's why she's the sept's wisewoman? Or did she get all the gifts because she *was* the wisewoman?"

"Good question. Turns out it's the chicken or the egg thing. God's work, that's all I can tell you." Aedan followed the blacktop road along the piers, maintaining the twenty-five miles per hour speed posted at the entrance to the marina. "But sorry. You can't marry Katy. She's taken."

"By who? Pete? That douche. They broke up last week."

"They break up every week. They've been doing it for hundreds of years." Aedan slowed down, checking the signs that indicated the slip numbers. He smiled and nodded at a woman in a big straw hat walking a peekapoo. "Seventeen. There it is."

"That's not right. Pete the douche gets Katy, and I get an old fire-starter?"

"She'll be reborn. And I gotta tell you, Peigi's a pretty hot sixteen-year-old."

Brian groaned and threw one foot up on the dashboard. "This sucks."

"It does," Aedan agreed, cutting the engine.

Brian turned to him after a moment. "Why don't you have a wife?"

Aedan loosened his grip on the steering wheel. "Because my wife died in childbirth just a few months before the *aota*."

"The curse that made us all vampires?"

Aedan nodded.

"So, you have a kid?"

"He died, too. A day old."

"Man, that really sucks."

Aedan smiled. The wound was old, a scar more than anything else. He and Elly had been married less than a year when she died. They were young, and while he had certainly loved her, his feelings had not been as deep as his love for Madeleine. He still thought of his little son, born too early to live in those days, but the pain had subsided until it was nothing more than an occasional tender spot.

"So now you can never get married because of the stupid sept rules about having to stay married to whomever you were married to when you were human?"

"Nope. I can't marry."

Brian looked at him. He was a cute kid. He'd grow to be a handsome man. "You got a girlfriend?"

Aedan opened the van door. "No."

"You gay?"

"No." He climbed out.

"But you don't have a girlfriend?"

"No," Aedan said, beginning to get a little testy. "She died, too." He paused. "Her name was Madeleine, and I loved her very much."

"She was a vampire who *died?*" Brian was actually becoming a little animated. "Did someone put a stake through her heart?"

Aedan leaned into the van, resting on the doorframe, his hands over his head. "Where are you getting your vampire information?"

Brian looked away. "Mostly the Internet. Some movies."

"Well, humans on the Internet or in the movie business don't know shit about vampires. Not real ones. There are different rules, depending on your situation and where in the world you live. It's complicated, being a Kahill. You have questions, you ask Peigi, or me. Kaleigh's probably safe." Aedan looked away. "The woman who died. The woman I loved." He hesitated. "She wasn't vampire."

"I thought that wasn't allowed."

"It's not." Aedan was done with twenty questions, at least for now. He wanted to get Victor and head home. He wanted to take care of sept business, and then he wanted to go to Brew and talk to Dallas. He wanted to know why his blocking his thoughts had made her so intrigued. And happy. "You stay here. Let me find Mary. I'll check on the Victor situation, and then I'll be back for you. Stay in the van. Don't speak to anyone."

"I've got no problem staying in the van." He adjusted his seat to a reclining position. "The sooner we get this done, the sooner I get back to 'Modern Warfare 3.' " He loaded a cartridge in an invisible rifle and let off a burst of invisible bullets.

Aedan closed the door and walked across the road to the dock. Mary was waiting for him on the deck of the boat they'd rented in slip seventeen; he'd called her after he left Walmart to say he'd be there in twenty minutes.

"Oh, Aedan." Mary McCathal was a plump woman with a pretty smile. She put out her arms to him as he boarded, and he hugged her.

"I'm very sorry about Victor, Mary."

She gave a little laugh, sniffed, and stepped back. "Happens to us all, doesn't it?" She waved him toward the main cabin. "He's downstairs in the salon. Waiting. I couldn't get him into the master bedroom cabin before he passed." She offered a brave smile.

"It'll all be okay, Mary." Aedan glanced over his shoulder in the direction of the van. He could see Brian's big feet on the dashboard, but not his face. "I brought Brian Ross. He's being a pain in the ass at home. You know, teenager stuff. But it's been pretty rough on Peigi. The age difference and all."

"Guess we'll be there for a while, too, won't we?" She smoothed her short-cropped curly hair with her hand. "But we'll deal with it, Victor and I." She glanced in the direction of the van. "You want to bring Brian down?"

"I will." The boat, a practically new forty footer, rocked gently as someone eased a jet ski through the canal. "He can help me carry Victor out. But I want to get the lay of the land first. Brian hasn't seen a dead body yet. Well, he doesn't remember that he has."

"You're going to do it in broad daylight?" she asked quietly, glancing around. The marina was small and quiet, but there were still a dozen people within viewing distance of Victor and Mary's boat.

"It won't be a problem. We've got it figured. Doing the old rug trick." He pointed to the panel van with the sign in the rear window.

She glanced at the van and nodded. "This way."

They took a narrow staircase below deck to the salon that opened into the galley. It was a pretty room, white with a bit of a tropical theme, but not overdone. Victor lay on a full-sized, tan-colored couch in the salon, his eyes closed, his hands folded as if he were taking a nap. He was wearing plaid green shorts to his knobby knees, a white polo, and a pair of sandals with white athletic socks.

"Here he is." Mary walked over to where the old man's body lay and smoothed his gray hair. "He's going to be angry when he realizes he never got to finish that bocce ball game. He was in first place."

Aedan smiled, taking a look around. It wouldn't be hard to get Victor out of there and into the van. Not at all. "Have you packed? I could drop you off at the airport on our way out of town."

"I'll call a shuttle van. My flight isn't until this afternoon. I'll still beat you home."

"Anything we need to take care of? Anything that needs to be wrapped up here?"

She shook her head. "I know no one approved of what we did, but we were careful. No one knows what we are. Nothing here in our names. Fake IDs," she explained. "Rent's paid through 'til June first. We can just walk away. You take care of Victor, and I'll see you Friday night at the church."

"You sure you'll be okay?"

"I always am, Aedan." She leaned over and kissed Victor on his leathery cheek. "I'm going to pack. You take care of Victor."

The transportation of the body went as well as it could have. Aedan and Brian arrived in Clare Point at dawn the next morning. They could have driven the distance in less time, but they had made a couple of pit stops. Brian got a kick out of South of the Border, despite its cheesy tourist atmosphere; he left wearing a big sombrero. The young man was surprisingly decent company, despite a couple of episodes of moodiness. They talked a lot, and Aedan felt as if the teen had a better understanding of himself and the sept by the time they pulled up in front of Peigi's cottage.

Two nights later, Aedan, along with many in Clare Point, attended Victor's rebirth. Brian surprised both Aedan and Peigi by making the suggestion that the teenager, Victor, still groggy from his transformation, go home with them. He even offered to share his bedroom with the new teen, if Peigi didn't want to bother making up the bed in the guest room. Aedan wasn't positive it was a great idea, but Peigi had seemed keen on it. Mary McCathal had no intention of "raising" Victor, so she was pleased with the arrangement.

Saturday evening when Aedan left for Rehoboth, Peigi was busy doing paperwork for the sept, and Brian, Victor, Pete, Kaleigh, Lia, and Katy were all in the den. The boys were playing video games, the girls talking amongst themselves while speed-texting on their phones.

Aedan parked on Rehoboth Avenue and took a stroll, watching for any sign that might suggest that Jay was on the prowl again. After his long slumber, Jay always seemed eager to get "back to work." There were often a series of attacks strung close together at first. Once satiated, Jay took his time. . . . The attacks became less frequent but more brutal.

There was nothing unusual happening on Rehoboth Avenue that night. There were people out strolling on the boardwalk and the avenue, relaxing, enjoying a quiet spring night at the beach. The bars and restaurants were busy. The traffic was nothing like it would be by July 1, but cars were actually jockeying for parking spots in front of the bigger places. It was such a nice evening that a few restaurants had set tables out on the sidewalks for al fresco dining. Everyone he passed seemed to be having a good time. He looked for Jay, hoping that even if he couldn't recognize him, he might be able to feel him. How could you be so close to evil and not *feel* it? The night Aedan had missed him by less than ten minutes, Aedan had been able to psychically smell his presence. The remnant of it. Jay smelled of rotting flesh and moldy leaves.

But if Jay was out tonight, Aedan couldn't tell. Aedan walked into Brew and was surprised to find his barstool taken by a twenty-something guy in a plaid shirt with a goofy smile. Dallas was standing next to him, a tray balanced on her hip, talking to him; the two of them were laughing. She wasn't flirting back, but she certainly wasn't knocking him on his ear, either.

Aedan stood in the doorway for a moment, then strolled up to the bar where surfer-dude was making his move. "Hey, hon, sorry I'm late." He grabbed Dallas's arm, turned her slightly, and kissed her on the mouth. When he stepped back, she was staring at him, her lips slightly parted.

"Aedan," was all she could manage in a breathy whisper.

"Got a minute?" He took her tray from her, set it on the bar, caught her hand, and led her to the nearest booth. "Sit with me." He gave her a little push, and her knees folded. He slid onto the bench seat beside her.

"Why did you do that?" she breathed. Her wits quickly returning to her, her words became more forceful. "You shouldn't have done that."

"Sorry. It's just that I've been thinking about kissing you since the first time I saw you."

She brushed her fingertips over her lips. "You did it again."

"I did what?" He glanced at the bar. The only waitress in the place was making her way toward them. "You want a drink?" he asked Dallas.

"No, I don't want a drink!" She grabbed his arm, touching him of her own free will for the first time. "Who are you? *What* are you? Why do you keep coming in here and bothering me?"

The waitress came to their table. "What can I get you to drink?" she asked, paying no attention to the fact that her boss was sitting at the table with a guy. The girl acted as if Dallas did it every night.

"Guinness," Aedan said. "You?" he turned to Dallas to ask.

"No drink!"

Aedan smiled up at the waitress. "Just the one, I guess."

"One Guinness, coming up." The waitress sashayed away.

Aedan turned to Dallas. "Tell me what happened the first time you touched me. You tell me what happened, and I'll tell you how I make it *not* happen."

Dallas had no intention of explaining herself or her *gift*. If he hadn't had her trapped against the wall, she'd have just gotten up and walked away. But there was something so earnest in his bluer-than-blue eyes. Something so trustworthy. And she was so damned lonely, so tired of fighting the good fight all alone. The words just came out. They came out so softly, so hesitantly, that he leaned closer to hear her.

"I see images. Of memories," she whispered, feeling as if this was one of the most intimate conversations she'd ever had with anyone. She'd told John of course, but looking back, either he hadn't believed her, or his drug-fogged brain hadn't understood what she had told him. He had never understood. "The memories people carry. I see them."

"When you touch someone?" He suddenly looked concerned. "A gift?"

Her brow furrowed. She felt woozy. Light-headed. Maybe it was the way he was looking at her, or the feel of his arm around her shoulders. Or maybe it was just the fact that the only thing she'd eaten today was half a cheese stick she'd shared with Kenzie. "That's what my mother called it, a gift. I call it a curse."

"Your mother had it, too?"

She nodded. "And her mother." She licked her lips. "The first time I touched you, I saw . . . stuff. But you made it stop. The other day. Just now when you kissed me you did it again." She looked up at him. "How do you do that?"

"I don't know," he said casually. He was rubbing her shoulders in a circular motion. "I just sort of clear my head."

"But how did you *know* to do it?" She looked into his eyes.

"How we doing here?"

Dallas was startled to see Tat tableside, serving Aedan his beer. "Everything okay?" Tat looked directly at her.

Aedan didn't move his hand from her shoulder. He didn't speak, either.

"I'm just taking five minutes. I'm fine." She looked at her bartender quickly, then away. "Can you check the ice machine? It was acting squirrely when I filled up the bins a few minutes ago."

Tat looked hard at Aedan, then walked away. "Can do."

"That your guard dog?" Aedan asked when Tat was out of earshot.

Dallas surprised herself by laughing. “Something like that.”

“Scary guy.” Aedan glanced at Tat, then back at her.

“I know.” She chuckled.

“So back to what we were talking about.” He took a sip of beer.

“What we were talking about,” she echoed.

“You can do this with anyone? Read his or her mind?”

“I don’t read minds.” She pointed at his Guinness. “You mind?” Her throat was dry.

“Not at all.” He slid the glass toward her.

Dallas took a sip of the rich, dark beer and wiped the little bubbles of foam off her upper lip before she went on. “I see images, like still photographs of things you’ve seen. Sometimes I pick up on . . . emotions. I think they’re mostly just attached to the images, not anything the person is feeling at the moment I make contact.”

“What did you see when you touched me that first time?”

She licked her lips, still tasting the beer. She wasn’t sure how much to say. “Yours were different.”

“Different how?” He suddenly seemed very serious.

She shook her head, not willing to come completely clean, not yet at least. “Just different.” She met his gaze. “I knew you were different.”

“You don’t have to be afraid of me, you know. I won’t hurt you.”

She thought for a moment. “I think I figured that out.”

He took a sip of his beer. “Can you control it? Stop it?”

She shook her head. “I wish. The easiest thing is to just not touch people.”

“Makes for a solitary life.”

“I have my daughter,” she said with a shrug.

“Guess that means you touched someone,” he teased.

She looked down at the table, averting her gaze. “I don’t want to talk about him. Ever.” A group of customers came into the bar. There must have been a dozen people, men and women. "I should get back to work." She said it with what seemed like conviction, but she made no move to rise.

"I'd rather you sat here with me."

"Kenzie would rather eat than not."

"Pretty name. How old is she?"

"Ten. We live upstairs. She has a nanny. Two of them, actually. Sisters who keep an eye on her when I can't. Kenzie is . . . special." Dallas didn't know what made her say that. She never talked to strangers about Kenzie.

"I bet she is. In what way in particular?"

She gave his arm a gentle push. He was muscular under the leather jacket. Very muscular. And big. Enormous. "Tat's going to be swamped behind the bar. You're going to have to let me out."

"Will you let me take you out?" he asked, not budging.

She couldn't bring herself to look at him. "I don't really date. I don't have time. Not with Kenzie and the bar and . . . all."

"Okay, but you must eat. Breakfast? Lunch?" He waited. "Or I could just sit here and wait until the bar closes."

She closed her eyes for a minute. What was she thinking? She could *not* go out with this man. She had no room in her life for this man. For any man. "Aedan, you don't want to go out with me."

"Your evil powers don't work with me," he whispered, his tone teasing and yet somehow protective. His breath was warm in her ear. "Come on. Brunch. With me, tomorrow. You can bring your daughter. She can be our chaperone."

Dallas couldn't make herself say no.

"Come on," Aedan dared. "Champagne brunch at Victoria's. You can meet me there. You don't even have to get in a car with me. How much safer could a date be?"

"I can't have a relationship with you, Aedan," she said quietly.

"I can't have one with you, either," he responded, with equal seriousness. "So how about we just make it two friends going out for brunch? And I'm serious. Bring your daughter."

"I really have to get back to work." She pushed hard on his shoulder this time, and he slid out of the booth.

"Eleven o'clock. Victoria's. You know where it is?"

She climbed out of the booth. "I know where it is."

"Eleven o'clock."

"You said that," she said with a smile.

He grabbed her hand, leaned down, and kissed her on the cheek. "See you tomorrow." He gave her hand a squeeze without relaying a single memory, and then he let her go.

*I was not certain traveling to America would be a good idea. The long plane ride, the tedious security measures. All of this just to taunt a vampire. The venue had not, at first, excited me. I know better places to hunt. I am of the world so infrequently that I do not like to waste precious time. I like familiar ground; I like large cities where it is easy to lose oneself among the humans. But now that I am here, now that I have had a taste of blood, I find that this place may offer a unique opportunity.*

*I like the beach that is nothing like the rocky, cold shore of home. The sunshine is warm on my face. And the women, they are so beautiful, so nubile, so . . . trusting. And they are not afraid to scream. Of course I cannot allow them to scream. But I like the idea of it. And I like the idea that the vampire pursues me. It adds a certain thrill to the hunt. I was lucky that I was able to find him so easily through contacts in Paris.*

*I do not know yet how I will handle him, ultimately.*

*For now I just want to mock him. Make him angry. He is no match for my cunning. I have already proved that. That does not mean he will not be fun.*

*So I sharpen my blades and make ready. The first girl was a delight, but I am still hungry after my long sleep, and so I must still find satisfaction.*

# Chapter 8

Aedan couldn't believe it, but he actually felt nervous as he got out of his car, locked it, and headed down the sidewalk toward the hotel on the boardwalk where Dallas had agreed to meet him for brunch.

What if she didn't show up?

What if she came and somehow, in the light of day, minus the ambience of the bar, there was nothing between them? But maybe that would be a good thing. He had no business meeting an HF for brunch. It wasn't right. Especially one with a kid. He'd be gone in a couple of months. Dallas needed someone who could take of her, someone who could be here for her. That's what partners were for, to be there for each other. And he'd obviously failed the test. Twice, big time.

He hadn't been there when Elly had gone into labor; he'd been off fighting. She was dead before he returned home. He hadn't been there for Madeleine, either. Not when Jay had cornered her, tortured her, mur—

"Hey there."

Aedan looked up to see Dallas rising from a bench on the boardwalk. She was wearing a jean skirt and a lavender top with a long string of wooden beads around her neck. Her hair fell loose down her back, reflecting the morning sunlight. She looked cute. *Hot.*

"I didn't know if we were supposed to meet you inside or outside." She gestured toward the Victorian hotel on the corner. "But Kenzie wanted to see the ocean, so we decided to wait out here. Kenzie!" she called toward the steps that led down to the beach. "Come on, let's go have breakfast."

"I'm glad you came. I was afraid"—he chuckled—"that you might stand me up." He put his hand on her waist and gave her a quick kiss. She reminded him so much of Madeleine, and yet she smelled nothing like her, *felt* nothing like her. Madeleine had had an earthy smell about her; Dallas smelled of jasmine and another flower he couldn't quite identify. Her lips were soft when he touched them with his. Smooth. She definitely kissed him back. Sort of.

"I thought about it. Not coming." It was her turn to chuckle. "I'm really not good at this dating thing, Aedan. I'm not sure I can do it for about a hundred reasons." She turned toward the stairs again.

The ocean was beautiful this morning, the tide washing in, hitting the beach, and retreating in a sheet of foam. A couple of storms over the last few years had taken a toll on the width of the beach between the water and the boardwalk and all its stores. But over the winter sand had been pumped in from out in the ocean, and the beach restored.

"Kenzie!" Dallas called.

A moment later, a blond girl bounced up the steps, carrying a pair of blue Crocs. The child was wearing blue jean capris and a T-shirt with a fire truck on it.

"Come meet my friend, Aedan, Kenzie. Remember, I told you we were going to have brunch together?" She grabbed the girl's hand and led her to the bench, pushing her down gently. "Let's get this sand off your feet."

"Hey, Kenzie, it's nice to meet you."

The little girl looked off into space over her mother's shoulder as Dallas squatted in front of her daughter and brushed the sand off her feet. Kenzie was pretty, the spit-

ting image of her mother: the same brown eyes, same white blond hair. At ten, it was obvious that the child would grow to be as lovely as her mother.

"I'm hungry." Aedan slipped his hands into the pockets of his khaki pants. He'd actually taken the time to iron a polo shirt this morning. "Are you hungry, Kenzie?" he asked casually, not wanting to put any pressure on the little girl. He was so big that sometimes little kids were intimidated by him.

Still, the girl didn't respond. In fact, she didn't really acknowledge her mother, either. She just sat there on the bench, hands at her sides, sort of vacant-eyed.

"She takes a while to warm up to people. Don't you, Kenzie?" Dallas explained. She stood, brushing sand off her skirt. "Put on your shoes and let's go."

Aedan hesitated, not exactly sure what was going on. He could sense Kenzie was different than the average ten-year-old. And Dallas, he recalled, had said something about her daughter being *special*. Dallas had given no further explanation then, and she didn't offer one now. So Aedan decided he'd just roll with it.

"I made a reservation. I didn't know how busy they'd be." He and Dallas walked side by side. Kenzie clomped behind them in her rubber Crocs. At the hotel door, he opened it and stepped back. Kenzie followed her mother in, but then fell in behind Dallas and Aedan.

When Aedan gave the hostess his name, Dallas spoke up. "Could we possibly have that corner table, near the windows? My daughter's a little uncomfortable in crowds."

The hostess led them to the table Dallas had requested, and Dallas pulled out the chair in the corner. "Slide in. I've got your books in my bag." She tapped the big, batik-patterned cloth purse on her shoulder.

Kenzie did as her mother asked. Once settled in the chair, she placed her hands in her lap and stared out the

window at the people walking by on the boardwalk. Dallas slid into the chair beside her.

Aedan took the chair across from Dallas. Once the waitress had taken their orders for juice and drinks, she suggested they could help themselves at the buffet.

"You coming with me or waiting here?" Dallas asked her daughter.

Kenzie made no move to get up, nor did she speak.

"You get something. I'll stay here with Kenzie," Aedan said.

Dallas hesitated, glancing at her daughter, then at the buffet set up on the other side of the dining room. "I'll be right back, girlfriend."

Aedan glanced around. He'd never been to the buffet at the Boardwalk Plaza Hotel; he'd just read a review in a newspaper that said it was one of the best breakfasts in town. The décor was a little gaudy for him—the patterned wallpaper and ornately carved furniture—but they knew their nineteenth century Victorian interior design.

Aedan watched Kenzie for a moment. The girl continued to stare out the window. Dallas had set several workbooks and a mechanical pencil down in front of her daughter. He was surprised when he leaned over to see that the workbook was a high school–level algebra book.

"Algebra, huh?" Aedan asked, casually. "Pretty tricky stuff for a girl your age."

The little girl never moved, but he heard a tiny voice in his head say, *Please don't look at me. It makes it too hard.*

Aedan's brow furrowed. His telepathy with his fellow vampires was good, especially when this close, but never, in all the years he had been alive, had he been able to hear human thoughts. But the girl was clearly speaking to him. It couldn't be anyone else. Aedan looked away.

Kenzie seemed startled for a moment, then hesitant.

*Thank you,* came the tiny voice. *It's scary, sometimes, you know. When people look.*

*I know,* he thought, not sure if she would hear him.

The tiniest smile touched her lips. *I didn't want to come for breakfast. I don't like people. They scare me. I like Ashley and Amanda. They just talk to each other and not me. I write if I have to tell them something.*

The waitress came back with mimosas for Aedan and Dallas and a Sprite for Kenzie. Kenzie seemed to withdraw as the waitress got closer to her.

Aedan glanced in Dallas's direction. She had two plates in her hands and was busy adding to both of them. It was all he could do not to look at Kenzie.

He thanked the waitress and waited until she was gone. *Can your mom hear you?* Aedan asked.

Kenzie giggled, her gaze still fixed on something beyond the window. *She thinks she can. She is always trying to guess what I want. But she can't hear me unless I talk out loud. I don't like to talk out loud.* She turned to look at Aedan. She didn't actually make eye contact, but she was looking at him. *Why can you hear me when no one else can?*

*I have no idea,* he answered honestly, averting his gaze again. *Can a lot of people hear you?*

*No.* She took a quick look at him, then fixed her gaze through the window again. *Are you a good man or a bad man?*

Aedan fiddled with his napkin, made a little uncomfortable by her question. The child didn't waste much time, did she? *A good man, I hope. I try to be.*

*Why do you bite people, then?*

He looked at her; he couldn't help it. *How do you know that?*

Dallas approached their table, and Aedan felt a sudden disconnect with the little girl. Kenzie didn't saying anything else to him.

"Look what I found, Kenzie," she said, carrying two plates. "Mashed potatoes *and* peaches for you." On her own plate, she had an omelet and home fries. Kenzie's plate, sure enough, held only peaches and mashed potatoes. "Move your books, hon." She glanced at Aedan as she took her seat. "Thanks for sitting with her. Go ahead, get something."

When Aedan returned with his plate, Kenzie was shoveling mashed potatoes into her mouth. Dallas had waited for him.

"You didn't have to wait," he said, sliding into his chair. He'd gotten a Belgian waffle and scrapple. He spread his white linen napkin on his lap and then lifted his glass.

Dallas raised hers.

"What shall we toast to?" he asked.

"To a good breakfast. Is there anything better?" She laughed.

He laughed and touched his glass to hers, making eye contact with her. She liked him. She didn't want to, but she did.

This was going to be complicated.

"To a good breakfast," he agreed.

*That's silly,* Kenzie's little voice said in his head. *Grown-ups are silly.*

Aedan smiled. "So tell me about Brown. That where you're going, Kenzie? That why you're brushing up on your algebra?"

Dallas laughed, and they started talking about Brown University. Kenzie ate her potatoes and peaches, and Aedan heard nothing more from her. His conversation with Dallas turned to Providence, Rhode Island, which led to a discussion of Boston and how the Sox were going to do this year. Aedan fully enjoyed his meal with her; she was easy to talk to, smart, but not snotty like some Ivy Leaguers could be. He'd been one himself once, at Harvard. In the nineteenth century. It hadn't been his thing, and he'd never tried it again.

Dallas seemed to be enjoying herself, too. They both had a second mimosa. Kenzie had a second helping of mashed potatoes, and they talked for a while after the last of the plates were cleared away. Kenzie never spoke to her mother or to Aedan. Once she finished eating, she opened a workbook and began to work on a page, obviously concentrating.

It wasn't until Aedan had called for the check that he heard Kenzie utter a word. The waitress had just left the check, and Aedan was fishing in his wallet for his credit card. Suddenly, Kenzie sat up very straight. Her pencil fell out of her hand.

"Kenzie? You okay?"

Dallas picked up her daughter's pencil, which was about to roll off the end of the table.

"Bad man," Kenzie said in a strange, guttural voice. It didn't sound at all like the voice he heard in his head.

"No," Dallas said. "Aedan's not a bad man. He's nice. He's been nice to us."

Kenzie turned her head, looking right at Aedan. *You have to get him,* she said inside his head.

"I'm really sorry about that, back at the restaurant, Aedan," Dallas apologized again. "I don't know what got into her. I can't believe she even spoke in front of you. I don't know what she was talking about. She acts like she likes you. I don't know why she would say that—say you were a bad man."

They walked side by side down the boardwalk. Aedan had offered to walk them home to their apartment over the bar, which was off the south end of Rehoboth Avenue on Wilmington Avenue, so he had left his car at the hotel. It was a nice day; he didn't mind walking, and he certainly enjoyed the company. He'd hoped Kenzie might say something more about the bad guy she had referred to back at the restaurant, but she wouldn't talk to him. He tried telepathy, but she either didn't hear him or was ignoring him.

"She never says things like that. She never says anything to anyone but me and a friend or two she's made at school." Dallas glanced behind her at her daughter who was walking a few steps behind them, clutching one of her math workbooks.

"It's fine. Don't worry about it. I'm not offended." He glanced over his shoulder at the little girl . . . who smiled at him. He smiled and looked forward again.

"She's autistic," Dallas went on, missing the interaction between him and Kenzie. "That's one of the reasons we came to Delaware. There's a great school here for autistic children."

"She seems very smart."

"She is. Super-smart. She just has a hard time communicating with people, especially verbally. That's what makes it so hard to be autistic. People assume you're stupid. She walked late; she talked late; even now, she barely talks. But she understands every word we say." She hesitated. "Is that a problem for you? Her disability?"

"Not at all." *I kind of like the fact that you're an odd duck, Kenzie. Quack. Quack,* he telepathed.

He heard a giggle in his head.

"She seems like she has a lot of potential," he went on, aloud. "I don't know much about autism, except that it's a very wide spectrum diagnosis."

"Exactly, and there's so much we don't know about it. Kenzie and children like her have so much potential, but we just have to—I'm sorry." Dallas laughed and ran her hand down his arm. "I get on my soapbox, and I can't shut up."

"I kind of like you on a soapbox," he teased, catching her hand.

*Mommy and Aedan sittin' in a tree,* Kenzie sang in his head. *K-I-S-S-I-N-G.*

*Mind your own beeswax, you little booger,* Aedan telepathed.

Kenzie broke into audible laughter, and Dallas whipped around, grinning. "I've never heard her laugh out loud in public." She looked to Aedan. "See, I told you she likes you. She never likes anyone."

"That's because I'm a likeable guy," he quipped. "So, what shall we do this afternoon? Make sandcastles? Rent bikes?"

"We're not going anywhere with you." Dallas laughed, swinging their hands. "I've got stuff to do at the bar. Brunch is over."

"You like to ride bikes, Kenzie? How about ice cream? Nice and smooth and not a lot of chewing involved. Bet you like ice cream. Maybe bikes, then ice cream? Then we can do what needs to be done at the bar, as a team. Or your mother can just kick me out. After ice cream."

Kenzie trotted up beside her mother and looked up at her expectantly. Dallas stared at her daughter, obviously pleasantly surprised. "Have you got her under some kind of spell? She wants to ride bikes." She shook her head. "This is crazy. She never opens up like this."

He leaned back so Dallas couldn't see him and winked at Kenzie. "Guess it's my charm."

Aedan returned to Peigi's late in the afternoon. When he entered the cottage, he heard the familiar sound of automatic weapon fire. He walked into the den and found it full of teenage vampires. Brian and Katy's Pete were both sitting on the floor in front of the TV with game controllers in their hands. Victor sat in a recliner, watching with obvious interest. Kaleigh, Katy, and Lia were all on the couch, cell phones in their hands.

"Get him!" Victor shouted. "Yes!" He pumped his arm.

Aedan hung in the doorway. Victor seemed to be adjusting pretty well to his rebirth; apparently Brian's idea of bringing him here had been a good one.

" 'Black Ops'?" Aedan asked, just wanting to make conversation with Victor.

"No, 'Modern Warfare 3.' The newer one." He watched the TV screen. "Grenade! Grenade! Pete, you gotta throw a grenade in those situations."

Aedan eyed the girls on the couch, an eyebrow raised. Lia giggled.

"You still here?" he asked her.

"I'm going back tomorrow. But just for exams. Then I can come home to Clare Point for the summer."

"Maybe for good," Katy put in. "If we can find someone here willing to be her guardian until she's twenty-one, she might be able to stay. She has one more year of high school, and then she could go to community college with me. Hey, you want to be her guardian?" she asked with sudden enthusiasm. "You know, anyone can do it. You just have to ask the General Council."

"I hear Mary Hall wouldn't vote to make him guardian of a puppy," Kaleigh quipped.

Aedan ignored the wisewoman. "I would if I could." He looked to Lia, whose face had brightened, then fallen. "But I'm just on hiatus. I'm scheduled to return to Paris in a few months."

"But that stuff's not written in stone. Fin's talking about going back on assignment so he doesn't have to stay on the police force. He could go in your place, and you could take his job," Katy suggested. "Then Lia could live here with you and Peigi."

"I think there are people here more qualified to be a guardian than I am."

"He wouldn't be that much fun, anyway." Katy looked at Lia. "We'll find someone, don't worry."

Aware he'd been dismissed, Aedan looked down at Kaleigh, who was speed-texting. "Peigi around?"

"Kitchen." Kaleigh looked up from her phone. "You missed taco night."

He frowned. "Do you have a home, little girl?"

Kaleigh grinned. "Yup. Just don't want to go there. I'm supposed to be cleaning my room. And Peigi's tacos are way better than my mom's. She's probably still in the kitchen. She's making cookies."

"School night," Aedan warned as he headed for the kitchen. "I want everyone out of here before midnight."

"Bring us cookies!" Kaleigh shouted after him.

He found Peigi in the kitchen, already in her plaid robe and slippers. She was seated at the kitchen table with paperwork spread all over the it.

She looked up when he walked in. "You have a good day?" she asked. "You didn't say where you were going. I thought you'd be home sooner."

The kitchen smelled of fresh chocolate chip cookies. He walked to the stove and slid a warm cookie off a baking sheet. "Just hung out with a friend. Victor looks good. Seems clearheaded. Kind of happy."

She looked down at a paper in front of her. "Pretty amazing, isn't it? Victor falls into line easy as pie, and my Brian has got to be a royal pain in my you-know-what." She checked something off with a pen. "This morning he asked me if he and Victor could go to Afghanistan. Something about being mercenary soldiers. Is he out of his mind?"

Aedan laughed and grabbed another cookie. "Hang in there. It'll get better. You know it will," he said, heading out of the kitchen. He thought he'd turn in early, surf the Internet for a while, and then go to sleep. "It always does."

"I hope you're right, because the way things are going right now, he's going to run me into an early grave." Realizing what she' d said, she chuckled, looking up. "Of course, that would solve all of our problems, wouldn't it?"

Not willing to justify that comment with an answer, Aedan left the kitchen. He ended up watching a movie via the Internet and turned off his light at eleven when he heard the three girls and Pete leaving.

Aedan's cell phone rang at twelve thirty-five.

"Yeah?" he said groggily. He hadn't even checked the caller ID, he'd been in such a deep sleep when the phone rang.

"It's Mark," his cousin said, his tone grim. "I need you at the hospital." He paused, sounding tired and discouraged. "He struck again, and I'm not sure this one is going to make it."

# Chapter 9

"Listen, I can't get you in right now." Mark rested his hand on Aedan's shoulder and steered him away from the emergency room registration desk. The toothpick in his mouth bobbed up and down as he spoke. "They won't even let me in yet."

Thinking of the injured girl behind those doors made Aedan feel small. Helpless. It pissed him off that Jay could make him feel this way. "She's that bad?"

They went around the corner so that they were near the doors that remained locked unless the receptionist at the desk, or someone inside, hit the buzzer to open them. Aedan could see the chairs in the waiting area. Some were occupied, but no one seemed to paying any attention to him or Mark.

"She's that bad," Mark said. "She's been sedated. No vital organs hit, but she lost an incredible amount of blood. She was just given a transfusion. She's apparently doing much better, but she's not out of the woods yet."

"Where was she when she was attacked?"

"First Street. In Rehoboth."

"Damn it," Aedan murmured, hanging his head. He and Dallas and Kenzie had walked down First Street today on their way back to Brew. It had been such a pretty, sunny, warm day. How could something like this happen on such a gorgeous day? He had felt so happy all day. Was this some sort of punishment for his happiness? He looked up at Mark. "You get to speak to her?"

"I don't think she'll be able to talk for a while. Her mouth is . . . pretty damaged." The police detective was quiet for a moment, both of them lost in their thoughts. "I think you need to see her. He got creative with his signature. I think he wanted to be sure you knew he was around."

"You think this is about me?" Aedan was stunned by the idea.

Mark plucked the toothpick from his mouth and tossed it in a nearby waste can. "I think it's a possibility we have to consider, Aedan. Looks like he's settled on Rehoboth Beach. Why else would he come here when he could have gone anywhere in the world?" He hesitated, seeming to want to choose his words wisely. "I'm not saying this is your fault, but I think he knew you'd returned home on hiatus. He knew you were here, and for whatever crazy-ass reason, he decided to make this place his hunting ground this time."

Aedan still couldn't get his head wrapped around the idea. "How could he have known I was here?"

"Who the hell knows? But I think he's making it into some kind of sick game."

"Because I've tracked him down twice and haven't been able to catch him?" Aedan thought out loud. "Because he wants to taunt me?"

"I don't know, Aedan." Mark clasped Aedan's shoulder. "Some days I don't feel like I know anything at all. Can you get in there?" He pointed toward the closed emergency room doors. "Just to have a look at her?"

Aedan glanced at the waiting room. The receptionist could see the locked doors, but not him. Some people in the waiting room could see him, but, still, no one was paying any attention to the two men near the doors. They were too caught up in their own personal traumas, whatever they were. "Where is she?"

"Curtain five. On the left. Just past the nurses' station."

"Got it."

Mark peeked around the corner at the receptionist. It was the same woman who had been there the night Teesha had been brought in. Tonight she was wearing hot pink scrubs. He turned back to Aedan.

Aedan was gone. In his place stood a woman somewhere in her early thirties, of average height, average weight, medium brown hair up in a twist with a pen stuck through it. She was wearing pale green scrubs and had a stethoscope around her neck. She would blend in anywhere in the hospital.

"Damn it, Aedan," Mark whispered under his breath. He looked away then back at him . . . her, again. "I hate it when you do that without warning me."

"Sorry," Aedan said in a woman's voice. "Where did he leave his signature?"

"Left side." He touched his abdomen.

Aedan leaned to one side, to see around Mark. "Can you hit the door?" he asked the receptionist in the same female voice.

The receptionist barely glanced up. She could never have identified the nurse she'd given access to the ER, if later asked. There was a loud buzz, and the automatic doors slowly swung open with a pneumatic hiss. Aedan strolled through them, walking with purpose, pretending he belonged there. Most times that was the trick—just look like you knew what you were doing and no human would question you.

The doors closed behind Aedan, and he went down the hall. The ER was busy, but not hectic, not like on a Saturday night, or worse, a full moon. The doctors, nurses, and technicians he saw were all actively engaged in caring for patients; no one was standing around shooting the breeze or waiting for coffee. Their movements were orderly and organized. The hall and open area around the nurses' station was alive with sounds: voices, the beep of monitors, the squeak of new sneakers, the moans of a patient in pain. A doctor and two nurses stood at the nurses' station, talking quietly as they looked over a chart. An orderly pushed a young man with a bandaged ankle up the hall in a wheelchair toward radiology. To his right, from behind the curtain of one of the examining rooms, Aedan heard an elderly woman gently reassuring someone; her husband, he guessed.

At exam room five, which was just a cubicle with a privacy curtain, Aedan stopped, checked to see if anyone was watching him, and quickly entered past the half-drawn curtain. He walked directly up to the IV machine on the patient's left side and rested his hand on it as if making an adjustment. He glanced at the woman lying in the bed. Her entire face was covered with loose pads of damp gauze, many of which were stained with blood. Both eyes were shut, but one was so swollen that he doubted she could have opened it if she tried.

"Ah, sweetheart," he murmured. With a sigh, he lifted the sheet. She was wearing a hospital gown, but it was draped over her so that her left side could be covered with saline-saturated gauze and yet the gown would still provide some modesty. He pulled a blue disposable glove from a box on the shelf above her head and snapped it on; he didn't want to risk compromising the wound in any way. He just needed to see it.

The wound was raw, but the J was easily visible. It was not, however, the crude initial Jay had left on Madeleine, or the hasty mark made on Teesha. Jay had taken his time with this signature; it was a large cursive J with an embellishment of scrolls around it. Cut with a knife.

"Jesus H. Christ," Aedan muttered, his hand instinctively going to the crucifix he knew was under his scrub top. He always wore it, no matter whom he morphed into. It helped ground him. Remind him of who and what he was.

Aedan gently covered the girl, arranging her gown and sheet, and pulled off the glove, dropping it into the nearest trash can on his way out. He strolled directly to the exit doors that led to the ER waiting room and hit the button on the wall that would open them. Mark was seated in one of the chairs on the end, but when the doors opened and Aedan walked through, he popped up, his face anxious.

"You get a look?" Mark whispered.

"Let's walk outside. I could use some air."

The police officer and the nurse in green scrubs walked past the reception desk, through the waiting room, and out into the well lit, covered entryway. Aedan moved to a shadowed area near a support pole, looked to be sure no one was watching, and morphed back into his own body. It made it easier for him to think.

"Jeez, that was awful," Aedan muttered, running his hand over his face.

"I hear you, buddy." Mark pulled a pack of cigarettes from his pocket. "Want one?"

Aedan frowned. "I thought you quit. I thought that was the point of the toothpicks."

"I cut down."

"You know how bad those things are for you?"

Mark lit up. "They're going to kill me?"

Aedan gave him a wry smile. *Vampire humor.*

"Listen, while you were back there," Mark said, exhaling a cumulus of smoke, "reception told me she's being transferred to Christiana Hospital. They're better equipped to handle this kind of trauma. They're going to send a helicopter."

"When?"

"Next few hours."

Aedan gazed into the darkness of the parking lot. "It could be days before you get a chance to interview her."

"I know." Mark inhaled. Exhaled. "So what do you make of it? Jay's artwork?"

"I don't know." Aedan shook his head. "It reminds me of the tattoos young girls are getting." He drew his hand down his ribcage. "You've probably noticed girls in their bathing suits on the boardwalk. The tattoos are getting bigger. More artistic."

"You think it means anything?"

Aedan grimaced. "To me? No. To him? Maybe. Like you said, he's a crazy killer. Who knows?"

Mark fell silent, enjoying the cancer stick that couldn't kill him. "Hey, I hear Victor was reborn. I couldn't make it the other night to the cemetery. How's he doing?"

"Well, actually. He's moved in with Peigi and Brian. He's adjusting better than Brian, although Brian went with me to retrieve Victor's body and the kid was decent company. He's just got some things to work through, you know?"

"We've all been there," Mark agreed. He exhaled and watched the smoke dissipate into the evening air. "So listen, I don't know when I'll get to talk to her." He tilted his head toward the ER. "I'll let you know when I get the go-ahead."

"What's her name?" Aedan asked, feeling guilty that he hadn't asked before. It was just that it was so hard after all these years. So many victims. Once he knew their names, they were with him forever. "I didn't even ask you her name."

"Maria Tolliver. She's twenty-five. We have no idea what she was doing on Rehoboth Avenue. She's from New Brunswick, New Jersey. Her parents are on their way now. They'll meet her up at Christiana. How about if we talk in the morning?"

"You want me to start checking hotels for guys staying alone?"

"No. Let my guys do it. You're on the case because you'll be the one to take care of him when we catch him. High Council approved the kill fifty years ago." He hesitated. "You want to meet me at the crime scene?"

"I might," Aedan agreed, "but you know nothing's going to be there. Because there never is," he finished quietly. He walked off into the dark, thinking of pretty Maria Tolliver, who would probably live but would never be pretty again.

"No, we're not going to brunch at Victoria's." Dallas snatched two waffles from the toaster and dropped them onto a paper plate. "Waffles, plain, no syrup, no butter, that's what you ordered." She pushed the plate in front of Kenzie, seated at the round plastic table bought at a local hardware store.

It was meant for a porch or patio, but it worked fine in the small apartment kitchen, and it was easy to clean. When they had left Rhode Island, they had left without much of anything, just clothing and a few personal items. No furniture, except for Kenzie's bed. The apartment was nice, freshly painted, hardwood floors. Dallas just hadn't had the time to furnish it. There was patio furniture in the living room, too. Purchased the same day, at the same hardware store. Big warehouse clearance.

Kenzie pushed the waffles with a plastic fork. "I want to go to brunch," she said in her gravelly voice.

"It's Monday." Dallas poured herself a big mug of coffee from a French press. "Victoria's doesn't have their fancy brunch on Mondays. Just Sundays. And if you don't eat your waffles quickly, you're going to be munching on them in the car. It's time for school."

Kenzie studied the waffles on the plate stubbornly. "Aedan likes brunch. He likes me."

Dallas added a big splash of half-and-half to her coffee. Cream, no sugar. "You're certainly the Chatty Patty," she remarked, a bit astonished. Kenzie could go days without speaking to anyone, including her. She rarely initiated conversations. Certainly not conversations like this. Like real conversations between a mother and her ten-year-old daughter. "Aedan does like you."

Kenzie put her hands in her lap, losing interest in the toaster waffles. "He wants to kiss you."

"Kenzie!" Dallas was surprised to feel her cheeks grow warm. What had gotten into this kid? Dallas was on one hand delighted, on the other completely perplexed by her daughter's communicative behavior.

"You *should* kiss him."

"Come on, let's go." Dallas scooped the waffles up off her daughter's plate, bit into one, and dropped the other into a Ziploc bag. Kenzie would have to eat it on the way to school.

Kenzie got out of her chair, running her hand over the bulldozer on the front of her T-shirt. No pink ruffles or Hello Kitty clothing for her. She liked motor vehicles and robots, particularly Transformer-type robots. She had a whole toy basket full of them.

Dallas mussed her daughter's hair as she walked by her. "You're weird, kid, you know that."

For once, Kenzie didn't push her away. "You're weird," she said, following her mother into the living room to get her book bag. "And you have a beard."

Dallas burst out laughing. She didn't know what had come over Kenzie. She'd been like this since yesterday, when Aedan had taken them bike riding, then for ice cream. Kenzie hadn't wanted him to go home. This morning, when she was brushing her teeth, the little girl had asked if Aedan could babysit her after school instead of one of the twins. She said she liked to *talk* to him, which was interesting because Kenzie hadn't said a word to him all day. Dallas had suggested she talk to Ashley and Amanda that they would love to talk with her, but Kenzie insisted, *only Aedan*. She said he *talked right*.

Dallas had no idea what Kenzie meant. Everything in Dallas's past warned her to stay away from this guy, that he'd mean nothing but heartache. But how could she tell him to take a hike? What if he had some kind of key to unlocking lines of communication with Kenzie?

Aedan parked his car on the Avenue just after dark. His intention was to cruise the streets on foot for a while and just take in the ambiance. He wasn't foolish enough to think Jay would walk up to him and introduce himself, but the more familiar Aedan became with the area, the better chance he had of finding Jay.

Later, he'd stop by Brew.

All day his thoughts had flip-flopped between images of Maria Tolliver lying in that hospital bed, and Dallas laughing, the sunlight shining through her blond hair just so.

He was going to ask her out on another date. She had already warned him that she didn't go out. She had told him that her free time was spent with Kenzie. He could deal with that. A date didn't have to be dinner and dancing. Maybe he'd suggest they get Chinese takeout and rent a movie.

Aedan passed a surf shop that was already closed for the evening, like most of the stores; mostly just bars and restaurants stayed open after nine. The feel of the ocean breeze on his face, he turned right, onto a narrow, pedestrians-only street that featured tiny shops on both sides for a full block. As he disappeared off the main avenue, he morphed into the same young woman he'd portrayed as the nurse in the middle of the night. She was one of his go-to personas.

None of the boutique shops were open yet; it was too early in the season. There were signs in the windows and on the doors advertising everything from henna tattoos to Beanie Babies. The darkness didn't bother him, of course. But the narrow street, enclosed by the shop fronts, made him feel claustrophobic. Uninhabited all winter, the street smelled musty, abandoned.

"Hey, sweet thing. Wanna party?"

A man in his late twenties stepped out of a doorway, blocking Aedan's passage. He was tall and thin with dilated pupils. Aedan couldn't tell what he was high on, but he was high all right.

"Leave me alone."

He grabbed Aedan's slender wrist. "Got any money? If you got money, I know a place we can party."

Aedan didn't resist. "You really don't want to do this," he said softly, in the young woman's voice.

"I think I do," the guy said. As he spoke, he yanked hard on Aedan's wrist, pulling Aedan's slighter body against his. As he leaned down, breathing bad breath on Aedan's face, the flash of light that always preceded a morph went through Aedan's head.

Aedan had no fangs in morphed states, unless he was a saber-toothed tiger or a rattlesnake. He seriously considered the tiger for a moment, but since the old ladies in the sept were already upset about the gorilla in the park in Paris, he went with *good old reliable*.

Big, badass vampire.

# Chapter 10

Aedan lost it.

There was no other way to describe it. All he could think of as he spun around, morphing into his own God-created-first body, was that this could be it. This could be Jay, and if it was, he was going to kill the bastard here and now in this dark, cold alley.

Aedan grasped his attacker's shoulders and let out a threatening animal-like growl. The guy stumbled back, producing a knife.

Somewhere in the back of his head, Aedan knew it wasn't the right kind of knife, that this wasn't Jay. Jay used something very sharp, refined—sometimes a filleting knife, other times, a scalpel. This was a rough, crude blade. The blade of a *punk*.

Aedan felt the knife's bite on his upper arm, a superficial cut that angered him more than it hurt. He threw the guy backward, against a shop door. The glass spidered behind the knife-wielding creep's head, cracking but not breaking.

Aedan's attacker cried out in pain. And probably fear. Even in his drugged-out state, he had to be wondering how the hell a five-foot-five brunette female had turned into a six-foot-five vampire.

Aedan held the guy back, bared his fangs, and sunk them into the soft, exposed flesh of the guy's neck. The guy howled with pain, slashing wildly at Aedan with the knife. Aedan hit his attacker's wrist so hard that his hand flew open, and the knife hit the pavement and slid away.

Just as the other guy came out of the next doorway.

This was definitely not Jay. Jay worked alone. That thought went through Aedan's head as the guy behind him swung something. Aedan turned just in time to keep from getting hit in the back of the head with a baseball bat, but not in time to keep from getting clipped on the corner of his eye. His skin split and burst open, bloody.

Pissing him off even further.

Aedan grabbed the first attacker by his collar and swung him around, throwing his body full force into attacker number two. They had to be a team. Maybe rolling over guys, trying to get lucky with the ladies.

They'd not gotten lucky this time.

The two men fell to the ground, one on top of the other. Bat guy took one more weak swing. Aedan caught the bat in his hand and sailed it over his shoulder, shattering a glass window behind him.

A burglar alarm blared. Lights flashed.

"Jesus! Jesus!" the second attacker swore, struggling to get to his feet. "Let's get the hell out of here."

The first guy must have hit his head on the paved walkway. Though he was still conscious, he didn't respond. He tried to get up, but, pinned by his partner, he lay down, surrendering.

Aedan eyed the second guy. There was no need to take blood, but Aedan was furious. And the blood of the first guy had whetted his appetite. There was nothing like human blood. . . .

It was wrong. Totally unnecessary.

Aedan stood the second guy up against a brick wall. He sank his fangs into his throat. The blood was sweet and hot and—

He only allowed himself a small amount. Or so he

thought. But time played out differently in the moments that the human side of his being became lost. The guy's head suddenly lolled. He'd passed out from lack of blood. It took all the restraint Aedan could muster to pull back. The guy had just lost consciousness. He'd come back around.

As Aedan got to his feet, he wiped the blood from his lips. His eye was smarting, as was one cheek. He wasn't even sure what had happened to the side of his face.

A police siren whined, and he saw a flash of blue lights. Still breathing hard, he walked away, pulling his cell phone out of his jacket. His heart rate slowly came down until he felt like himself again. He dialed Mark.

"Hey," Aedan said when his cousin picked up. "Just wanted to let you know I ran into two hoodlums off Rehoboth Avenue. One had a knife."

"Jeez, please tell me it's Jay," Mark said.

"Unfortunately not." Aedan walked fast. Reaching the end of the alley of shops, he turned in the direction of Baltimore Avenue. "Just two punks looking for trouble. The first one was strung out. Probably the second one, too. We broke a store window setting off an alarm."

"So Rehoboth police are on their way."

He could probably hear the sirens in the background. "Yeah."

"You take any blood?" Mark asked.

Already, Aedan was feeling guilty. He wiped his mouth with the back of his hand again. "A little."

"Aedan. You're not supposed to do that."

"They took me by surprise," Aedan confessed. "They'll be fine. They won't remember a thing." Fortunately, bloodletting usually did that.

"Just one night I'd like to come home, put my feet up, and have a peaceful evening," Mark muttered. "All right. I'll take care of it. You okay?" he asked, almost as an afterthought.

"Took a baseball bat to the eye." Aedan touched his brow gingerly. The blood was already clotting, making a crusty mess. "I'll be fine."

"Call me in the morning." Mark hung up.

On the street, Aedan hurried along the sidewalk, head down. He could hear more sirens behind him. He ducked into Brew, and, keeping his head down, walked to *his* stool.

Dallas was at the cash register, her back to him, ringing up a customer's tab. Tat saw Aedan and nodded as he shook up a mixed drink in a cocktail shaker. Then he did a double take.

"Bleedin'," he remarked, indicating Aedan's eye.

"Yeah."

"Might need some stitches," he observed as he poured the drink into a martini glass and added a cocktail onion.

"Nah."

Tat carried the drink to a woman in her forties sitting alone at the other end of the bar.

Aedan glanced at Dallas. If she knew he was there, she hadn't indicated so.

As always, when in the bar, she was wearing worn jeans and a tight black T-shirt that he knew would feature the bar's logo on the front. The jeans fit her derrière just right, with the strings of her small waitress's apron hanging down the back. Tonight he thought about pulling the string of the apron, removing it. But he wouldn't stop there. Her hair was piled on top of her head, and he knew that when she turned around, she would be wearing no makeup. Just like Madeleine.

Except for the honey-flavored lip balm Dallas was partial to.

Even at this distance, he could smell the sweet berry scent of her drugstore shampoo. He could imagine how soft her hair would feel.

He shouldn't be here. It was wrong. A betrayal of

Madeleine. Of the love they had shared. He didn't deserve to be happy, not after what he had done. What he had allowed to happen. Aedan had himself almost convinced. Then she turned around, saw him, and smiled.

And all was lost.

Then she saw the blood, and her smile fell. But she didn't panic like some women might. Which he liked. But she didn't fawn over him, either. Which he might have liked.

"What happened to you?" she asked, walking from the cash register to the bar. She glanced in Tat's direction. "Can you take this to table seven?" she asked, sliding a credit card and receipt across the polished wood.

"Can do." Tat eyed Aedan but said nothing.

"Get into a fight?" Dallas asked Aedan, leaning on the bar to get a better look.

"'Fraid so."

"Hope the other guy looks worse."

He grinned. "They do."

*"They?"* She squinted, looking closer at his eye. "You were just walking down the street, minding your own business, and—"

"Wham," he finished for her, giving her his best "isn't that the damnedest thing" look.

"Seriously?" she asked. "You weren't in some other bar drinking someone else's Guinness?"

"I drink no one's Guinness but yours," he said, lowering his pitch, knowing how alluring a human could find a vampire's voice.

"You call the police?" She gently touched his temple.

"I'm okay," he said, hanging his head. He suddenly found himself thinking about the girl he'd seen in the ER last night. She'd been flown to Christiana and had undergone surgery. Mark hadn't had much more information. So that girl was lying in her hospital bed, her face cut up so badly that her parents probably wouldn't recognize her, and here he was, flirting in a bar. "I should go," he mumbled.

"Like hell." Dallas turned to Tat who was headed back, credit card receipt in his hand.

"I'm going to get Mike Tyson here cleaned up. I know it's early." She rested her hand on Aedan's, looking at her employee. "But do you mind closing?"

Tat glanced at Aedan, then back at her. "Not a problem," he said, sounding like maybe it *was* a problem. He was making it pretty clear he didn't care for Dallas's new admirer, and she was making it pretty clear she didn't care what he thought.

"Give me a holler if you need . . . anything," Tat said.

Dallas looked at Aedan and tilted her head in the direction of the swinging door that led from behind the bar to the kitchen. Aedan hopped off the barstool quicker than any fifteen-hundred-year-old man ought to be able to. He stepped behind the bar and followed her into the kitchen. It looked like any other small restaurant kitchen: a griddle top, a deep fryer, a salamander, some sinks, and an industrial dishwasher. There were two guys who looked like brothers working, one loading a dish tray to go into the washer, another dumping freshly fried onion rings into a plastic serving basket.

"Carlos and Miguel," Dallas introduced as they walked around a prep table, headed for a narrow hallway off the kitchen. "They see you following me upstairs. I holler; they come with baseball bats."

Aedan touched his eyebrow gingerly. "Been there, done that already tonight."

She cut her eyes at him but didn't say anything. It wasn't until they reached a staircase in the hall that she turned around to face him. "I'm not kidding," she warned. "You mess with me, you'll be sorry." She was standing on the bottom step.

He walked up to her. With her on the step and him still on the floor, they were almost the same height. "I like you, Dallas. I wouldn't do anything to hurt you . . . or risk another encounter with a baseball bat." He spoke slowly, softly. She was watching his lips.

It would have been so easy to kiss her.

She acted as if she was going to say something, then turned and took the steps two at a time. He knew he scared her. Which wasn't such a bad thing, because she scared the crap out of him.

She used a key in a door at the top of the stairs. "Amanda?" she called as she walked in.

"In the living room," a young woman hollered back.

Aedan could hear the sound of a TV in the background. The apartment was small, but nice, with hardwood floors and thick, craftsman-like trim around the doors and windows. It looked like Dallas had just moved in. There were boxes in the hallway. More in the doorway of the kitchen. She led him down the hallway to the room where Amanda was watching TV.

"Amanda, Aedan. Aedan, Amanda," Dallas introduced awkwardly from the doorway of the living room.

The woman, who Aedan assumed was one of Kenzie's babysitters, rose from the couch. . . . which was actually a piece of porch furniture with tribal print, brown indoor/outdoor cushions on it. There was a matching glider chair.

"Nice to meet you." She glanced at the TV, then back at Dallas.

She was watching a rerun of an HBO show that Aedan was familiar with. He wasn't big on TV, but he knew this show because it featured vampires. The show was a constant source of amusement among his friends and family.

"Everything okay?" the slender woman in her early twenties asked.

"Yup. Everything's good."

Amanda checked out Aedan's eye.

"He got into a fight," Dallas explained. "Boys."

Amanda chuckled.

"So, I thought you might want to go home early. I'm going to help him clean up his face and then we might . . . kick back," Dallas said, as if she needed to explain herself to her babysitter.

"Sure. Cool." The young woman grabbed a textbook off the tile top coffee table, which also appeared to have come from Lowes. She tucked the book into a backpack on the floor and heaved the bag onto her shoulder. "Ashley's coming tomorrow."

"Good. Great." Dallas followed Amanda down the hall.

"Nice to meet you," Amanda called back to Aedan.

"Nice to meet you. Be safe going home."

"Have Tat or one of the guys in the kitchen walk you to your car," Aedan heard Dallas say.

The door closed, but Dallas didn't come right back. He heard her go into the kitchen and open and close cabinets. She got ice from the icemaker. He sat down on one end of the couch, which was surprisingly comfortable. Shifting his weight, he touched his eyebrow. It was really beginning to swell. Damn, but it hurt.

Aedan closed his eyes. He felt weird, sitting here in Dallas's apartment. It smelled like her: fresh, clean . . . mysterious.

He shouldn't be here. But he couldn't make himself get up off the couch. He couldn't leave.

He thought about Kenzie, asleep in her bedroom. He liked the little girl. She was unusual. Not that her autism made her unusual, though he'd never met anyone with autism before. What made her even more unusual was that he didn't meet many humans with her kind of telepathic power. But it was worrisome, too. What she had said about *him* being out there. Aedan had tried to question Kenzie later that day about what she had said, verbally as well as telepathically. She had ignored him, leaving him with more questions than answers.

"Please tell me you're not the kind of guy who gets into bar fights," Dallas said, walking into the living room carrying a Ziploc bag of ice, some paper towels, and a tube of ointment.

"I'm not the kind of guy who gets into bar fights," he repeated.

Dropping the things onto the coffee table, she sat down beside him and grabbed a paper towel. It was wet. She turned to him, paper towel poised. "I'm serious. My husband had a brother who used to get into fights all the time. I hated it. I can't tell you how many times we bailed him out of jail or picked him up at the ER."

"You have a husband?" Aedan asked, suddenly feeling uncomfortable. He didn't do that.

"You ask now?"

He shrugged. "You've made references to Kenzie's father, but you didn't really say if you were—"

"A loose woman?" Raising an eyebrow, she hesitated, then pressed the wet paper towel to the cut above his eye, none too gingerly.

He made certain she wouldn't be able to see into his past. It was easy with her, a lot easier than with nosy vampires.

"Ouch." He flinched. The coldness and the pressure of her hand stung.

"Big man can get into a fight in a bar, but he can't take a little warm water?"

"Back to the part about your having a husband," he said, squinting from the bad eye.

"Kenzie's father, my husband. Deceased." She rubbed the cut with the paper towel.

He cursed under his breath. "Ouch. Damn it! That hurts

more than getting hit did." He grabbed her wrist and lowered her hand.

She looked into his eyes.

"You want to tell me about Kenzie's father?"

"Nope. Not ever. You want to tell me about this fight you got into?"

"I can explain," he said quietly, still holding on to her wrist. "I don't usually do things like that." Which was sort of a lie, wasn't it? But he couldn't explain the whole "protecting God's humans" thing, could he? And the whole stalking, death sentences, and ceremonial killing knives would really muddy the waters.

"I don't want to hear it."

"You don't?" He leaned over her, pulling her close until her lips were a breath from his.

"No," she whispered as his mouth touched hers. Her eyes were open wide, as if she was scared. But she couldn't resist him any more than he could resist her.

"Just don't fuck this up," she whispered. "You do, and I swear I'll—"

"You'll what?" he dared. And then he covered her mouth with his, ending the conversation.

# Chapter 11

Dallas felt as if she were falling as Aedan wrapped her in his arms and covered her mouth with his.

But it was a good falling . . . if that was possible. Like closing your eyes and letting yourself go, tumbling onto a soft, down mattress or into a bed of leaves on a fall afternoon.

He was a good kisser . . . just enough pressure with his lips. Teasing with his tongue.

It was so glorious to feel a man's touch, to taste a man's lips and not see images of his past in her head. For once, she felt unencumbered by, untethered from another's emotions. For just a moment, the briefest moment, her life was about her. About the intense feelings he was stirring in her.

When Aedan pushed her down onto the couch cushion, she didn't resist. She had no intention of resisting. She'd known that, somewhere in the back of her head, since the second time she'd touched him.

Dallas slipped her hands around his neck, her fingers finding the soft fringe of hair at the nape of his neck. He smelled good: woodsy, so male, and not at all artificial. He wore no cologne. He didn't need it. Not with all the natural pheromones this guy was putting out.

When he slid his mouth from hers, they were both panting. But one breath of air was all she needed. She inhaled his scent and guided his mouth to hers again. Now that this freight train was headed downhill, she fully intended to stay on it. It had been more than two years since she'd felt a man's touch or been touched by a man, beyond passing a fried shrimp basket.

Kissing the curve of her jawline, Aedan slid his hand up her ribcage and cupped her breast. A soft moan escaped her lips. What had ever made her think she should remain celibate? She liked this, liked it way too much.

She liked this guy too much.

Dallas pushed on his chest with both hands, and he lifted up, looking down at her. "You okay?" he whispered, gazing into her eyes with those big gorgeous blues of his. He stroked her cheek and brushed her hair back. "We can slow down if you want."

"Slow down?" She reached down, grabbed the hemline of her Brew T-shirt, and shimmied out of it. "I was thinking speed up."

He looked down at her, a playful half smile on his lips. "It's okay? Kenzie, I mean."

"Sleeps like a rock." She threaded her fingers through his hair and met his mouth hungrily.

His shirt came off next. Then, her black, lacy bra. She'd always been one for nice underclothes . . . even when she knew no one would ever see them.

His chest was broad and rippled with muscles, genuine muscles, not the kind that came from steroids and a needle. With just a sprinkling of red man-hair.

He stroked her shoulder, caressed her breast, and then drew his thumb over her hard nipple, sending waves of sweet heat through her entire body.

Dallas knew she didn't have room for a man in her life right now. She didn't have the time or the energy. But no matter how hard she tried to reason him off her and out of her apartment, she couldn't reason away the fact that she was more sexually aroused at this moment than she ever recalled in her life. She'd always enjoyed sex. Sex had been good with John, but never like this.

Every time Aedan kissed her, touched her, licked her, she felt like she was melting, spinning, hurtling into a forbidden place she hadn't known existed. Had only fantasized about.

When Dallas tried to kick off her sneakers and couldn't get one dislodged, Aedan sat up and gazed into her eyes as he grasped her foot and slowly worked off the shoe. He helped her wiggle out of her jeans and then leaned down and kissed her flat belly.

It occurred to Dallas at some point that they might have been more comfortable in her bed. Or at least on the floor. After all, he was several inches taller than the couch was long. But she could barely form a complete thought; a sentence seemed beyond possibility.

The first time she came, he had barely touched her. She laughed out loud, surprised, relieved . . . she wasn't sure what. He held her for a moment, giving her a chance to catch her breath, and then he began to stroke her again, taking his sweet time, giving her *her* sweet time.

The second orgasm came on more slowly, but a lot more intensely. This time, tears filled her eyes.

Dallas caught one breath and began to fumble with the top button of his jeans, which were button up, not zipper fly. Why did that not surprise her?

Boxer briefs, of course. No surprise there. But pink elephants? She laughed as he swung his legs over the edge of the couch, stood, and slowly stripped for her. At that point, she could barely keep her eyes open, her lids were so heavy with passion, still unspent.

Clothes discarded, Aedan leaned down, kissed her again, and she scooted up on the couch, and leaned on the padded arm, making room for him over her. She parted her legs . . . and gasped as flesh met flesh.

Dallas was overwhelmed by the feel of him. The fullness

of her pleasure that seemed to ebb and flow like the tide on the beach. As they moved together, easily finding a rhythm, he tried to hold on . . . to hold back and prolong the sweet agony of it. But she couldn't help but move faster beneath him, pulling her heels into his back, sinking her nails into his broad shoulders.

She came again and heard him groan . . . but withhold. A few quick breaths and they were moving again. Her heart was pounding, swelling with the joy of feeling so close to another human again.

As Aedan moved faster, knowing Dallas was close to orgasm again, he tried to think of something else. Anything to keep from crossing the finish line too soon. Or biting her. Bloodletting was a part of healthy vampire sex, which was why he wasn't supposed to be having sex with a human in the first place. At this point, he didn't want to commit either *sin*.

He thought about the fact that he needed to change the oil in his car. He concentrated on Mary Kay's banana nut bread, at home on Peigi's counter. This technique usually worked, at least for a couple of seconds.

But not this time.

He pressed his mouth to Dallas's one last time, squeezing her breast. One stroke, another, and she was crying out, clawing at his back. He moaned with pleasure and released, still trying to keep his full weight up, off her smaller frame. They both shuddered, and he rested his head against the back of the couch, his eyes closed.

The moment was so intense, so utterly satisfying, that it took Aedan another moment to realize Dallas had stiffened beneath him. That her entire body was suddenly taut and quaking. He opened his eyes to see her staring at him. What was it he saw in her eyes? Fear? Not fear exactly. Something more complicated.

"Get off me," she whispered, her voice not sounding right.

*What the hell?* Aedan moved as gently as he could, separating their damp, hot bodies. "Dallas—"

"Don't say anything." She sat up. Her hands were shaking as she reached for her T-shirt on the floor. "Just . . . just get dressed and go."

"D—"

"Aedan! Please."

She sounded as if she might burst into tears, and he knew her well enough to know she wasn't the kind of woman who cried easily.

"Don't say anything." She pulled her shirt over her head, over her perfect, small, round breasts. "Just get dressed and let yourself out." Then she got up and walked out of the living room and down the hall.

Aedan reached for his underwear. He wanted to pretend he had no idea what had just happened. He wanted to pretend she was just embarrassed by the fact that she'd just had a sexual encounter with a man she barely knew. In the same apartment with her sleeping daughter.

But he knew what had happened. He knew all right. And it had nothing to do with the fact that she'd made the conscious decision to have sex with him.

This was his fault.

At that last moment, he'd been so wrapped up in his own pleasure, he'd let down his guard, and she'd seen something in his head. Who knew what? Did it matter?

As he stepped into his boxer briefs, he realized he was still wearing his socks. What kind of man made love to a woman stark naked, but wearing socks?

He pulled on his jeans and buttoned his fly, contemplating what to do next. He knew what he *should* do. He should go down the hall and enter Dallas's bedroom on the pretense of wanting to know what had upset her. When he got close enough, he would grab her, throw her onto her bed, sink his fangs into her, and drink her hot blood. It was what he had wanted to do all along anyway, wasn't it? The nature of the beast and all that?

Just the right amount of blood and she would become unconscious. He would then tuck her into bed, and when she woke in the morning, she would have no memory of the couch. Or of him even coming upstairs with her. If anyone said anything to her later—the babysitter, the bartender—when she realized she couldn't remember what had happened, she'd be too embarrassed to say so. It was always that way with HFs. They never trusted their own senses.

He fished his shirt out from under the coffee table, spotting the ice bag she'd made. The ice was melting, sweating on her table. He picked it up, along with the blood-tinged paper towel, and carried them to the kitchen. Buttoning his shirt with one hand, he stood in the dark kitchen and poured the ice into the sink. Back in the living room, he sat on the living room couch that should have been on a deck or a patio and put on his shoes. He shrugged on his leather jacket and went down the hall.

He should have ended his relationship with Dallas then and there. Instead, he went out, locking the door behind him, and wondered what she would say to him if he dared ever show his face in her bar again.

*I am bored tonight. I sit in front of the TV in the rented condo and flip through the channels. A few days ago, the TV fascinated me. So bizarre, so mesmerizing. Not only wildlife shows, music videos, and reality venues, but pornography. Channels and channels of pornography.*

*But pornography does not hold my focus long. My attention strays. I think of the girl with the honey brown hair. How unsuspecting she was. How frightened and big her eyes became when she realized what was happening. When she saw the knife.*

*I smile.*

*The thought of the knife makes me smile. It makes my heart pound.*

*Her heart pounded. I felt it through her clothing.*

*I told her not to scream, and unlike the first, she did not. She must have had it in her pretty little head that if she did what I said, it would go better for her. That was, of course, not the case.*

*By the time she did scream, I had already gagged her. Her blood had already begun to trickle . . . then to flow, as I did that which I must do.*

*The women struggle at first, but it never lasts long. Eventually they become too weak, or they pass out from the pain.*

*I am always disappointed when they go too soon. This one did not, however. She was strong and brave . . . and in the end, very ugly like all the others.*

*I hit the Off button on the TV remote, and the room goes black. I like the velvety darkness. It reminds me of home.*

*But I will be home soon enough. Soon enough, for it always seems to go too quickly. Like the blink of an eye. So many females to choose from. So little time to choose.*

*My thoughts turn from the humans to the others. Curious creatures, the vampires. This one in particular. Big and brave and strong, and yet so weak. So malleable in my hands.*

*I saw him tonight when I took a stroll. Was he looking for me, I wonder, or going somewhere?*

*Where might he be going?*

Aedan walked into the mostly dark house and followed the only light to the den, where the TV flashed. For once, there were no wayward teens there. Just Brian. Without speaking, Aedan plopped down beside him.

Brian glanced at him, then back at the screen. The volume was down low, for once. When bombs exploded and soldiers fell, the walls of the room didn't vibrate.

Aedan watched the TV screen sullenly. He was getting so he could recognize the games. "Modern Warfare 3." This game was too graphic for him, too. Too much like the real thing. He'd been on a few battlefields over the years: in the Americas, in Europe, in the East. Good guys, bad guys, it didn't matter. The blood was always the same. The tragedy of the loss of so much human life so deeply overwhelming.

"Victor gone to bed?" Aedan asked, watching Russian soldiers rush across the screen. *Russians invading America?*

Brian nodded.

Aedan nodded.

After a few minutes the explosions stopped, and Brian turned to Aedan. "Bad night?"

"Something like that," Aedan said glumly.

The thing was, it had started out so well. Maybe not the guys in the alley part, but all of the Dallas part. Aedan really felt as if they had connected, as if maybe they could have shared something, if only for a few weeks.

And he'd had to blow it by not keeping his sense about him at the big moment. What? Was he seventeen again and having forbidden sex for the very first time?

"Wanna . . . talk about it?" Brian asked.

Aedan glanced at the teen, completely taken by surprise by Brian's . . . momentary unselfishness. "Nah." He sighed. He wasn't even supposed to be seeing an HF; he certainly wasn't supposed to be *knowing* her, in the biblical sense. It was his responsibility to be a good role model to Brian, not show him just how many ways a man could screw things up. "Lady trouble," he explained.

"Ah, got some of that of my own." Brian set the game

controller beside him, on the end table. "You want a Coke or something?"

Still in shock that Brian was behaving so . . . normally, Aedan nodded. "Sure." He pointed at the TV screen. "I thought you couldn't pause this thing."

"I'm outta lives. I have to start a new game." He shrugged as he got up. "No biggie."

Brian was back momentarily. He handed Aedan a can of Coke and popped the tab on his own and took a loud slurp. "I guess we can't do without them."

Aedan glanced at the teen vampire, not following.

"The ladies." Brian shook his head and took another slurp of soda.

Aedan had to contain his amusement. "I know I can't. As much as I'd like to." He paused. "You get into it with Peigi again tonight?"

"Sort of." Brian sighed. "Peigi said we should do something. You know. Together." He sounded slightly embarrassed. "So I said okay. Kaleigh said I had to at least be nice to her, you know, because we're married and all."

Aedan nodded and sipped his drink.

"So, I was being nice." Brian burped loudly and then went on. "She wanted to go to a movie." Again, a shrug. "So we went to Rehoboth. I even let her pick the movie. Some *chick flick*."

"The ladies love their chick flicks," Aedan commiserated.

"So we got popcorn and soda and stuff and went to the dumb movie. About halfway through, I had to take a leak." He frowned. "On my way back to the theater, I heard all this noise from another theater. You know, cool explosions and flaming fireballs and stuff. So I went in. Just to see. It was this movie where these alien robots come down to earth and try to wipe out mankind," he explained, getting more animated. "It was really amazing. I didn't mean to stay. I just sat down for a minute. Next thing I know, the movie's over."

Brian was quiet for a minute. Aedan waited.

"So, the movie's over, and I go out in the lobby, and Peigi's there, all upset." He brushed back his shaggy hair. "Like, crying upset." He rolled his eyes. "She thought I was lost or I left or something. Like I could get lost at the movies." He crushed his empty soda can against his forehead. "I told her I was sorry. I didn't mean to like, scare her or anything. I just wanted to see if the robots were going to kill all the humans. They didn't." He set the can on the end table where there were several other empties. "She was really mad. She didn't talk to me all the way home in the car. Then she just went upstairs. And now . . ." He sighed, picking up his game controller. "I don't know what I'm supposed to do. I should never have agreed to go to the stupid movies with her in the first place."

Brian punched a button on the game controller, and the TV screen changed. BLACK TUESDAY flashed on the screen.

Guessing the conversation was over, Aedan got up, taking his can with him. "Guess I'm going to bed."

"Later, man."

Avatars spun on the TV screen as Aedan left the den for the quiet darkness of his room to worry over his own lady trouble.

*Aedan held Dallas close in his arms, her naked body, still dewy with their lovemaking, pressed against his. He kissed her bare shoulder, and her long, blond hair tickled his nose.*

*"It's all right, you know," she said, covering his hand with hers. She pressed her bare, curvy buttocks into his groin.*

*"Mmm?" he murmured, sleepily. They'd nap and then make love again.*

*"That life changes."*

*"No," he argued, closing his eyes. "I want nothing to change. I want to lie here forever." He stroked her breast. "I'm never going to let you go."*

*She laughed and rolled over in his arms until they were nose to nose. "Life always changes,* mon amour. *It can never stay the same."*

*He opened his eyes and saw that he was not looking into Dallas's face, but Madeleine's. He let go of her in surprise. "Madeleine."*

*"You'll not forget me." Her tone was kind, rather than jealous or condemning.*

*"No, I never will."*

*He felt her lips on his, and then she faded away into the darkness of his dreams.*

The next morning when Aedan came downstairs around nine, Peigi was gone, and Brian was asleep on the couch in the den. Aedan shut the TV and game station off to give them both a rest and went into the kitchen to make himself a protein shake. Mark called just as he was loading the dirty dishes into the dishwasher. Mark was headed up to Christiana Hospital, hoping to speak to Jay's latest victim. He promised to give Aedan a call later in the day.

Antsy and not sure how he was going to spend his day, Aedan headed to the gym. It was new in town; Tavia, owner of the vampire bar in town, had just opened it in the spring. He hit the elliptical for forty-five minutes, headphones in his ears, and then headed for the free weights.

Aedan wasn't big on cardio. In fact, he hated it. He did it to keep his body in decent shape so he could deal with jackasses like the ones last night, and with more dangerous enemies. But he liked lifting weights. It gave him time to think, or not think, depending on what he needed. This morning, he just wanted to listen to his music. He was zoning out on the bench press, working his way through a set, when someone jerked one earbud out of his ear from behind.

It startled him more than anything else.

"What the hell?" Still holding the barbell over his head, he arched his neck. "Dallas?"

# Chapter 12

"What are you doing here?" Aedan asked, surprised as hell to see her. "How did you find me?" He lowered the dumbbell to the safety rack and slid off the bench, coming to his feet. He grabbed the white towel next to his water bottle and wiped the back of his neck as he let his nerves settle. He didn't like people sneaking up on him, and he didn't like people in places they didn't belong. *Dallas didn't belong in his gym.* And she certainly didn't belong in *Clare Point*.

She put one hand on her hip. She was wearing jeans, flip-flops, and a cute top. With her hair down, she was mesmerizingly beautiful. And obviously not happy with him. "You want to talk here or you want to go somewhere else?"

Petey Hill, one of the cops on the Clare Point force, was working out on an abs machine. And watching Aedan and Dallas pretty closely.

*Problem?* Petey telepathed, obviously amused.

*No problem, Officer,* Aedan shot back, trying to sound casual and cool. He wasn't feeling all that casual or cool right now. Dallas was one pissed off HF.

Other people were looking at them, other vampires. The gym was open to visitors in the summer, but there were only locals today. He saw Rob Hill jogging on a treadmill. Eva, a redhead like him, was working a leg press and making no attempt to pretend to be watching the CNN program on the TV over her head.

*Tsk, tsk,* she telepathed. *Aren't you already in enough trouble with the General Council? Wait 'til they hear Aedan's got a hottie girlfriend. A hottie human girlfriend.*

*She's not my girlfriend,* he shot back. He looked at Dallas. "Somewhere else." He grabbed his water bottle. Now that his initial surprise had passed, he wondered why she was here. Well, he probably knew, but he was still surprised to see her. Most women would have waited for the man to come to them. "Give me a few minutes to shower. I'll meet you out front."

"You try to slip out the back and get away from me, Aedan, I'll find you," Dallas warned.

For once, Aedan felt a little like the hunted. He took a quick shower and walked out through the main doors and onto the sidewalk, carrying a gym bag. Dallas was waiting for him. Pacing.

"You want to go get a cup of coffee?" he asked her. "There's a little diner—"

"You probably don't want me in an enclosed place right now," she warned.

He didn't know what to say. What had she seen in his head last night? Now he was curious. Wary . . . but still curious.

"How about if we grab a cup of coffee and take a walk on the boardwalk?" He motioned toward the bay. "It's only two blocks."

She nodded her consent. He threw his bag into his car. They stopped for the coffee and then walked the last block to the boardwalk in silence. By the time they got there, he was nearly bursting with curiosity.

"Okay. First, how did you find me?" he asked. They

took the steps up to the wooden promenade that ran several blocks and started walking north. "I never told you where I lived."

"You told me Clare Point. I asked at the diner." She sipped from her cup.

"Someone told you where I lived?" he asked, incredulous.

They walked along the boardwalk, with closed stores on their left, the beach and the bay on their right. Most of the businesses weren't open on weekdays yet. It was a warm day; the breeze was pleasant.

"I look innocent enough." She gave him a fake smile.

He wondered which waitress it had been; there were no humans working in Clare Point. He was surprised, because Kahills were very private people, for obvious reasons. Vampires didn't give intel on other vampires, especially not to humans. "Someone told you where I lived?" he repeated.

"Apparently I was convincing."

He took a sip of coffee from the paper cup. He didn't even like coffee. It had just been the first thing that had come to mind when she said she wanted to talk to him. "And you found me at the gym by . . ."

"Brian, at your house, told me where to find you. He said he was sorry *we'd had a fight*. Exactly what did you tell that kid?" she asked.

"I didn't tell him anything about you," Aedan defended. Brian had answered the door? The day was filled with one surprise after another. "So cut to the chase."

She stopped, turning to him, coffee cup at her side. "You lied to me."

"About what?"

She brushed a piece of hair from her mouth. The wind off the bay was whipping it in every direction. "About who you are."

"I am a PI. Of sorts." He ran his hand across his forehead. "Look, I don't usually work in the U.S., so it's complicated."

"I'm not talking to you about being a PI."

"Then, Dallas, I have no idea—"

"You should have told me you were a vampire."

Aedan did a double take. He wouldn't have been more surprised if she'd turned into a water buffalo and charged off across the beach. "What?" he said under his breath.

She glanced around. There was no one around to hear them. The boardwalk was pretty much deserted. It would be crazy busy in six weeks, but it was dead on a Tuesday morning.

She looked up at him, her eyes teary. "You should have warned me you were a vampire." She sniffed and looked away, wiping her nose with the back of her hand. "I had a right to know, Aedan."

So shocked he didn't know what to say, he walked over to a wooden bench facing the water and sat down. She sat down beside him.

He wasn't sure what to do. Deny it? That seemed silly, at this point. Last night she had obviously seen something in his head. Seen him in his true state, maybe?

"Dallas, I—"

"I don't want your lies. Not even for my own good." She looked at him. "Aedan, I know they exist. That you exist . . . I met one once. In a bar in Boston." She pressed her lips together. "My . . . ability. It apparently opens me up to . . . I don't know what you want to call them. *Supernatural beings*." She met his gaze. "You should have told me."

He set his paper cup near his foot. "How?" he asked, suddenly feeling very old and . . . very vulnerable. "How was I supposed to tell you? I'm not supposed to be with you, you know that, right?"

"I could guess," she said softly.

He looked at her, not sure what to say next. Where to go from here. Did he just take her now and get the bloodletting over with? Obviously he couldn't just let her walk around Rehoboth Beach *knowing* he was a vampire.

But Madeleine had known. The world had been different then: less modern, more superstitious. It had been a time when humans believed in vampires and werewolves and such.

"I didn't mean to take advantage of you," he said, surprised by the emotion that welled in his throat. He looked down at his hands, helpless, in his lap. "I guess there's something about you that . . ."

He didn't know how to explain it. The connection he felt to Madeleine through her. The guilt. The profound loneliness he sometimes felt, a loneliness that went to the depths of his very soul. And the ray of sunshine she seemed to be.

"I understand."

"Understand?"

"What it's like to be an outsider." She slid her hand tentatively across the wooden bench seat and touched his hand.

He raised the wall in his head before her hand made contact with his, and when she looked into his eyes, she seemed grateful.

"I don't think I would have even minded—your being a vampire—if you'd just told me." She gave a little laugh and looked away. "I can't believe I'm having this conversation."

He gazed out over the bay, taking her hand in his. "Me neither." He frowned. His thoughts were bouncing all over the place. "So this vampire you met in a bar in Boston. He have a name?"

She chuckled. "Asher."

"Rousseau," he finished for her.

"You know him?" she asked.

He rubbed her hand between his. "It's a relatively small world, the world of vampires."

To his surprise, she laughed.

"I'm sorry Asher was the first of us you met. He's not typical. Not a typical Kahill, at least." He touched his chest. "I'm a Kahill. Originally, many centuries ago, from Ireland. The Rousseau brothers, they're dangerous vampires."

"Aren't you all?" she asked quietly.

He took in her gaze. "You're not afraid of me, are you?"

"You afraid of me?" she asked. "Of what I know about you? Of what I've seen? What I *could* potentially see?"

He sensed that while she might know that vampires existed, she probably didn't know the details of that existence. Not the truth, at least. He doubted she knew he could erase her memory. Of course the longer they knew each other, the less likely it would be that he could erase all memory of himself from her mind. It worked best on short-term memory.

He gazed out onto the water again, thinking of a day he had spent with Madeleine on the shore. It had been a day of laughter and swimming naked and making love on a rocky beach.

Was that what this infatuation with Dallas was all about? Trying to relive his short, sweet time with Madeleine?

Except that Dallas wasn't Madeleine. He knew that. And he knew he could never relive those days.

"Tell me what you saw last night . . . in my head."

She sighed and sat back, but still allowed him to hold her hand. "This is not getting you out of trouble with me," she warned. "You being all kind and sensitive."

He didn't say anything, and she went on. "The first time . . . I just saw lots of flashes of people, places. I knew something was different about you right away, from the overwhelming number of memories. And the clothing. People were wearing period clothing."

"Maybe I'd just been to Colonial Williamsburg."

She cut her eyes at him. "Authentic clothing. From different countries, different time periods. Not just you, but other people. Lots of other people. Which was odd."

"That doesn't make me a vampire."

"It makes you something not human."

"And last night?"

She hesitated. "I saw the man with the baseball bat. In that alley or somewhere. Somewhere close." She bit down on her lower lip. "It was just a flash, but I saw you attack him. I saw your . . . your fangs."

"And you weren't afraid?"

"No, not really. Emotions come with the flashes. I already knew you were a good man. Mostly, I was just pissed." She pulled her hand from his. "Because you lied to me."

"I didn't lie. I just didn't fully disclose. And again, how was I supposed to tell you? Why would I? You think I can walk around telling every woman I meet, 'Hi, I'm Aedan Brigid and by the way, I'm a vampire?' "

She looked away without answering.

"Do you think I can do that?" he repeated. "How many people would believe me?"

She smiled at that comment. "Not many I suppose."

"Not many." He smoothed the legs of his jeans. "I can't really go into the details, Dallas, but this is not just about me. It's about my family and my responsibility to protect them. And to conceal their identities."

Again, she didn't respond.

"Look, if you want an apology, Dallas, I'm willing to give it. I just—"

"I'm a witch," she interrupted.

"What?" He stared at her.

She brushed a lock of hair off her cheek. "In the spirit of full disclosure, I need to be honest with you. I was keeping something from you, too. Probably for many of the same reasons. And that is . . . I'm a witch."

"Are you sure?" he asked, scrutinizing her. "Because I've known some witches, and they were all hags with long, hooked noses and big, hairy warts on their chins."

She rolled her eyes.

"I'm not kidding," he said. "Where do you think stereotypes come from?"

He could tell she still wasn't sure if he was kidding or not.

"There are different kinds of witches . . . apparently. I'm not even sure I'm a witch, *per se*." She encircled her waist with her arms. "It's just what people said. Back in Rhode Island."

He sensed something tender about the subject, but decided not to push it right now. "Damned New Englanders," he muttered.

She smiled, and they were silent for several minutes, both watching the incoming tide, both lost in their own thoughts.

"So what are we going to do?" he finally said, turning to her.

"Do?"

"You know, *do?* Are you going to break up with me?"

She frowned. "I wasn't aware we were a couple going steady."

It was his turn to smile. "You know what I mean. I really like you, Dallas. I like Kenzie. And you and I . . . I think we could both use a friend right now."

"And there is the fact that the sex was mind-blowing."

Now he was grinning. "Definitely." He waited. "So, can I see you again?"

"I'll have to think about it." She rose. "I need to go. I've got errands to run and the fish guy to meet at the bar at two."

He got up, getting that he wasn't invited to walk her back to her car. "So can I come by the bar? Tonight?"

"It's a free country."

"I mean, can I see you?"

She turned around, walking backwards so she could face him, the wind whipping at her long, blond hair. "No, what you mean is, *can you have sex with me?*"

He thought for a second. "Okay. Can I?"

She laughed and turned away. "You vampires are pretty ballsy."

"I was going to say the same thing about you witches," he called after her.

"I appreciate your stopping by," Mary McCathal said, setting the teakettle full of water on the stove. "But I really am okay. Victor and I knew this was coming. I felt like we were ready." She measured loose tea into a china teapot. "If you can ever really be ready," she mused aloud.

"I know you're okay." Peigi took two mugs, one green, one yellow, off a mug tree on the counter and carried them to the small kitchen table. "That doesn't mean you can't use a friend."

Mary turned to Peigi with a smile. "I also really appreciate your being willing to take Victor in. That was one part of the plan we weren't sure about. I knew it would be better if he weren't here with me, but I wasn't sure who would be willing to let bygones be bygones and accept him into their house. People were pretty upset with us when we left. A lot of people are still upset."

"They care about you." Peigi pulled out a chair at the table and sat down. Mary's kitchen was cozy and had always made Peigi feel good. Maybe the wallpaper was a little worn or the appliances were a little old, but Mary's had always been a welcoming kitchen. Sitting here, Peigi realized how much she'd missed Mary while she was off on her adventure with Victor.

"That was Victor's chair." Mary's voice turned nostalgic. "He always took that seat."

"I'm sorry." Peigi started to rise. "Should I—"

"Oh, don't be silly." Mary gave a wave. "I was just thinking. That was Victor's chair. It's funny how we get possessive of such things. Bobby always took this chair." She rested her hand on the back of the chair across from Peigi and pulled it out to sit down. "Which I started sitting in after he was gone." She looked across the table at Peigi. "Victor never knew that. That it was Bobby's. I just . . . didn't want to hurt his feelings. You know?"

Mary stood back up and turned away. "How about a piece of key lime pie?" She opened the refrigerator. "I found key limes at the big grocery store in Rehoboth." She pulled a pie from the refrigerator. "I made two. I thought you could take one home. It's Victor's favorite."

"I'd be happy to take a pie home. There's no telling who will be there. Sometimes I've got an extra four or even six for dinner. Of course I never know if Aedan will be home or not."

"How is Aedan?" Mary took two small plates from the cupboard. "I know he's got to be upset about that monster's reappearing here."

"He is upset," Peigi agreed, thinking about the last couple of times she had seen Aedan. "But . . . I think he's handling the pressure pretty well."

Mary cut into the pie. "You don't sound so sure."

Peigi sat back, thoughtfully. "Something's going on with him. Something other than the case. I just don't know what."

"You ask him?" Mary slid a perfect slice of lime green pie with a graham cracker crust onto a plate.

"No."

"You . . . dig around in his head?"

Peigi glanced at Mary. "Most certainly not. It's not my place. I think we all need to do a better job of minding our own business in this town and staying out of other people's heads when we're not invited." She paused, knowing there was no need to go off on Mary. Mary was one of the smallest offenders. "I'm sorry. That annoyance wasn't directed at you, Mary. I'm just on edge about *everything* lately." She took a breath. "Aedan will tell me what's going on when he wants to. *If* he wants to. When he comes home, my house is supposed to be a haven. He's supposed to be resting. Recharging his batteries, regaining his chi . . . that sort of thing." She accepted both plates Mary handed her and placed one on her placemat, one on Mary's. " 'Course, I doubt he's getting too much rest in my house, the way Brian plays those video games all day and night."

The teakettle whistled, and Mary poured hot water into the teapot. "Aedan mentioned that Brian was having a little difficulty . . . transitioning. Is he doing any better?"

"Yes," Peigi said, trying to sound positive. She got up to get forks. Then, "No. Not really." She shook her head. We had a terrible . . . misunderstanding last night. I got upset." She took two forks from a drawer and sat down again. "I shouldn't have gotten so upset." She clenched her fists in her lap. "I just don't understand him."

"It's like that at first. You know that."

"Not like this." Peigi sighed. "We're so far apart. We don't seem to be able to communicate at all. On any level. The age difference feels overwhelming this time."

Mary covered the teapot with a quilted green tea cozy that said THE SUNSHINE STATE and carried it to the table.

"And he makes me so angry that I just want to—" Peigi cut herself off, angry with herself for feeling this way, but not knowing how to change it. Feelings were always like that. No matter how you *wanted* to feel, you couldn't control how you actually felt.

"Makes you feel like you want to what?" Mary asked.

Peigi dug her fork into the pie and pushed a cold, tart

piece into her mouth. She knew it would be delicious; Mary's pies were always delicious. But it tasted like stale bread in her mouth. "Do you ever think of . . ." She looked up, knowing she shouldn't be saying it, but feeling like she had to talk to someone before she burst. "*Re-adjustment?*"

# Chapter 13

"*Readjustment?*" Aedan repeated into his cell phone. He lowered his voice and glanced around. He was in the market in town, and he didn't want anyone to overhear. Fortunately, none of the customers, though all sept members, seemed to be paying any attention to him. "She used the word *readjustment?*" He put a large jar of chunky peanut butter into his cart.

With Victor in the house, it seemed as though they were going through a grocery cart of food a day. Aedan was trying to make things easier on his aunt in any way he could. He couldn't solve the problems between her and her husband, but he could shop for groceries.

"That's what she said," Mary McCathal repeated. "I shouldn't even have called you. You know me. I'm not a tattletale. I try to stay out of other people's business, but I'm worried, Aedan. I didn't know who else to call. She sounded serious."

He turned the corner into the junk food aisle and began to load up: corn chips, potato chips, pretzels . . . and cheddar cheese popcorn. Kaleigh's request. Apparently, there was no school the following day, and the teens in town were staging an *intervention* tonight. They were taking Brian's TV over at precisely 11 p.m. and were having a Harry Potter movie marathon.

"So exactly what did Peigi say about *readjustment?*"

"Nothing really. Just that she was considering it. I tried to get her to elaborate, but she changed the subject. Probably because of the look on my face. She wasn't really asking my opinion. I'm afraid she's already formed one of her own. You know your Aunt Peigi, she can be as stubborn as a wart on a troll when she wants to be."

Aedan sighed. This was bad. Bad for Peigi. Bad for the sept. Readjustment just wasn't done; the Kahills believed it was against God's will and that there could be serious consequences to the soul. He picked up two jars of salsa. Medium or mild? He added both and one of queso dip to the cart. "I appreciate your calling me about this," he said, pushing his cart down the aisle.

"I didn't know what else to do." She hesitated. "In normal circumstances, I would have talked to Victor, but . . ." She sighed. "Obviously that wouldn't be appropriate right now."

"Has she said anything to Brian?"

"I don't think so." Mary had sounded sad a moment ago, but now her voice was once again filled with concern for her friend. "I get the impression they're not talking much right now. She's very upset about some of Brian's attitudes and behaviors, but you're living there so you know that. I don't know why she's being so sensitive. These things take time. I tried to tell her that, but she didn't want to hear it." She hesitated. "What do you think we should do? She spoke in confidence when she mentioned . . . *it.*"

"I won't say a word to her, or anyone else, about our conversation," Aedan promised. "I'll just try to feel her out when I have the opportunity. See what's really going on in that head of hers."

Mary chuckled. "Good luck with that."

"Thanks for calling, Mary. I'll keep you posted." Aedan rocketed a bag of marshmallows into the cart and disconnected from Mary. He still needed sports drinks, chocolate bars, and graham crackers. Katy and Kaleigh had high hopes for a campfire in the backyard so they could make s'mores. It didn't seem like a guy thing to him, but if the girls could get Brian off the couch and into the backyard, Aedan was willing to support their efforts with a whole host of high calorie, high sugar-content foods.

As Aedan stood in front of a sea of cookie options, he thought about Peigi. He wanted to tell himself that she wasn't serious about considering readjustment. He wanted to believe that Peigi was too logical, too responsible to do such a thing. What scared him was that she was also passionate. Passionate about her centuries-long love affair with Brian.

He grabbed a box of graham crackers. Honey cinnamon? He returned those to the shelf. Chocolate graham crackers? Low fat? Where the hell were the plain old graham crackers?

His phone rang and half expecting it to be Mary again, he answered it. "Can you buy plain old graham crackers?" he asked.

"I . . . I suppose so," Mark answered.

Aedan scowled and threw a box of honey graham crackers into the grocery cart. He didn't know if he had everything he needed. What he did know was that he had completed his shopping experience. Next time, he'd just give one of the girls fifty bucks and send them shopping. Less frustrating, and from the look of the cart, it would have come out cheaper.

"Sorry, I thought you were someone else," Aedan said into the phone. "Did you get to speak to Maria Tolliver?"

"Nope." Mark sounded tired and frustrated.

Aedan headed for the checkout line. "I thought her doctor said she could talk with you today."

"He did. But by the time I reached Christiana, her parents had gotten her a lawyer, and they said she wouldn't be speaking to the police again without *representation present.*"

"What? Why the hell not? She didn't do anything wrong." Aedan grabbed a bag of mini Snickers bars and tossed them into the cart. For himself, not the teens. "She's not being charged with anything. She doesn't need a lawyer."

"I explained that to her parents. For forty-five minutes."

"Does she . . . do *they* realize this guy is going to attack another woman? That what she says might—"

"You're preaching to the choir," Mark interrupted. "And her parents are having her transferred to their local hospital, so if I do want to interview her, with her lawyer—"

"You'll be driving on the Garden State Parkway," Aedan finished for him. He began to load his items onto the conveyer belt at a register. "So you've got nothing."

"Nothing but what she told the uniform in the ambulance on the way to the hospital the night it happened. She was walking on the street, stopped to look at the heel on her shoe, next thing she knows, he's dragging her off behind a Dumpster. Oh! The one new thing I *did* get was that, according to her mother, he put something smelly over her face that made her woozy temporarily."

"He, meaning Jay."

"Yes."

"You think she was confused? She might have been given oxygen in the ambulance."

"The mother seemed sure it was her attacker."

"So she was unconscious when the assailant raped and cut her?" Aedan asked, putting the marshmallows on top of the crackers, instead of the other way around, to send them down the belt. "That doesn't sound like our guy."

"She wasn't unconscious per se when he did what he did," Mark explained.

Aedan sighed. "Just more easily controlled."

"And quieter. Our door-to-door got a report after Teesha's attack that someone in an apartment off the parking lot thought she heard a scream about the time of the attack. She actually considered calling the police, but her boyfriend insisted it was the neighbors' TV. Apparently over the winter she had called in a report of a woman screaming—"

"And it was a neighbor's TV?"

"Better," Mark intoned. "It was the neighbors making whoopee."

Aedan grinned. He was dry, his cousin; he still liked him. "Mark. People don't say 'making whoopee' anymore."

"Just repeating what was told to me."

Aedan watched the last of his groceries ease down the conveyor belt, and he pulled his wallet from his jacket. "So you'll keep me up to date?"

"Will do," Mark said. "Anything on your end? Got both of your bozos for crystal meth possession, by the way."

"They weren't *my* bozos. And I can pretty much guarantee you, Jay isn't on meth. Or any other mind-altering drug."

"Yeah. He's a creep all on his own." Mark hesitated. "You know it's not like me to stick my nose into other people's personal business, but that woman at the bar. The one I interviewed. Tell me you're not—"

"That whole not sticking your nose in other people's business," Aedan interrupted. "One of your finest qualities, Mark. Talk to you soon."

They disconnected. Aedan paid for the groceries and then headed home. The evening was quiet, until the teens started arriving around nine-thirty. Aedan stuck around to say hello and then wandered around the house, looking for Peigi. He found her outside in the backyard. She was already in her flannel bathrobe and slippers, but wore a down vest over the ensemble, to ward off the evening chill. A storm was brewing; Aedan could smell the rain coming.

"Don't know if they're going to get a chance to sit around a fire tonight," he said. Peigi was carrying sticks from a pile behind the shed to a place in the middle of the yard. "Looks like it might rain." He gazed off into the dark western sky.

Peigi didn't say anything; she just started dumping sticks into his arms.

"I was going to head out for a while. If you don't need me here." He chuckled. "I think Katy and Kaleigh have got things pretty much under control in the house. They've got some kind of countdown going, giving Brian ample time to prepare to have to turn off his game."

Peggy pointed at the pile of sticks she'd already made in the middle of the yard, and Aedan carried his bundle over. He dropped the armful and was just stepping back when searing flames shot up from the pile, into the sky, a good twenty-five-feet high.

"Damn, Peigi. A little warning, maybe?" He rubbed his forehead, taking another step back, the temperature was so intense. "I think you singed my eyebrows."

"They want to make s'mores. You need good coals. The fire needs to burn up, then down." She walked back to the shed and came up with a decent-sized log. She offered it to him.

"You're not going to light this while I'm carrying it, are you?" he joked.

She didn't even crack a smile.

Peigi had pyrokinetic abilities. She could light a bonfire in her yard or throw flaming fireballs across a battlefield with just a thought. The gift wasn't as helpful on the domestic front as it had been in war, but it was nice to never need a lighter to light a birthday candle.

Aedan carried the log to the fire and dropped it in. Peigi added another and stood beside him watching the flames lick at the dry wood, then pop and snap. The smell was heavenly.

"What's the fascination?" Aedan mused. "With fire? Not just for vampires, humans, too."

"Werewolves don't like fire," she observed.

He thought for a moment. "Good point."

She glanced at him. "I don't know what you're doing every night or who you're doing it with, but I do know you shouldn't be."

He glanced at her. "I'm working the Jay case."

"You didn't smell like serial killer last night when you came home. You smelled like human female. It's wrong, and you know it's wrong. Human/vampire relationships never work out. They don't understand us. They *can't* understand us."

He stared into the fire, trying not to let the guilt take hold in his chest. He wanted to go to Dallas tonight. He wanted to see her. Hold her. Make love to her.

"If it's sex and blood you're looking for, there's plenty of willing women in town," Peigi observed.

"It's not like that with her."

"It always ends up being *like that*. We're vampires. We drink blood. We crave human blood most of all. The cravings never go away, Aedan. You know it. I know it. Sometimes those feelings sleep." She crossed her arms stubbornly over her bosom. "But they never go away. We all fight the burning desire for human blood. Even old ladies like me."

Aedan grasped a stick protruding from the fire and used it to push one of the logs. "This woman, Aunt Peigi . . . she's special."

"She's human."

He exhaled. "Yes, she is . . . I think."

"You think?" Peigi stared at him.

"You ever know any witches?"

"A couple. An ugly cuss in Cork. A couple in London. And there's that coven in Dover."

He smiled. "I mean, have you ever *known* one? Like been friends with one?"

"Witch is a broad term. Humans like to throw it around."

"I don't think she's really a witch. She doesn't cast spells."

"Sounds like she's cast one over you."

He smirked. "She has . . . a kind of *sight*."

"I don't care if she flies on a solar-powered broomstick." Peigi walked back to the woodpile, grabbed another log, carried it to the fire pit, and tossed it in. "She'll only leave you and break your heart, just like the last one."

"Peigi, that's hardly fair." He looked at her. "Madeleine was murdered. She didn't *leave* me."

"A broken heart is a broken heart." She turned and started for the back porch. "Throw a few more logs on before you go. Don't worry about waking me when you come home, whatever time the cat drags you in . . . or kicks you out." She opened the back door. "I have a feeling this bunch will keep me up all night, anyway."

The door slammed shut behind her, and Aedan did as he was told.

"Tat doesn't think I should let you upstairs again," Dallas said, tossing Aedan her bar rag.

It was midnight, and the crowd was light. A couple sat at one table, engrossed in an argument. Three young guys were laughing and carrying on and playing pool. Four women sat around a table commiserating on someone's breakup with her significant other. Them, and a guy and two girls at the bar, and that was it.

Aedan eyed Tat, who was rinsing glasses at the sink under the bar and racking them to carry them back to the dishwasher. Aedan wasn't sure if he was supposed to comment or not. After all, Tat was standing right there. He'd obviously heard Dallas.

Aedan played it safe, kept quiet, and began to wipe

down the bar. He assumed that was why Dallas had passed the rag to him. She was putting him to work, which he kind of liked. He wasn't just a customer anymore. Or the guy she'd had sex with on her couch the night before. He was something more to her. What, he didn't know.

"Tat doesn't think good-looking guys like you can be trusted. He thinks you're a love 'em and leave 'em kind of guy." She was lining up liquor bottles along the back of the bar, putting them in order for the next day's business: whiskeys together, vodkas together, and so on.

"I tried to tell him that was exactly what I was looking for," Dallas continued. "Someone to love me and then leave me the hell alone." She glanced over her shoulder at Aedan.

"I told you I would only be in town a few months," Aedan ventured, quietly.

"Hear that, Tat? A few months and he'll be out of our hair."

"I told you," Tat said testily. "It's your business what you do." He lifted the rack of glasses and headed for the kitchen, the tattooed muscles of his arms bulging with anger and effort. "I just don't . . . I don't fucking want . . ."

He couldn't seem to get out what he wanted to say, so Aedan said it for him. "He doesn't want me to hurt you. And that's nice, Dallas. That he's looking out for you."

Tat went through the door and into the kitchen.

"You shouldn't encourage him," Dallas said. "I don't need him to look after me."

"You don't need anyone, right?" Aedan said, half-teasing, half-serious. "Just you against the world."

She eyed him. "What can I say? My ex did a number on me. I found out my friends weren't really my friends. I've got no family. I've got no one to rely on but myself."

"You've got Kenzie."

"Who needs to rely on *me*," she pointed out, moving a

bottle of single malt from the group of Scotch whiskey blends to its proper place.

"She's one smart cookie." He walked around behind the bar to rinse out the rag. It was that easy. One minute he was at the bar, the next minute cleaning up behind it. "You might be surprised what she has to offer."

"You've never been a parent. You don't understand."

He stuck the bar mop under the running water and thought of the infant son he had lost. He thought of all the people he had lost over the years, vampire and human. He didn't say anything. He took the clean rag and went to wipe down the tables. Without any more serious talk, he and Tat and Dallas closed down the bar. It wasn't until Dallas was locking the front door behind Tat that she spoke again directly to Aedan.

"You coming upstairs?" She checked the double bolt a second time.

"That depends."

"On what?" She strolled across the dim barroom, keys jingling on her finger.

"Am I invited?"

She leaned against a wooden support beam in the middle of the barroom. "I wouldn't be asking if you weren't invited."

He stepped in front of her, caught both of her wrists, and pressed his mouth roughly to hers. "You're not afraid of me, are you?" he asked, as he drew his lips across her cheek to her earlobe.

She relaxed against the wooden beam. "No."

Her smell was intoxicating. Her neck throbbed where blood rushed through the carotid artery. He thought about what Peigi had said about the fact that their desire for human blood never went away. He couldn't deny that he wanted her blood, but he felt . . . in control. "Why aren't you afraid of me, Dallas? You know what I am. You saw what I could do. What I do. With those two guys."

"You won't hurt me," she whispered, breathing hard. She pulled one hand away from his, used it to guide his mouth to hers. Her kiss was hungry, aggressive for an HF.

"You don't know that," he panted when their lips parted again. "I've hurt people before. People I didn't want to hurt."

"But I have the sight," she whispered, then nipped at his earlobe.

"But not the ability to see into the future."

She teased his upper lip with the tip of her tongue. "What I have is better," she told him, still speaking softly. She rested her hand over his left breast. "I can see what's in your heart."

Then, before he could respond, she ducked under his arm and escaped. "I'll send Ashley down. You mind walking her to her car? Then come up." She headed into the kitchen.

Aedan waited in the semi-darkness of the barroom and wondered what he was doing there.

# Chapter 14

*I stand in the shadows of the inky night and watch the young woman walk out of the bar. It is late, and she should not be unescorted. But she is young and stupid. Someone closes the door behind her. Locks it. Locks her out and she walks down the sidewalk. She is on her cell phone and pays little attention to what is happening around her. She does not see the car pass and the three young men inside look at her with lasciviousness in their eyes. She does not feel my presence.*

*I am fascinated by cell phones, one of the many technologies that did not exist when last I walked this earth. I watch her for a moment and then fall into step behind her. She is pretty: tall, slender, with a certain sashay of her hips that emotes a young and tender age, but not so young that she cannot be plucked.*

*At first, it makes me happy to merely follow her. To watch. But then the anger comes. It comes almost out of nowhere, so intense that I feel my muscles clench. She makes me angry.*

*I wish I had my blade. If I had my blade, I could plunge it into her. Carve her flesh. I could taste the freshness of her cunny.*

*But, alas, it is too soon. I must be careful. Be smart.*

*And sadly, I must pace myself. My initial desire somewhat satiated, I can take a step back.*

*I am in a new country, a place I have never been before. So much to experience in so short a period of time. And what better way to taunt the vampire than to keep him off-balance, keep him guessing what I will do next?*

*That Statue of Liberty, of all things, interests me. Maybe I will go sightseeing.*

Aedan and Dallas made it to the bed this time. She didn't like doing it on the couch. It was bad on her back and made her feel cheap. Maybe she was cheap; so far, all he'd bought her was brunch and an ice cream cone. But this was no ordinary relationship under any circumstances. The witch and the vampire. Maybe HBO would make a series about them, and her money worries would be over.

Dallas had her T-shirt off by the time they made it into her dark bedroom. Her bra came off right after. She couldn't get enough of the feel of his hands, his mouth. She couldn't get enough of the feeling of not having to worry about what she saw because, when they touched, she saw nothing. Nothing but sweet darkness, almost like a wall.

Logic told her this was crazy. Even warned her that it was dangerous. Sex with a vampire? The logical portion of her brain, which was quickly growing numb, warned her of the danger.

But he didn't *feel* dangerous. He felt . . . safe. And Dallas needed so desperately to feel safe.

Aedan pushed her T-shirt aside with his foot and took her in his arms, kissing her mouth as he cupped her breast with his big, warm hand. The room was cold, and her nipple hardened even before he touched it with his fingertips.

When she pulled back a little, needing to catch her breath, she leaned against a set of plastic shelves on the wall inside the doorway. He kissed a path from the tip of her chin, along her jawline, to her earlobe. He tugged on her earring with his teeth, and she smiled. He'd unbuttoned his shirt, and she could feel his chest hair against her bare breasts, rough, but not too much so. It was just the right amount of sensation to make her heart beat faster and her breath come in little short bursts.

"How about the bed?" she suggested.

He pulled off his shirt and threw it on the floor. "I can accommodate that."

He crushed his mouth against hers; he tasted of Guinness. She liked the way he was playful when he made love to her. He wasn't too macho, keeping the testosterone at a reasonable level. He knew very well this was just a fling.

She almost laughed aloud at the thought. She was having a fling with a vampire? Had she known they were as well-endowed as Aedan was, maybe she'd have sought one out sooner.

She did laugh.

"What's so funny?" he asked in her ear. Then he looked down at her. Looked into her eyes.

"Me. Us. I was thinking that I'm in my bedroom about to have sex with a vampire. Do you know how crazy that sounds? Even to me, who has seen some pretty crazy things."

"Technically, I think you're already having sex with a vampire," he teased, unbuttoning her jeans.

She pushed him gently, both hands on his bare chest. "You know what I mean." She narrowed her gaze. "How do I know you're really a vampire? What if that's just your line?"

He closed the bedroom door, locked it, then caught her hand and led her to the bed. It was almost pitch-dark in the room without the glow of the hallway light, yet he seemed to have no problem navigating his way. "You know I'm a vampire, Dallas. You saw me that night."

"I saw what *you* think you saw," she challenged.

He spun her around and pushed her back. Her calves

caught on the mattress and she tumbled back, enjoying the momentary feel of weightlessness.

"An air mattress?" he teased. "Lawn furniture in your living room, patio furniture in your kitchen, and you don't have a real bed?"

She laughed with him. "What can I say? I left Rhode Island in a bit of a hurry. I haven't had time to shop."

"Fair enough." He flopped down beside her, kicking off his shoes, then sitting up to pull off her sneakers. "So back to this notion of yours that I'm not really a vampire," he said. "I'm intrigued. What would make you say that?"

"I don't know. What if you're crazy?" she said. "What if that was all in your head, literally? What if you just *think* you're a vampire, so those are the memories I saw?"

He stretched out beside her again, up on one elbow. She couldn't see him, but she could feel the warmth of his body next to hers and the weight of his body on the air bed. He drew the palm of his hand across her hips, hip bone to hip bone, and she shuddered with the pleasure of his touch.

"I cannot believe I actually confessed to a human that I'm a vampire and she challenges me as to the truth of it."

She reached out in the darkness and touched her hand to his cheek. He had a couple days of beard growth. "Do you have fangs?"

"Yes."

She dared to touch her index finger to his lips. "Will you show them to me?"

He leaned over her and she instinctively flinched, realizing she'd practically invited him to take a bite out of her. Instead, he gently kissed her chastely. "No. I will not." He stroked her thigh less chastely.

"Why not?"

He leaned over farther and kissed the swell of her breast. "Because it's a bad idea."

She ran her fingers through his hair. It was thick and soft, not wiry like some red hair. "Why?"

"Because . . ." He caught her nipple between his teeth and tugged. She moaned.

"Because," he repeated, "it makes me want to—"

"Bite me?"

He lathed her nipple with his tongue, his hand moving to her inner thigh. She could feel herself already wet for him. Truth was, she'd been wet since he had walked into the bar tonight.

"Something like that," he said.

"Would it hurt?"

"It depends how it's done. Why?" he said, resting his cheek on her hip.

He was playing with the pale tuft of hair between her thighs, making it difficult for her to think. "I don't understand."

"If I drink out of anger . . . or as a defense mechanism, there is pain for the victim. But . . . among vampires, when we . . . have sex, it becomes pleasurable in the act."

"With vampires?"

"We're only supposed to do it with other vampires. *Willing* vampires, of course."

"And it's pleasurable for them? For you, when you bite them and suck their blood?"

"Definitely."

"Could you make it pleasurable for me?" she asked with genuine curiosity.

He kissed the place where his hand had been, and she moaned again. His tongue darted out.

"I know other ways to give you pleasure," he said.

Which was completely true. By the time she climbed onto his lap, hot and sweaty, and stretched out over him, she'd come twice. She took him fully inside her.

Dallas reveled not just in the physical act as she rose and

fell over him, but in the emotional pleasure of a connection that didn't scare her or make her sad. How ironic that it would take someone not human to give her the human connection she had craved for so long. She certainly wasn't naïve enough to think this was love that she and Aedan were sharing on her air mattress, but it felt so damned good. So good, that she didn't want it to end.

Twice, when Dallas sensed that Aedan was coming too close to his grand finale, she slowed the pace. She moved fast enough, hard enough to bring herself pleasure, but not quite enough to give him his. Not that he wasn't having a good time. The way he groaned made her thankful for Kenzie's nature-sounds machine beside her bed and the fact that she slept like a log.

"What are you trying to do to me?" Aedan panted as she sat perfectly still on his lap, giving his pounding heart, which she could feel beneath her palm, a chance to slow.

"Trying to be a good partner," she whispered, brushing her love-swollen lips against his.

"Trying to get greedy is what you're doing!"

Aedan grabbed her so quickly that she couldn't put up much of a fight. Not that she really wanted to. She was all for trying different positions, but there was nothing better than the good old man on top scenario. He was good at maneuvering without losing ground. One second she was king of the mountain; the next she was flat on her back and he was penetrating her.

She cried out, sinking her nails into his back. He pushed harder, faster, and she literally saw sparks of white light as she came one last time as he enthusiastically crossed the finish line.

Lack of oxygen to her brain, maybe? Vampire voodoo? All Dallas knew, as Aedan rolled off her onto the mattress beside her, was that this was the best sex she'd ever had in her life.

"Sweet Mary, it's hot in here," she panted, resting her

hand on her forehead. "I need water, but I think I'm too tired to get up. You wore me out."

He rose, crossed the room, and opened the door. He was back a minute later with a glass of cold water.

"That's the sweetest thing anyone's ever done for me," Dallas said, sitting up as he offered the glass.

"I find that hard to believe."

"You've never met any of the losers I dated." She drank half of it before she gave the glass back to him and he finished it. Then he set the glass on the bedside table, which was definitely a moving box covered by a sheet, and drew her into his arms.

Dallas knew she needed to tell Aedan to go. She was so sleepy all of a sudden that she couldn't keep her eyes open. "I don't want Kenzie to see you here," she murmured, her eyes drifting shut.

"I understand." He kissed her temple.

She just couldn't keep her eyes open. She snuggled against him, feeling completely satiated; she couldn't move a muscle. "I'm serious, Aedan."

"So am I. I totally get it. We don't want Kenzie getting the wrong idea. Thinking I like you or anything."

"It's more complicated than that, and you know it." She rested her cheek on his bare chest. He smelled so good, even better now than before.

"Go to sleep," he whispered, kissing her again, as if she was special. As if she was loved. "I'll stay a while, and then I'll let myself out."

"Promise?" Her voice came out as nothing more than an exhalation.

"I swear it on sweet Madeleine's grave."

She wanted to ask who Madeleine was, but she fell asleep in his arms before she could get the words out.

The next morning, Dallas poured some Cheerios into Kenzie's plastic cereal bowl.

"Where is he?" Kenzie asked.

"Where's who?"

"Aedan."

Kenzie was wearing her favorite Batman T-shirt. This was the third appearance of the shirt this week, but at least she'd let Dallas wash it. "Aedan's not here."

"He was." She straightened her spoon up where it rested beside her bowl. She then sat back, looked at it, and moved it again, trying to get it just so.

"Sorry." Dallas reached over her daughter's shoulder and lined the spoon up parallel with the Spider Man placemat.

Kenzie liked certain things certain ways, and Dallas was learning to comply with some of her idiosyncrasies, those that were harmless, while not reinforcing others, those that were repetitive or antisocial. It was a subject being explored in the weekly parenting class she was attending at her daughter's school.

"Aedan wasn't here last night," Dallas lied, though why, she didn't know. It was nearly impossible to keep things from her daughter. Dallas never knew what Kenzie would pick up on and what she wouldn't.

At last satisfied with the spoon's position, Kenzie picked it up and dug into her Cheerios, which she ate with vanilla soy milk. Dallas poured herself a cup of coffee. She wanted to question Kenzie as to why she thought Aedan had been there, but she didn't dare. What if her daughter had heard the sex?

Dallas cringed at the thought. Kenzie knew nothing about sex. Her daughter didn't even understand relationships. The child had no relationship with anyone but Dallas, and sometimes Dallas feared that was an illusion, based on her need to see Kenzie as normal. But things seemed to be improving on that front; these morning conversations were proof of that, weren't they?

Seeing that Kenzie was almost done with the little bit of

cereal Dallas had put in her bowl, she held up the box. "More?"

"I don't like the bad man." Kenzie put her spoon down, in precisely the right place.

"We've been over this. Aedan is not a bad man."

"Not Aedan. The bad man." Kenzie stared off into space, using her mechanical "robot voice," as Dallas called it. She wasn't really talking to Dallas; she wasn't talking to anyone.

"What—"

"Tell Aedan," Kenzie interrupted, suddenly sounding angry.

"I don't understand—"

"Tell him!" the little girl screeched. Then she picked up her bowl and hurled it through the air, spraying the table and floor with soy milk.

# Chapter 15

Late morning the next day, Aedan stood at the sink in the upstairs bathroom, brushing his teeth. And smiling. Brushing his teeth and smiling. He'd stayed with Dallas until three in the morning, then kissed her forehead, tucked her sheet over her shoulders, and let himself out. He'd only slept a few hours, but he felt good. Clear-headed.

"I said I'd clean them up in a minute," Brian shouted from downstairs.

Aedan halted mid-upper right molars, then started brushing again.

"I know what you said. The same thing you said the night before about your dirty dishes," Peigi said. She wasn't shouting, but she certainly wasn't her calm self, either. "The same thing you said about your dirty clothes lying all over your room!" Her last words came close to shouting.

"It's my room! I don't see why you care where I throw my clothes!"

Aedan rinsed out his mouth and shut off the water, dropping his brush into the cup on the sink.

"Because it's my house," Peigi said.

Aedan walked out into the hallway, in jeans, but still barefoot and shirtless. He eyed the bedroom Brian and

Victor shared. The door was ajar, and Aedan could see Victor still asleep, sprawled in one of the two single beds.

"I thought it was my house, too!" Brian shouted.

Aedan closed Victor's bedroom door and went down the staircase. "Everything okay down here?" he asked.

"Does it sound like everything is okay?" Peigi, still in her robe, stood in the downstairs hallway outside the den, her hands perched on her hips.

Brian sat, surprise, surprise, on the couch in the den, game controller in hand. The TV was on, but he wasn't actively playing a game. Screens flashed, giving the player options in weapons: AK-47, AA-12, G36, ACR. Aedan wouldn't have known what half the weapons were, if pictures of them hadn't rolled by.

"I just asked Brian to clean up the dishes he and his friends left in the sink last night, and on the kitchen table and counters. And I asked him to take the garbage out." Peigi turned on Aedan. "Is that too much to ask?"

"How about if you put some clothes on?" Brian demanded, throwing his game controller onto the couch. "Could you maybe not walk around in your bathrobe in front of my friends? Is *that* too much to ask?"

Peigi grabbed the lapels of her robe and pulled them tight. "I'm not indecent."

"No." Brian barreled out of the den, headed for the kitchen. "But you sure are ugly, aren't you, you old b—"

Vampires are fast. Faster than humans. Much faster. And among vampires, Aedan was fast. He clamped his hand over Brian's mouth before the kid could finish another word.

"Hey man! Get off me!" Brian grunted from under Aedan's hand.

Aedan half pushed, half dragged the teen to the wall and pushed him up against it. He put one massive arm under each armpit and lifted Brian a good three inches off the floor. "That's enough. Do you hear me? I don't care how angry you are with Peigi, you don't speak to her that way."

"Why? Because she's supposed to be my stupid wife?" Brian said. He gave Aedan the slightest push.

Aedan pushed him hard enough to knock him against the wall. Then he did it again. He didn't hurt him, just got his attention. "No," he growled. "Because she's one of us and because if you continue to speak that way to her, I'm going to beat the shit out of you, that's why."

"Aedan," Peigi said, her voice filled with emotion.

"I've got this, Peigi." Aedan glanced over his shoulder at her. He was pissed, but she had nothing to worry about. He was completely in control. He hadn't really lost his temper; he just wanted Brian to know he had put him in his place. Sometimes a young vampire male needed to be pushed around a little. God knew there had been times when he'd needed it, and there had always been an elder to comply. "How about some tea, Peigi? I could use some tea."

She hesitated.

"Peigi," Aedan repeated. "Give us a minute."

Brian just hung there, back against the wall, cheek to the wall, looking in the opposite direction.

Peigi walked away, retying her plaid bathrobe.

Aedan waited until she stepped into the kitchen, gave the kid another gentle shove, and then he lowered him to the floor, took his hands off him, and backed off.

Brian just stood there.

"That was mean," Aedan said.

Brian chewed on his lower lip.

"You hurt her feelings."

"I'm sorry. I didn't mean to," he muttered.

He was quiet for a few seconds. Aedan waited.

"It's just that she acts like she's my mother or something," Brian finally said. "All she does is tell me what I'm doing wrong, what I ought to be doing."

Aedan exhaled. "I know this is rough on you. But you have to remember it's rough on her, too. Only a few months ago, she was taking care of you when you were ill."

"I didn't ask her to do that!"

"Actually, you did." Aedan hesitated. "Maybe we need to think about moving you. To another house. For a few months. Maybe a year."

"I don't want to go somewhere else." He eyed Aedan angrily. "This is my house. I like it here. I remember it," he said in a smaller voice.

Aedan studied the gangly kid for a minute. "When was the last time you slept?"

Brian shrugged.

"If you stay up all night, that's fine," Aedan explained. "It will take you a while to acclimate to a human's schedule, and even then, you'll struggle your whole life cycle not to fall into sleeping all day and prowling all night. But for now, if you're going to stay up all night, you *have to sleep during the day*. Like Victor. It's important that you get enough sleep, Brian. Plenty of sleep. Particularly right now. You're under a lot of stress. Your body and your brain are still going through the transformation."

"I wish you'd tell her that," he muttered.

Aedan just stood there.

"Okay," Brian gestured. "So, I'm sorry. I *am* tired." He rubbed his eyes. "I'll try to get more sleep. It's just hard. I've got so many things going on in my head." He brushed his hair out of his eyes. He looked exhausted. "And I'll try to do better about cleaning up. I told those guys not to leave that crap all over."

He started for the kitchen, but Aedan put his hand on Brian's back. "Why don't you head upstairs? Get some sleep and then clean up your room, take out the garbage, and clean up out back. *Before* you play video games. I'll take care of the kitchen."

Brian turned and went the other way. "Thanks," he said quietly, as he walked by.

"No problem." Aedan waited until he heard the bedroom door close, then walked into the kitchen.

Peigi was rinsing dishes in the sink and loading them in the dishwasher. The teakettle was on a burner on the stove.

"I'll do that."

"You don't have to," she muttered, lining up two plates on the bottom rack. "He's my problem."

"He's *our* problem." Aedan came up behind her, turned off the water, and gently escorted her to her chair at the kitchen table. "Sit," he ordered.

She sat.

"Irish breakfast or Earl Grey?" he asked.

"Earl Grey. And a shot of whiskey."

He chuckled as he retrieved the teapot and two mugs and set them on the counter. "Little early for that, maybe?"

"Early?" She rested her face in her hands. "Hell, Aedan. I haven't been to sleep yet."

He flipped on the faucet and began to rinse off the dishes and place them in the dishwasher. "If the teens were keeping you awake, you should have told them to pipe down. I'm glad they're taking an interest in Brian, and now Victor, but they don't have the right to take advantage of you."

"It wasn't them." She let her hands fall to her lap. "I feel as if I've lost my bearings. As if I don't know which way to turn, what to pursue next. And don't tell me it's just the *adjustment period,* because I'll not be pandered to, not about this. We've been through this before, Brian and

I, too many times to count. But it's different this time. *I'm* different this time."

The teakettle on the stove whistled, and Aedan put the last cereal bowl into the dishwasher, closed it up, and wiped his hands on a dishtowel with a robin on it. Sensing his aunt just needed him to listen for now, instead of offering the platitudes she didn't want to hear, he made a pot of tea.

"Ever since Brian was reborn, I haven't felt as if I was running the Council well. I'm impatient, disorganized . . ." She paused, thinking. "I feel like I don't want the damned job anymore."

He carried the porcelain teapot to the table and sat down. "So tell Gair you're ready to pass the position to someone else. You've been doing it for years. Someone else can take his or her turn."

"You?"

"Not me." He laughed, but it was no laughing matter. He loved his job as an investigator on a kill team. He'd never give it up voluntarily and certainly not to be a sept administrator.

"And I told Gair I'd had enough."

"What did he say?"

"That I was going through my adjustment period with Brian and that it would all be fine in a few months."

"But you don't believe that?"

She was quiet for a moment, and when she looked at him, Aedan found himself concerned. Her eyes were so sad. . . .

"I can't explain how I feel, Aedan. It's as if everything is off-balance, but I don't know how to find my feet again."

He poured tea for her, then himself. "Would you consider talking with Dr. Kettleman?"

"Me? A shrink?"

He shrugged. "Okay, so she's got the fancy psychiatric

education now, but she's always been our counselor." He reached for the honey pot on the table. "She helped me after I lost Madeleine."

"Madeleine, is it? Is that who's gotten in your head?" Peigi dumped a spoon of raw sugar into her cup, sipped it, and added another spoonful. She started to get up, but Aedan rested his hand on her shoulder.

"I'll get your cream."

"I'm not an invalid," she complained. "I just lost my temper and hollered at my husband is all."

He went to the refrigerator. "You've done so much for me over the years, Aunt Peigi. I like being able to do something for you once in a while." He returned to the table with a carton of half-and-half.

She thanked him and added the milk to her tea. "I want to ask you about something. Hypothetically speaking," she said, and then looked up, eyeing him.

"Okay . . ." He drew the word out, having a pretty good idea what was coming next.

"What's your gut feeling about readjustment?"

"It's a sin against God," he said without thinking. "And it's wrong."

"Easy for you to say. You don't have this issue."

He felt a tightness in his chest and was surprised by the surge of emotion he, again, felt for his long dead wife who he'd barely known. But maybe the feelings weren't about her, but about Madeleine and the guilt he felt creeping up on him like some unknown beast of the night.

An undefined beast, like Jay.

"Just because I don't have a wife, because I'm not in your same situation, doesn't mean I don't have empathy for you."

"I don't want empathy." She slapped her spoon on the table. "I want a solution. I *have* a solution."

His hand went to the crucifix around his neck. "Readjustment is not a solution."

"Damn if it's not."

He stirred his tea, his jaw set stubbornly. "It's dangerous."

"Not if it's done right."

"It's against sept law. There would be serious repercussions. You'd be punished, Peigi."

"I was thinking I could ask for . . . a one-time dispensation. I could petition the General Council."

He shook his head and sipped his tea. "They'll never go for it."

"It's time we relaxed some of our rules. We never thought this would go on this long. All these centuries. We thought we would be redeemed by now."

He stirred his tea again; it didn't taste sweet enough, but he knew he'd added enough honey. Maybe it was the conversation.

"They regretted not giving Mary and Victor a dispensation and allowing them to marry, you know," Peigi pointed out. "Several members came to me after Mary and Victor disappeared and said we'd made a mistake. That letting them marry would have been harmless."

"This isn't the same thing," he argued. "It's not even in the same realm."

"Venial sins. Mortal sins." She gave a wave as if what they were talking about was inconsequential. "Kind of hard to punish a person already suffering the ultimate punishment."

"Peigi, please tell me you're not serious about this. We could be talking about your ultimate salvation."

"I'm serious. About asking permission from the Council to readjust the age difference between me and my husband."

"What you mean is that you're going to ask them if you can commit suicide."

They were quiet for a minute, and then she got up. "Would you like some ham and eggs?"

"No, I don't want ham and eggs. I want you to be sensible."

"I *am* being sensible, and you know it. It's a perfect solution to my problem. To our problem. Brian's and mine. If I were sixteen or seventeen again, I would *totally get him*." She walked to the refrigerator and pulled out a carton of eggs. "Now, what wouldn't be sensible is for you to sit there hungry and not eat my ham and eggs."

# Chapter 16

"Come on. It's only dinner," Aedan cajoled a week later.

"I told you." Dallas took packages out of the cardboard box he was holding for her and stacked them on the refrigerator shelves: buffalo mozzarella, fresh basil, two bags of lemons, two bags of limes, and so on. "Kenzie and I have a routine on weeknights. She hates it when we break her routine."

"But she likes me."

Dallas glanced at him, saw his grin, and couldn't resist him. She smiled. "She has homework. Chores to do. We don't usually go out for dinner on school nights."

"So I'll make dinner for us at your place while you guys get the homework and such done."

She grabbed the empty box from him and tossed it on the floor next to several others. "She's picky about what she eats."

He opened his arms wide. "I'll make whatever she wants."

"Filet mignon and lobster tail." She closed the refrigerator.

"Done and done."

Dallas shook her head. "You're so gullible. She likes frozen French fries, fresh cauliflower overcooked until it's mushy, and chicken breast plain, a hint of lemon if you catch her in an adventurous mood."

"You like French fries, plain chicken breast, and mushy cauliflower?" he asked. "I can make that for you, too."

"What do *you* think?" She grabbed a clipboard with her order information on it off the work counter and began to check off items with a pen she plucked from behind her ear.

"How about this?" he said, still trying to win her over, but pretty certain he had her. "Lobster tails for us, and chicken breast for Kenzie."

"Lobster's expensive." She frowned. "You don't have to buy me lobster. I already let you in my pants."

They were alone in the kitchen. Both cooks were out front shooting the breeze with Tat. They only had two customers, and those guys were both drinking their lunch. Aedan grabbed her and pulled her into his arms. She didn't put up much of a fight.

"This isn't about getting into your pants, Dallas."

"Please don't say it's about our *relationship,*" she groaned, refusing to make eye contact with him. "You *know* that's the kiss of death with mind-blowing casual sex."

He caught her chin between his thumb and forefinger and gently turned her head until she was looking up at him. "Why is it so hard for you to believe I *like* you?"

"Because I'm a bitch. *And* a witch." She laughed, and he laughed with her.

He leaned over her and kissed her hard on the mouth. "I don't believe you're a bitch," he murmured against her lips. "I don't mind if you're a witch."

She groaned and kissed him again. "God, for a dollar I'd take you upstairs right now, Aedan Brigid."

"I got a dollar here somewhere." As he drew his lips along the corner of her mouth, he patted his pockets.

"You're funny."

He kissed his way to her ear and then, unsurprisingly, moved to her throat.

Dallas arched her neck, closing her eyes. "God, that feels good. Is that why so many women are willing to let you bite them and suck their blood?"

"Something like that," he whispered, trying not to focus too long on the pulse at her neck. He had pretty good control, but a human like Dallas was always dangerous. He tried not to think about how sweet and rich her blood would be. "So, come on, let me make you two dinner."

"This is against my better judgment."

"So noted." He gave her another light kiss on the lips and let go of her. "See you at what? Six?"

"Depends on how long it takes you to make mushy cauliflower. Kenzie goes to bed at eight, and we read together. She needs a lot of sleep to make out okay at school."

On his way out, he grabbed three empty cardboard boxes off the floor to toss into the recycling bin in the alley. "See you at six."

"When is six?" Kenzie asked from the couch where she was working on her homework.

Dallas was running around the house, trying to pick up a little. Even if she didn't have time to vacuum the area rug in the living room—a sort of indoor/outdoor jute rectangle—she wanted to at least get the dirty panties off the bathroom floor. The Spiderman boys' briefs that Kenzie was partial to *and* the lacy thong numbers.

"It's in about fifteen minutes." Dallas halted, laundry basket in her arms. Kenzie couldn't tell time. Dallas, along with a whole host of teachers, had tried to teach her, but she was never interested enough to even attempt to learn. Kenzie was strong-willed and stubborn. She was improving academically, as well as socially, every week at the consortium, but it was very difficult to teach her anything she didn't want to learn. "You want me to show you on the clock in the kitchen?" Dallas asked nonchalantly.

It was the only place in the house where they had an analog clock; the others—on the microwave, on the stove, on the cable box, and in Dallas's room—were digital.

Kenzie set her workbook on the coffee table and got up stiffly. Her movements were always a little stiff, another telltale sign of autism, Dallas had been told. "Yes."

"So you'll know when Aedan is coming?" Dallas asked. "That's why you want to know?"

Kenzie led the way to the kitchen.

Dallas set the laundry basket down inside the kitchen doorway and walked over to the wall where she'd hung a simple black-and-white clock she'd picked up years ago at a rummage sale. She'd always liked the simplicity of it. "See the six?"

Kenzie stood solemnly in front of her mother and nodded. Today she was wearing a Disney *Cars* T-shirt.

"It will be six o'clock when the little hand is on the six and the big hand is on the twelve."

Kenzie stared up at the clock for so long that Dallas reached over her head and took it off the wall, bringing it closer to her daughter. Kenzie silently put her finger on the six and then the twelve. She knew her numbers; it was the concept of time she had difficulty with. Dallas could feel her heart beating in her chest. Kenzie's movement was a simple gesture, but somehow, it felt like a breakthrough.

Dallas held her breath as Kenzie touched the glass over the little hand and pretended to move it until it was precisely over the six. Then she did the same with the longer hand, making a wider sweeping motion.

"That's it!" Dallas said. "You've got it."

"Can we wait for him?" Kenzie deadpanned.

"For Aedan? Sure." Dallas chuckled as she hung the clock back on the wall. "He's making dinner for us. French fries and cauliflower, remember? We won't get our dinner if we don't wait for him."

"No." Kenzie shook her head. "Can we *watch?*" She pointed to the clock. "Wait."

"You want to stand here and watch the clock until Aedan comes?" Dallas glanced over her shoulder at the laundry basket.

Kenzie nodded. "I want to wait for Aedan. Aedan has to get the bad man."

Dallas caught her daughter's hand and crouched beside her, looking into her face, even though Kenzie wouldn't look into hers. That was a lot of words strung together at one time for her.

"Kenzie, you have to tell me about this bad man. You're starting to scare Mommy."

"Aedan knows." Kenzie stared at the clock. "Six."

Fortunately for Dallas, Aedan was right on time. She buzzed him in through the rear, downstairs door that would let him into the kitchen, then opened the door into the apartment for him at the top of the stairs. She carried the laundry basket on her hip.

"Hey," Aedan said, leaning down to kiss her on the cheek. He was carrying cloth sacks of groceries in both hands.

"Hey," she echoed. "Kenzie's in the kitchen waiting for you." She motioned with a tilt of her head. "She's watching the clock. She wanted me to show her how to tell time so she would know when you would be here. She can't tell time, Aedan."

He closed the door behind him. "That's great news, then. Right?"

"Yeah, it is. Her teachers will be pleased." Dallas remained standing in the hall instead of leading him to the kitchen . . . or heading for panty clean-up duty. "Aedan . . ." She lowered her voice. "Kenzie has mentioned to me a couple of times now that there's a *bad man*."

He didn't say anything, which worried her a little.

"Do you know who she's talking about? A bad man, who she's afraid of?"

"Dallas," he said quietly. "There are a lot of bad men in this world."

"I know. But she seems to think you know who she's talking about."

He was quiet, and Dallas went on. "It doesn't make sense. I don't allow her to have contact with strangers. There are just her teachers. She's better than me at controlling—" She stopped and then went on, glancing up at him. "You don't think she could be talking about one of her teachers, do you? Could there be a bad man at school, maybe? But that doesn't make any sense either," she went on, thinking aloud. "Because all of her teachers are women."

"What did she say about this bad man?" he asked quietly.

"She won't give me any details. I don't know that she knows any." She chewed on her lower lip. "That case you're working on . . . the guy who attacked those two women?"

"Yeah?"

"You don't know who he is, do you? I mean, I know that sometimes cops know somebody's a criminal but they don't have enough evidence to arrest him. Is it someone . . . living near here?"

"We don't know who the attacker is."

"You wouldn't lie to me, would you?" she asked.

"About something like this?" He met her gaze earnestly. "No, Dallas. We don't know who attacked those women, but there are several men and women on the case, both on the state police force and privately."

"Like you. A private investigator?" she asked.

"I'm not at liberty to say."

"Of course you're not." She frowned. "Exactly how

does a vampire find himself in the *private investigation* business?"

"Long story. And I've got vanilla ice cream melting." He held up one of the bags.

"Right." She took a step back. "Well, I'm just giving you a heads-up, in case she starts talking crazy about a bad man. It could just be something in her head. Just before we moved to Delaware, she became adamant that there was a bad dog. I ended up going door-to-door, looking for this pit bull she was afraid of. Turned out, she'd been talking about a picture of a dog she saw at school that scared her." Dallas turned and went down the hallway. "She's in the kitchen. You better go find her. She's probably getting tired of standing in front of that clock." She passed the kitchen door. "Give me a few minutes and I'll be in."

Aedan stepped into the kitchen. Sure enough, Kenzie was standing ramrod straight in front of a wall that sported a big, black-and-white, old school clock. "Hey, Kenzie," he said aloud.

*Aedan,* she telepathed.

*Let's use words so your mom doesn't get worried,* he suggested as he put the groceries down on the counter.

*But what if I want to tell you something I don't want her to hear?*

Aedan noted that the little girl spoke much better telepathically than she did aloud. *About what? The bad man?*

*The bad man,* she echoed in his head. She still stood facing the clock, her back to Aedan.

*Honey, your mom's a little worried. Where is this bad man? Can you tell me so I can go talk to him?*

*I don't know where he is. He's outside. He watches.*

*He watches you? Us?* Aedan telepathed. He set some items on the counter, others in the fridge or freezer.

*He watches ladies.*

Aedan walked over to Kenzie, remembering not to touch

her; Dallas said that made her uncomfortable. He crouched beside her so they were eye level, even though the little girl wouldn't turn to look at him. "What makes you say that, Kenzie?" he said quietly. "How do you know about this bad man?"

*I don't know,* she responded telepathically, then out loud, "French fries." She walked away.

Aedan knew when he was being dismissed. He set the temperature for the oven, glancing over his shoulder at Kenzie as she left the kitchen.

Did the little girl somehow have some connection with Jay? Was that who she was talking about? But that was impossible, wasn't it? How could she? Maybe Dallas was right. Maybe the "bad man" was similar to the "bad dog" at school. It was just a coincidence, and Aedan was reading too much into things. He felt too much guilt over too many issues. Peigi said it was a Catholic thing. Aedan thought it was more a vampire thing. He looked for evil in every shadow, but the truth was that sometimes there was nothing there but the shadow.

"Heard you were looking for me." Kaleigh perched beside Aedan on the bumper of his car.

He was parked in a gravel lot on the edge of the federal game reserve that bordered Clare Point. Kahill vampires didn't need to feed often. Once or twice a month. Because the blood of humans had been prohibited since shortly after their arrival in the New World, they'd had to get creative. They were permitted to drink from other vampires, but due to the sexual nature of those encounters, they'd needed a more practical, less personal way. They'd begun feeding on deer, and the system had evolved over the years. With their surreptitious connections in Washington, D.C., they'd managed to have the Clare Point forest declared a national wildlife refuge, protecting the area from sale and development. The Kahills cared for the wildlife on the reserve and fed on them to keep themselves nourished. They could feed on the deer without killing them.

"Going for a run?" Kaleigh asked when Aedan, lost in his thoughts, didn't answer. *Going for a run* was a euphemism for feeding. The tricky thing about drinking blood from deer was that you had to catch them first.

"Thinking about it."

She studied him in the fading light. "When was the last time you fed? You're looking a little peaked."

He half smiled.

"You know," she said, "if you wanted to talk to me, you could have called me on my cell or texted me. Hell, we're telepathic. You could have shot me a message." She drew her finger from her temple outward as if shooting lightening bolts from her brain. "You didn't need to keep asking people where I was. Asking my mom, who then tracked me down at Katy's."

"I ran into her at the mini-mart," he defended. "How was I supposed to know you were skipping school again? You're supposed to be in school," he admonished.

She shrugged. "Senioritis. Cut me a break. I'm third in my class."

"Not valedictorian?" he asked.

"Nah. You know how it is. I didn't want to draw too much attention to myself. No one likes it when a vampire beats out humans in a race for the top."

Aedan stared straight ahead, into the woods line. It was an ancient forest, once occupied by the Lenni-Lenape Indians, thousands of years ago. Intersected by game paths, it was made up of both deciduous and coniferous trees: pin oak and poplar, longleaf and loblolly pine. Along the edge, here, scraggly holly bushes and ragweeds grew. He could hear a rabbit or something creeping around in the brush.

"I know you're pretty familiar with our library," he started. "I heard that the text you found to save Lia's soul last summer was pretty obscure."

"I had this feeling that there was a precedent. It was just a matter of finding it in all those old books." She plucked ChapStick from her jeans pocket and rubbed it over her lips. "It makes me freakin' crazy that I have to relearn this crap every single life cycle. I mean, I'm the wisewoman, right? Shouldn't I get—"

"Favors?" he suggested.

"Exactly." She punched him none too gently. "Favors from God. That's exactly what I deserve." She tucked the grape-smelling ChapStick back into her pocket. "So what do you need from the library?"

"I was wondering if you could dig around for some information for me." With the arrival of darkness came the evening insect song. A bullfrog croaked somewhere in the distance. Over the centuries, Aedan felt as if he had become a city boy. It was where most serial criminals lurked; it was where he spent most of his time, tracking them. But it always felt good to come home and experience the earthiness of the forest, the seashore, and the wetlands that dotted the area.

"Okaaay." She drew out the word, encouraging him to go on.

He pressed both hands to the tops of his thighs. He was getting antsy. Things were going great with Dallas. Despite hesitation on both their parts, they were seeing a lot of each other. Aedan was enjoying getting to know her and her daughter.

It was Jay who was worrying him. It had been two weeks since his attack on Maria Tolliver. Something was up, and with every passing day, Aedan became more worried. He hadn't been able to get anything else out of Kenzie about the bad man. Dallas had inquired at her daughter's school, and the guidance counselor had confirmed that Kenzie didn't really have any contact with any males in her small circle of teachers and assistants.

Jay had another month before he'd go dormant again, if

he followed his previous pattern. So where the hell was he? Why hadn't he attacked again?

"Where's who?" Kaleigh asked.

Aedan frowned. "I forget that I can't just put up any old wall with you. It's gotta be brick and mortar." He glanced at her. "Didn't your mother teach you it was rude to listen in, uninvited, on other people's thoughts?"

"She did. What she didn't tell me was that people would come to me all the time asking for my help, but I'd have to drag the details out of them."

He chuckled. "It's this case I'm on. Jay. He's attacked two women in the Rehoboth Beach area. I'm sure it's him. He's left his signature. Literally."

"This is the creep you've chased before. The one who signs his name in women's flesh."

"An initial. J."

"That's disgusting."

"So, if it's the same guy, which I'm assuming it is, in a month he'll disappear, and he won't prey on humans again for another fifty years."

"And you'll be a teen again or toothless, so it will be a hundred years before you have a chance to catch him again, and you might be using a cane by then."

Aedan didn't care for the cane remark, but she got the point. "I was wondering if there's some record of crazy, weird creatures we don't encounter often. This isn't your run-of-the-mill vampire, werewolf, or zombie. It's got some kind of serious hibernation clause in its contract. Could be a shifter of some sort, but I don't know about that."

"He appears as human, not as an animal or a creature?" Kaleigh questioned, thinking.

"Every woman describes him as a man, but the descriptions are vague; they rarely get a good look at him. I don't know what this son of a bitch is, but I need to catch him, Kaleigh, this time around."

She was quiet for a minute, and he left her to her thoughts, in the hopes she might be digging up something from the dregs of her mind.

"You sure you're not too close to this?" she asked, finally.

He glanced over to meet her gaze. She was a pretty girl who was no longer really a girl, but a young woman. She was one of those women whose beauty truly shone from within. "I don't know what you mean. Of course not."

"You *do* know what I mean. I haven't forgotten about Madeleine, and I know you haven't either."

He was quiet for a minute. "He *did* kill Madeleine, but not because of me. It was a coincidence. A bad one. I was in her town following up on another case. Jay happened to see her and . . ." He stopped and started again. "It was after he killed Madeleine that he appeared on our radar."

"I think you're pushing your luck here a little, buddy, but okay."

"So you'll see what you can find out?" He stood. "There's probably nothing there, but just in case." He slipped out of his leather jacket and tossed it into the car through the open window. He'd be too hot in it in the woods.

"So you are going for a run?" she asked.

"I think so. You want to go with?" he asked, sort of hoping she wouldn't want to. It was only polite to invite another vampire along, when you crossed his or her path in the forest. The hunting went faster. Cleaner. But he really felt like he wanted to be alone.

"Nah, I already ate this week." She jumped up off the bumper. "I'll let you know if I find anything. Be safe."

"Always," he called over his shoulder as he took off into the forest, his fangs bared.

# Chapter 17

"Fancy meeting you here." Dallas stood behind the bar in her usual uniform of the evening: jeans, black tee, and little white apron around her hips, with the string tied in the front in a bow.

"It's only been a couple of days. I had stuff to do. Family stuff." *Like keeping my aunt from killing her teenage husband . . . or herself.* "If you gave me your cell number like a normal woman, I could call you and tell you when I'm coming. I could even ask you out. Like on a date. *You* could even have *my* phone number."

"A normal woman?" She arched a brow. "Is that what you're looking for?" Her tone was sarcastic, but she was glad to see him.

"What's a man have to do to get a Guinness around here?"

She grabbed a clean pilsner glass and pulled back the lever on the tap. She studied the rubber mat on the bar rather than looking him in the eye. He realized then that something was up. This wasn't their usual evening, pre-sex banter.

"Kenzie's been asking for you. She brought a picture she drew in school home today."

"Did she?" he asked, genuinely interested. He knew he

couldn't . . . *shouldn't* get attached to Dallas. The same went for the little girl, but he couldn't help it. Her disability didn't bother him; he liked Kenzie. As for her quirks, he just thought they made her different. A more interesting soul.

"A picture of her standing between me and a guy wearing a black leather jacket and a crucifix around his neck," she intoned. "Stick figures, but a lot of detail: our blond hair, the boardwalk with the ocean behind it. Her Transformers T-shirt."

"Really?"

"It's the first time she's ever drawn a self-portrait. Her teacher called to tell me it was a breakthrough."

"That's wonderful news."

"It is," Dallas agreed, setting the glass in front of him.

Aedan took a sip of cool beer; it went down well. "So why don't you look happier?"

"When the teacher asked Kenzie who the man was, she actually answered. She told her you were her *daddy*."

"Her *daddy?*" He almost choked on the next swallow of beer. "You're kidding."

Dallas frowned. "I didn't know what to say to the teacher."

"What *did* you say?"

She leaned against the bar and wiped it with a bar mop. "I said . . . I told her you were my boyfriend." She met his gaze. "I didn't know *what* to say."

Now Aedan didn't know what to say. A part of him liked the idea that Dallas would say he was her boyfriend. It had been a long time since anyone had claimed him; he liked to feel needed, like any other guy. But now she wasn't talking about casual sex. She hadn't told the teacher he was "a friend with benefits." She was making a reference to a relationship, which scared him in more ways than he could count.

"At least she didn't draw me with fangs," he quipped.

Dallas frowned. "She doesn't know about *that,*" she whispered. "At least I hope she doesn't."

Aedan grabbed her hand as she started to turn away. "What's that supposed to mean? You didn't tell her—"

"Of course not," she interrupted, withdrawing her hand. "What kind of mother would terrorize her child with stories of vampires, even if they are true?"

He held up a finger. "And no witch hat on your head."

"There but for the grace of God," she muttered under her breath. She began to hang wine glasses on a rack that hung above the bar.

Tat walked over to stand beside Aedan. "That's the last ones," he said, indicating the patrons walking out the door. He glanced at his watch. "It's a little early, but I say we pull the plug and call it a night. An hour of cleanup and we'll be out of here."

"Sounds good to me." Dallas slid the last two clean glasses into the rack. "But why don't you go on home? Kitchen's already closed. We'll finish up here." She nodded in Aedan's direction.

Aedan had been studying the tattoos on one of Tat's arms. Every time he looked, he found something he hadn't noticed before amid the curlicues and vines. Tonight he was checking out a whale swallowing a man on Tat's left forearm. Whoever had done the tattoos was a true artist. The depiction was eerily realistic, and when Tat moved his arm, the water around the whale rippled.

"You sure?" Tat asked, tugging on his ear. The gauge of his earring was so big that you could see his thumb through the hole in his ear. "I don't mind staying."

Aedan eased off the barstool, taking another long pull on his beer. He didn't mind that Tat didn't like him. In fact, he liked the idea that the guy was looking out for Dallas. Tat would still be here when Aedan went back to work in Paris, or Barcelona, or wherever he'd be sent next. "I'll lock up behind you."

"I got my keys." Tat touched a long chain on his belt from which various keys dangled. "Night."

"Good night," Dallas and Aedan echoed.

She came around the bar and started wiping down the tables and turning the chairs upside down on top of them. Aedan went to the front door behind Tat and unplugged the neon sign in the window, officially closing Brew for the night.

Aedan and Dallas chatted as they worked. He didn't mind at all, helping her out. It sure beat his usual work, which involved dark alleys and bad men. He brought a broom and a dustpan from the kitchen and started at one end of the barroom, sweeping toward the other.

"Tell me about being a witch," he said.

She chuckled. "Pretty direct, you vampires."

He shrugged and continued to sweep, occasionally stopping to push the dirt and stray French fries and pieces of napkin into the dustpan, which he dumped. "As I said before, I haven't known many witches and the ones I did know, I had no desire to sleep with. I mean, what if she didn't deem me decent in the sack? She might shrink my willy or something."

Dallas burst out laughing. "Shrink your *willy?*"

"You know, with a spell." He made an abracadabra motion with his hands, then took up the broom again. "They can do that, you know. Witches. Cast spells."

"I'm not the spell kind of witch. I don't think I'm really a witch at all." She was refilling salt and pepper shakers. Corey had left early to take care of her sick kid, so Dallas was finishing up her work for her. "It's just what people said. You know, people who knew I saw things."

"Like who?" he asked.

She shrugged. "People. My dad. You know how it is; we're scared of what we don't know."

"Your *dad* called you a witch?"

"I scared him a couple of times. Before I got smart

about keeping my mouth shut and keeping my hands to myself. I think I scared him, as a teenager, when it got pretty strong. He came from an old family in Massachusetts. I think maybe some family member of his was hexed by a witch or something back in the Puritan days," she joked.

"But you said your mom had it, too. He wasn't afraid of her?"

"Apparently not. She didn't get pictures like me, though. Just fuzzy images, a feeling once in a while. She was fascinated by my ability. She wanted me to *develop* it, whatever the hell that means." She slid a saltshaker across a table and moved to the next one. "I was a rebellious teen. She didn't get what she wanted out of me. Then she died. Car crash. Both of them."

"My mom died, too, about two hundred years ago. I never knew my dad. He died before we were cursed."

"I thought vampires were immortal, unless they got tangled up in a bunch of garlic or something."

"We're not easy to kill, but it's not impossible."

The salt and pepper shakers refilled, Dallas went into the pool room, which was more of an alcove than a room, and began to put the cues back in the rack on the wall. "I'm sorry to hear that. About your mom. Sounds like you were close."

"We were," he agreed, thinking of her beautiful red hair, her rich, dark eyes. "She was killed on vampire business."

"Vampire business?" She rested her hands on her hips. "I know we sort of agreed, without actually saying so, that we weren't going to pry into each other's business, but . . . *vampire business?* How does someone's mom die on *vampire business?*"

He leaned on the broom, thinking of how pretty Dallas was. How fresh, clean. Her spirit seemed clean and pure to him. "I can't tell you what we do, Dallas. You're not supposed to know about me in the first place." He leaned the broom against the wall and walked over to her. "We're not bad people. I can tell you that. In fact, I like to think we're doing some good in the world with our *vampire business.*"

She turned around to face him, leaning back against the pool table. "Top secret, is it?"

He smiled, taking a step closer to her. "Something like that."

"If you told me, you'd have to bite me? Mind-erase me?"

He was still smiling as he rested one hand on each side of her hips, on the pool table. "Something like that." He leaned forward and brushed his lips against hers.

"Mmm," she murmured. "I've been thinking about that all day."

"Have you?" He teased her lower lip with the tip of his tongue. "And how about that?"

She slipped her arms around him and looked up into his eyes. "That, too."

Their kiss deepened, tongue to tongue, as he explored the sweet coolness of her mouth.

She took his breath away . . . and in its place, it seemed as if she left hope.

Dallas slipped her hands under his T-shirt and stroked his back. When she had to catch her breath, and pulled away, he drew his lips across her cheek. She slid her hands over his broad shoulders, appreciating his trips to the gym.

Grasping the backs of her thighs, just beneath her butt cheeks, he lifted her onto the pool table so that she was sitting, her legs open. He stole one kiss after another, and one thing led to another.

"You want to go upstairs?" Aedan whispered huskily in her ear. Her long, blond hair fell around their faces in a curtain. He loved her hair. It was as bright as sunshine.

"Very gentlemanly of you." She stroked his cheek, teasing his lower lip with her thumb. "But I'm kind of comfy right here, if you are."

His fingers found the bar apron, and he tossed it on the floor. She pulled her T-shirt over her head to reveal her pink, lacy bra. In a few minutes, she'd show him the panties that matched.

"Mmm," he sighed, pressing his mouth between her breasts.

Dallas threaded her fingers through his hair, encouraging him to kiss the swell of her breasts, the firm ridge of her rib cage. She tugged on his shirt and pulled it over his head. This was exactly what Tat had been warning her against. It was guys like Aedan who made girls like her want to have sex on pool tables.

He unhooked her bra with an ease she didn't want to contemplate. The air in the room was cool against her naked breasts. She gasped as he closed his mouth over her nipple, and she leaned back on the pool table, wrapping her legs around his. He kissed her again, gently squeezing her breast, rolling her nipple under his thumb.

She was eager to feel him inside her. She didn't want wooing. She didn't need all that much foreplay. She was already hot for him. Wet. What was it about this man, who wasn't really a man, that made her feel this way?

Dallas fumbled with the button on her jeans. The zipper. He followed her lead and eased her jeans and panties down. She kicked off her sneakers. Her mouth was hungry for his, and she kissed him again and again as she unbuttoned his jeans and slid them and his boxers down over his hips.

"You sure you don't want to—"

She silenced him with another kiss.

"We can—"

She grasped his willy in the palm of her hand, and that shut him right up. She stroked and he moaned, kissing her temple, whispering to her. Free of her shoes, her jeans, and her panties, she opened her legs to him. She clung to him as she slid forward, meeting his first thrust.

Maybe it was the naughtiness of it all—having sex in her bar, with the babysitter upstairs watching TV. On the pool table. With a vampire. Or maybe it was just that she needed Aedan. Either way, she didn't last long. She cried out, burying her face in his shoulder so she wouldn't make too much noise, her hands on his buttocks, squeezing, pulling him deeper.

Aedan slowed down, and she caught her breath. But she didn't want her breath. She wanted him. Again. Dallas drew her short fingernails down the small of his back in a bit of a frenzy. She thrust her hips.

When she opened her eyes, his were closed. She raised one hand to stroke his cheek, and he opened his eyes, gazing into hers. For just an instant, as their gazes locked, she felt, far more than she saw, flashes of Aedan. Of the man he had been, the lives he had led. This time it didn't scare her. She welcomed the images.

She saw a good man. A good soul, desperate to right his wrongs. Her heart went out to him for the curse he bore.

Tears suddenly filled Dallas's eyes, and she squeezed them shut, embarrassed.

"Dallas," he whispered. What's—"

She pulled him deep, lifting her hips off the pool table, holding him tightly. He groaned, giving in to the moment, and together they rode out the last waves of pleasure.

When it was over, Dallas collapsed forward against him, her cheek to his chest. She didn't know why she was crying . . . why his pain, and the goodness in his heart, cut her so deeply.

She did know.

Because she wanted to be with this man forever . . .

Aedan didn't know exactly what was going on with Dallas. He wasn't used to women crying mid-coitus. She'd seemed to be having a good time, even after the tears started.

"Hey, you okay?" he asked, sheepishly, as he stepped back to pull up his jeans.

"Ignore me. I'm an idiot," was all she said as she slid off the pool table, wiping her eyes, and began to gather her clothing. She pulled on her panties. He offered her her jeans. She slipped her shirt over her head, sans bra.

Aedan found one sneaker on the other side of the table and brought it to her, feeling totally awkward. "You sure you're okay?"

She brushed her hair, from the crown back, and it fell over her shoulders. "I'm fine. You were . . . fantastic. Seen my other sneaker?" She took the one from his hand.

He found the missing shoe and brought it to her. He watched her as he pulled his T-shirt over his head. He'd left his jacket on the barstool.

"You . . . you want me to go? To stay?" he asked. "Walk you upstairs?"

She sighed and looked up at him. She was no longer crying, but her eyes were red. "You wanna come up? Just . . . to sleep?"

"You mean 'til morning?"

"I don't know what I mean." She balled up her bra and stuffed it in the pocket of her apron, which she also balled up. "At least stay a while?"

He was glad to hear he wasn't getting kicked to the curb. At least not tonight. "Sure." He glanced around the room. "Should we finish cleaning up?"

She gazed around the pool room. "Nah. I'm beat. I'll finish in the morning." She flipped a switch, and the light hanging over the pool table went out.

Aedan grabbed his leather jacket, and they walked through the bar, through the kitchen, turning off lights behind them. Upstairs, Amanda gathered her belongings while Aedan waited for her at the door.

Dallas was in the kitchen, getting a glass of water.

"I'm just going to walk Amanda out and then I'll be

back up," Aedan called as he held the door open for the babysitter.

"You don't have to walk me out," the college student said with a shy giggle. She looked up at Aedan, then quickly away. Dallas had warned Aedan, the other day, that both of her babysitters had serious crushes on him. "We took a self-defense class, Ashley and I."

"Dallas will feel better if I see you get to your car."

"It's right outside," Amanda tee-heed. As she spoke, her ponytail swung back and forth. "I always park under a street lamp."

Aedan glanced down the hall. He could see Dallas in the kitchen. She was leaning against the counter, glass of water poised, but she wasn't drinking. She was lost in her thoughts. He knew it was conceited of him, but he wondered if she was thinking about him. He certainly spent a hell of a lot of time zoning out, thinking about her.

"Be right back," he called again as he followed Amanda out the door.

# Chapter 18

*I stroll down the dark street off Rehoboth Avenue, the one with the bars and restaurants, blending in as I always do. I am in a good mood this evening, despite the threat of rain I feel in the air and the distant rumble of thunder.*

*I enjoyed my holiday. I saw the Statue of Liberty and Ellis Island. I rode the elevator to the top floor of the Empire State Building and stood at Ground Zero where the World Trade Center Towers once stood. The story was so sad, the loss of so many lives to terrorism.*

*It was a pleasant trip. Not only did I take in the sights of New York City, educating myself, but I managed to take a little pleasure as well. The attacks were, no doubt, cited as random and unconnected, in the local papers. The two young women, in two different boroughs, one still in the hospital with an unfortunate internal injury, would never know that I had just been visiting, or that there were other connected incidences.*

*Which is the way it is supposed to be. This was the way it had been until the vampire took a personal interest in me. Which now has caused me to take a personal interest in him.*

*I know I should not care that he is out there looking for*

*me. He won't find me in time; in less than another phase of the moon, I will be gone again. Asleep again. But it is galling that he believes he is in any way a challenge to me.*

*So what if I killed his silly little girlfriend in France? She was a harlot. A harlot like all women. She needed to be taught a lesson. It certainly wasn't my fault that she fought me the way she did, or that she was so weak-willed and died so easily. Had she not struggled so, perhaps she would not have bled out, but merely been disfigured. Humans are amazingly frail creatures; it is something I have come to accept over the years.*

*I walk faster, my pleasant mood fading as I think of the girl named Madeleine in France. The little whore. She had screamed. She had fought me. She bit me!*

*Obviously, something the filthy vampire taught her.*

*The street is mostly empty. The businesses have closed. I notice that the Open light is off in the window of the establishment across the street. I remember the waitress I saw the last time I walked down this street.*

*And then, as if by a miracle, I see her. She is at her car.*

*I stop on the sidewalk and look one way up the street and down the other. The couple I passed half a block ago is gone.*

*The young woman is alone.*

*I wonder if I can catch her before she gets into her car, but she is dim-witted, like all women, and makes it easy for me. She stands at her car door, but instead of unlocking it, she pulls her cell phone out of her backpack. She punches buttons by the light of the streetlamp over her head, without checking the area around her.*

*I sniff. The smell of rain is heavy in the air. I will have to hurry if I don't want to get caught in the downpour. I cross the street quickly, hands shoved in my jacket pockets, fingers curled around the bone handle of the handy little switchblade I picked up in New York City.*

* * *

"Thanks for meeting me," Peigi said. She sat on a beach towel in the sand, staring out into the quiet, dark bay. There was no one else on the beach, as far as the eye could see.

"Thanks for asking." Mary McCathal eased down onto the towel beside her. "I think." She smiled with her usual good humor. "It's been years since I've been invited to a clandestine meeting."

"Weatherman's calling for rain," Peigi mused, drawing up her knees to hug them.

Mary looked up into the dark sky, then over her shoulder. "Clouds coming in from the west. But I wore my rain jacket. We won't melt."

"That we won't."

"And if we get too chilly, you can light a bonfire for us," Mary suggested. "No matter how many times I see you set things on fire, I still think it's a good trick."

Peigi smiled. Mary was a good egg. It was funny how her husband's death and her subsequent affair with Victor had been what it took for Peigi to really notice her. To realize how much she liked her.

"Victor said to tell you hello," Peigi said.

Mary smiled.

"He said he was looking forward to dinner tomorrow night."

"I hope you don't mind." Mary zipped up her yellow rain slicker. "I invited Victor and Brian and Kaleigh and Katy and some of the others over for spaghetti."

Peigi glanced at Mary. "And Brian agreed to come?"

"Victor said he didn't say he wouldn't come." Her tone was hopeful; Mary was the kind of woman who always saw the glass as half-full.

Peigi had used to be that way. She sighed, hunkering down against the chill. "Mary Kay stopped by to speak to me today, about my request. You know, she's heading up the committee."

"She tell you you'd lost your mind?"

"She did not." Peigi turned to Mary. "She was actually very professional. Of course she *thinks* I'm out of my mind, and she tried to talk me out of it."

"She succeed?"

Peigi returned her gaze to the ocean. "Of course not."

Mary was quiet for a moment. "She bring you anything good?"

"Banana chocolate muffins and cinnamon raisin buns."

"Mmm, Mary Kay is the best cook. Far better than me." Mary looked at Peigi. "You *know* they're going to deny your request."

"I know. That's why I asked you to meet me." She hesitated. "I know you understand what I'm . . . what Brian and I are going through. Because you and Victor, you're in the same situation.

"I think we should make a pact." Peigi rubbed her hands together; they were cold. "In case . . . for when the Council denies my request for readjustment."

"A pact?" Mary asked, alarmed. "Exactly what kind of pact are we talking about?"

Aedan lay in the dark on his back, Dallas asleep on his shoulder. He'd fallen asleep for a while after they'd made love again, this time in bed. He smiled to himself in the darkness. He wasn't sure the air mattress was any more comfortable than the pool table downstairs. Maybe less. Dallas's air mattress was so bouncy that he had threatened to buy her a real bed.

He'd woken around two forty-five, and now he couldn't get back to sleep. His muscles were all tense. He felt keyed up and worried. About what, he wasn't sure.

Things had been pretty calm when he'd left the house that evening. Peigi had been on the phone, talking with Mary McCathal. The women had been friends for centuries, but they seemed even closer now. Maybe because of what they were both going through, having young husbands. Peigi had submitted her ridiculous request to the General Council. A special committee had been formed to handle the matter and make a recommendation to the General Council. Mary Kay had offered to head up the committee, which was a pleasant surprise to Peigi. She had told Aedan that Mary Kay had never been interested in politics before, but she had been expressing an interest in the working of the Council lately, and had volunteered for several jobs.

Aedan glanced at the digital clock on the cardboard box beside Dallas's bed. It was ten after three.

When they'd gone to bed, he'd seriously been considering staying the night. Dallas hadn't mentioned the idea again. She was a strange woman. Most women he knew needed to talk everything out, say everything that went through their minds. Not Dallas. He never knew what she was thinking.

So he didn't know if Dallas wanted Kenzie to find him at the breakfast table in the morning or not. And now . . . he wasn't sure if *he* wanted her to find him there. The fact that the girl had told her teacher he was her new "daddy" spooked him. He couldn't be Kenzie's *daddy*. He couldn't be anyone's *daddy*.

Aedan kissed Dallas's forehead and very gently slid out from beside her. Without waking, she rolled over on her opposite side, wrapping a pillow in her arms. He carefully got out of the bed, which wasn't easy to do. When he pushed his hands down, the air in the mattress shifted. Dallas gently rose, then fell, as if riding a wave on the ocean.

He didn't need a light to dress by. He pulled on his underwear, jeans, and shirt. He slipped out into the hall, shoes in his hand, and carefully closed the door behind him. He found his jacket in the living room. He sat down on the couch and put on his socks and shoes. A sound caught his attention; it took him a second to realize what it was.

It was his phone, vibrating. He found it in his jacket pocket. For a second, he contemplated not answering it. Maybe he'd just stick his head in the sand. The fact that Jay had been silent for more than two weeks had been plucking at his nerves. But this wasn't what he wanted, either.

"Mark," he said quietly into the phone.

"You ought to answer your damned phone, Aedan. I called twice in the last fifteen minutes."

"I'm sorry. It's Jay?"

"Yes, Jesus H. Christ, it's Jay. I'm on my way to the hospital now."

"I can be there in twenty minutes."

"No need to hurry. She's dead."

He hung up.

Aedan arrived at the ER about the same time as Mark. He was standing on the sidewalk smoking a cigarette. Mark had never learned to smoke the way Americans did, with their fingers extended. He held the cancer stick between his thumb and forefinger and puffed on it.

To keep anyone from getting suspicious about the tall redhead hanging out in the emergency room, Aedan morphed into a forty-something male EMT in a jumpsuit. His nametag identified him as Joseph Oaks. He wore a wedding band on his left hand. Why, he had no idea. His morphs were both conscious and subconscious. He didn't have the time or the energy to contemplate that detail right now.

Aedan, aka Joe, approached Mark, and nodded. *It's me,* he telepathed.

*Gotcha.* Mark ground out the cigarette in a standing ashtray in an alcove near the EMPLOYEES ONLY entrance.

"What happened?" Aedan asked, walking beside Mark. An ambulance had just pulled up to the bay, its siren blaring, lights flashing.

"Christ Almighty, I'm sick of this," Mark muttered. He was wearing wrinkled khakis and a white polo shirt with a Delaware State Police emblem. "She was found on the sidewalk, right next to her fucking car." He kicked a cement support pole and then winced when his toe made contact.

"In Rehoboth?"

"Yes. On Baltimore Street."

"Christ," Aedan whispered. "That's near where I was when you called."

Mark glanced at him, but didn't say anything. Aedan knew he knew he had been with Dallas. Fortunately, Mark also knew to stick to the issue at hand.

"How long ago did it happen?" Aedan asked.

"A couple of hours. I don't know what time. I don't have any information yet. Just that she was DOA."

"But it was him?"

A nurse, talking on her cell phone, walked out the door. Mark caught the door before it swung shut, and they went inside. "Left his handiwork on her abdomen."

The employee entrance opened into a small hallway just outside the ER. Mark flashed his badge at the nurse behind the desk; she was on the phone and trying to pull out a piece of paper jammed in a printer. "Female DOA," he intoned.

Aedan just stood there like he belonged there. No one noticed him.

She covered the mouthpiece on the phone. "Seven."

"Anything been done?"

The woman shook her head, ripping the piece of paper from the printer. "Declared at the scene. Waiting on you guys and the coroner."

Mark slid his badge back into his pants pocket and

walked down the corridor on the far side of the nurses' station. Two EMTs wheeling an unconscious, elderly man on a gurney hurried by. Aedan and Mark stepped back against the wall to let them get by. A nurse in a bright green smock rushed past.

The girl was alone in number seven. Covered with a sheet. The sheet had slid so that her ponytail, but not her face, was exposed on the pillow. Her hair was sandy blond brown.

Mark and Aedan both stood over the body for a moment and stared at the sheet, smudged with blood. Aedan wondered if Mark still prayed. After all these centuries, some of them didn't anymore. Aedan found his crucifix through his jumpsuit, rubbed it with his thumb, and then pulled back the sheet. "Christ." He looked away, turned his head, clenching his eyes shut, still holding the sheet between his fingers.

"You know her?" Mark asked, catching the other corner of the sheet.

Aedan took a deep breath and looked at her cut-up face. "No. She's just so young."

A plastic bag with a backpack and a phone inside it lay on the table, beside the bed. Mark laid the sheet down gently and opened the bag, then the backpack. He pulled out a wallet.

Aedan drew his side of the sheet back farther to get a better look. The woman's clothing was covered in blood. She was wearing jeans, which hung around her knees, exposing her private parts. She still wore a black waitress's apron, now around her knees as well. Her bloody T-shirt said MACKY'S BAR AND GRILL and featured a swordfish. It was a little place down the street from Brew.

Aedan's gaze drifted downward for just a moment. He wished he could pull up her panties for her; they had pink polka dots. But he couldn't tamper with the evidence. Not until a rape kit was done on her. Jay's signature was big across her stomach. "He got sloppy," he said quietly. "Why was he sloppy?"

"Catherine Ponds," Mark read from the girl's driver's license. "She turned twenty-one . . . last week. Lives in Milton."

"Works at Macky's on Baltimore. She's wearing a waitress's uniform." Aedan carefully pulled the sheet over her, covering her completely. He'd seen enough.

"You said you were right there?" Mark asked, setting her license aside to look through the rest of her belongings. "What did you say you were doing there at three in the morning?"

"I didn't." Aedan walked out of the exam room and down the hall. Mark let him go.

Aedan felt as if his head had just hit his pillow when his phone started vibrating again. He fumbled for it on the bedside table, where he'd plugged it into the charger when he'd gotten home from the hospital.

"You still asleep?" Mark said in his ear.

Aedan glanced at the clock beside the bed. It was twelve twenty-five. Past noon. He couldn't believe he'd slept this late. Of, course he hadn't gotten home until 5 a.m., when the sky was already beginning to grow pink in the east. "No." He unplugged the phone from the wall so he wasn't tethered.

"I just got a call at my desk at work. Came right in through the main switchboard, pretty as you like."

Aedan swung his long legs over the bed and scratched his bare chest. His crucifix swung when he hit it. "Okay."

"It was Jay."

Aedan bolted upright. "You've got to be fucking kidding me. It was really him?"

"It was him. Had a little bit of an accent. Scottish."

"You're sure?" Aedan got out of bed and went to the window to open the heavy drapes. It was a beautiful, sunny May day. How could the sun shine so brightly when pretty Catherine Ponds lay in the morgue and her parents sat somewhere weeping?

"About the fact that it was him or that the accent was Scottish? Yes, I'm fucking sure," Mark snapped. "On both counts."

Aedan was quiet for a second. He didn't take Mark's shortness with him personally. Mark was a good guy. Big heart. He took every one of these cases personally, not just Jay's murders, but every murder in the area. Maybe in the world. "What did he say?"

"He wanted to apologize," Mark said, putting emphasis on each word. "For getting heavy-handed. He said he didn't mean to kill her."

"You hear what did kill her?"

"Bled out, internally. When he was carving her up, after he had raped her against her car, he slipped, his knife went too deep, and he nicked some artery in her abdomen," Mark explained.

Aedan grabbed a clean pair of jeans from a laundry basket Peigi had left on the floor at the end of his bed. He found a shirt, underwear, and socks and set them all on the bed. "An accent," he said, thinking out loud. "A Scottish accent. No one's ever said he had an accent."

"It was very slight. Could be no one noticed."

"Maybe no one but an Irishman would," Aedan said, making a bad joke. There had been a time when the Irish couldn't stand the Scots and vice versa. Some might say the dislike was still there.

"So, did you get a trace on the call?" Aedan walked out into the hallway, headed for the bathroom.

"Working on it."

"Look, I'm going to jump in the shower. Make some phone calls." Aedan closed the door to the boys' room. Both Brian and Victor were asleep in their beds, long limbs dangling from beneath sheets. "I'll call you back later, but if you hear anything on the trace before then, give me a ring."

"There's one more thing, Aedan."

Aedan walked into the bathroom, closing the door behind him. "Yeah?"

"Jay said to tell you he said hello."

# Chapter 19

"How about dinner?" Aedan said into his Bluetooth. It had taken him three tries to call Dallas while driving, but the fact that she had put her number in his phone last night pretty much demanded that he try it. "And maybe I can grab a movie for after Kenzie goes to bed. You could use a night off."

"How about you slow down a little, Romeo," she answered. She was pleased he had called, though. He could hear it in her voice.

"You're the one who gave me your number," he defended.

"I don't know if dinner is a good idea. You know, the whole *family* illusion." She groaned in obvious indecision. "But Kenzie would like it."

He signaled and got into the lane to make the left-hand turn into Rehoboth. He was only a mile or so from Brew, but he wasn't headed there. Not now. Mark had called. Jay's call had been traced to a popular pizza place on Rehoboth Avenue. Aedan was meeting Mark there. "We can go out or stay in."

"School night," Dallas said.

"I make a mean mushy cauliflower." The light turned green, and he turned off Route 1.

"I was thinking sushi."

"Kenzie eats sushi?"

"Of course not. I've got something here she'll eat. She doesn't care about dinner. It's you she wants to see." There was a little resentment in her tone.

"Okay, so sushi for us, Rice Krispies for Kenzie." He hesitated. "Last night, Dallas, it was—"

"It *was,*" she cut in. "I was surprised you didn't stay."

"Yeah . . . I wasn't sure that was such a good idea," he admitted.

"Because you can't *stay* stay."

He pressed his lips together. He liked his job; he was good at it. He liked the fact that he traveled, that he never stayed in one place long. The last time he had wished he could have stayed somewhere, it had been in a little town in the south of France. "You're right. I can't *stay* stay."

She was quiet for a minute, quiet long enough that he wondered if he'd accidently disconnected her on the Bluetooth. Then she said, "It's okay, Aedan. That there's no future. I mean that . . . I just think . . . I think—God, this is hard to say. I think we need you right now. Kenzie and I." She paused again. "That too heavy for you?"

Tears stung the backs of his eyelids. Lack of sleep, probably. "I'm sorry it can't be different. I just . . . I don't want to make promises. To you *or* Kenzie. And I've got this case, and . . ." He let his sentence fade into silence.

"Come on, we're just talking about dinner," she joked. "Not eternity. Look, I'm at Kenzie's school. I gotta go."

"Yeah. I gotta go, too." He pulled into a parking spot. After this weekend, after Memorial Day, he'd have to feed the meter, which had actually been swapped out for a fancy parking kiosk in some places in Rehoboth. "I'll call you later about dinner?" he said.

"Sounds good."

As Aedan was getting out of the car, his phone rang. It

took him a second to switch the call from the Bluetooth to the phone. Kaleigh's name came up on the caller ID. She was calling him back.

"So, you actually went to school today?" he asked, walking down the sidewalk.

"Calculus final," she groaned. "And my last week of high school *ever,* so I thought I'd *give it my all.*"

"So you make a decision?"

"On what essay to write for my English final due tomorrow? Nah. I thought I'd give it 'til midnight. It's not due 'til morning."

"On college."

"You didn't hear? I thought for sure someone would have told you in the diner or the gym. It's a wonder my mom didn't have it posted at the post office. I'm going to the University of Delaware. It's not too far away, so if anyone needs me to do any wisewoman stuff, I can come home. But I'm going to college."

"Good choice," Aedan said. "I'm proud of you."

"You didn't call me to tell me you're proud of me," she said dryly. "What's up?"

"I've got a little info for you on this nut job we're looking for."

"Okay, cool. I was headed to the library tonight. Premidnight, I gotta clean my room first, then I was going to the library, then to Peigi's to check on my peeps. I might see you there."

"Maybe," he said noncommittally, hoping he'd be lying on an air mattress tonight. "I don't know if this will be any help, but the creep called Mark today."

"He called him? Eww. Gross. Didn't he attack another girl last night? I heard it on the radio."

He hesitated. "She's dead."

"We gotta get this guy, Aedan. I know you're not really supposed to be doing anything, but—"

"Mark's trying. I've been doing a little undercover work,

trying to bait him, walking around looking like a twenty-one-year-old girl."

"I'd like to see that."

He looked both ways, then crossed in the crosswalk, against the light. "So Mark spoke to him, and Mark thinks he has a Scottish accent."

"He *thinks?*"

"He said it was pretty subtle, but—"

"An Irishman can always pick out a Scot."

"Something like that." Aedan approached the pizza place, which was famous in the area. He spotted Mark at a table in an outside seating area. "You'll let me know if you find anything?"

"Sure. It might take me a few days. I can't promise there's anything there."

"I know. We're just trying every angle."

"Later," Kaleigh said.

"Later." Aedan walked past the hostess station to Mark and took a chair beside him.

"I ordered four-cheese. Iced tea." Mark pointed at one of the two paper cups on the table.

"I'd rather have a beer."

"I'm on duty." Mark took a sip from his straw and nodded at the counter in the front of the restaurant that served takeout to passersby. "The call was traced to a line typically used for takeout orders."

"The calls taken there?"

"Depends on the time of day and how busy they are. There are four other phones available that can use that line."

"The phone call could have been made from any one of those phones." Aedan took a sip of his tea.

"It could have, but any of the phones inside would be hard to get to unless you were a employee."

"Jay's not an employee."

"Not likely," Mark agreed. "There are only a couple of

new hires at this location. I'm going to have them all checked out, but there was street noise in the background when Jay called."

Aedan glanced at the carryout counter, then at the street, then back at the counter. There was a young man in a uniform T-shirt on the cordless phone. When he hung up, he set it on the end of the counter and walked to the other end to serve a customer.

"I could pick that phone up and make a phone call," Aedan observed.

Mark sucked on his straw. "You think?"

"Oh, yeah." Aedan got out of his seat.

"Where you going?" Mark asked.

Aedan pushed in his chair. "Men's room. Wanna come?"

Mark made an obscene gesture, involving a particular finger.

Aedan grinned and walked away, weaving a path between tables outside the restaurant, then inside. He walked into the men's room, into a stall. A few seconds later, he walked out of the stall. He glanced at the mirror over the sink as he went out the door.

He was a thirty-year-old, clean-shaven, Caucasian male, average height, average weight, with brown hair. He wore khakis, an oxford shirt, and Docksider shoes. Jay apparently was an average-looking, nondescript guy with nothing about his looks or behavior that stood out to his victims.

Aedan walked out of the bathroom and through the restaurant and out onto the sidewalk. He walked half a block and then turned around and went back to the pizza place. As he approached the carryout counter, he slowed his pace. Two teenage girls in jeans and tank tops got in line; it was still a little cool for tank tops this time of day, but the kid behind the counter seemed to be appreciating their choice in after-school attire.

"Ladies," the guy behind the counter said with a big grin. "What can I get for you?"

Aedan walked to the end of the counter, putting out his hand. He swept the cordless phone up and kept walking. He stopped behind a sign advertising their specials and punched a number. From his spot between the sign and a support pole for the restaurant awning, he saw Mark take his cell phone out of his pocket.

"Restaurant name come up on your caller ID?" Aedan asked, using his own voice rather than his morph's.

Mark looked up, then around. "No," he said, sounding completely confused. "Just the number."

"Look to your right." Aedan stepped into view and waved the phone at him.

"Point made," Mark muttered.

Aedan carried the phone back to the counter. The kid was still talking to the teenage girls. Aedan set the phone where he'd found it and strolled over to Mark.

"Anyone could have done that."

"Just about," Aedan agreed.

A waitress approached the table, carrying a large cheese pizza. "Anything else I can get you guys?" she asked, setting the pizza on the metal frame on the table.

"A to-go box?" Aedan asked pleasantly. "I have to run."

"No problem." The girl walked away.

"You're not going to sit here with me and eat the pizza I'm paying for?"

"Nope." Aedan remained standing. He grabbed his cup and sipped his tea, imagining Jay strolling up to the counter and picking up the phone and calling Mark. Brilliant. Amazingly easy.

"But you *are* going to eat my pizza?" Mark asked, incredulously.

"Actually I'm taking it to someone. A little girl who likes white things, including cheese pizza."

Mark shook his head, biting into a slice of gooey pizza. "You're a piece of work, Aedan, you know that?"

"Here you go." The waitress reappeared with a takeout box. "And your check. For whenever you're ready," she said cheerfully.

As she walked away, Aedan slid another piece of pizza onto Mark's plate and put the rest in the box. He closed up the box and pushed the check across the table toward Mark. "I owe you one," he said as he walked away, carrying the drink and the pizza box.

"Keep your money," Mark called after him. "Just find this guy."

Brian glanced at the den doorway. One game of "Modern Warfare 3" had ended, but they hadn't started the next. "Exactly what did she say?" he asked, quietly.

Victor hesitated.

Brian didn't know why he was curious. What did he care what Peigi said or did, so long as she didn't ride his ass? "Come on, man, you're the one who brought it up."

"Where is she?" Victor looked at the doorway.

"I don't know. Somewhere." Brian shrugged. "In the kitchen maybe. She's been doing a lot of stuff for the Council. More than usual."

"You can't *tell* where she is?" Victor set his controller on the couch and reached for his can of Coke. "It's weird, but I know when Mary's nearby. Like I was walking down the street the other day, Katy and I were going for a bagel, and I just like *felt* Mary. She walked right out of the bagel shop. She was getting Old Bay bagels. She knows I like them." His smile was goofy.

Brian rolled his eyes. "You know, you're not really married to her. Not according to the sept. You guys aren't like mated for life like wolves or something."

Victor looked away, taking another drink of soda. "I know."

"So what did Mary say? You heard her on the phone with Peigi, right?"

"Yeah."

"And she said Peigi should talk about something with me? What?"

"I don't know. She didn't say. I can't read her mind yet. I can't read anyone's mind." Victor frowned. "Can you?"

"Not really," Brian said, feeling a little uncomfortable with the subject. Actually, he *was* kind of starting to get feelings from Peigi. No words, just . . . emotions. And he didn't like it. He didn't like getting sucked in to her problems. All that angst. It made him feel weird. Like sad for her . . . and for himself.

"But Mary sounded, like, whatever it was," Victor went on, "it was a big deal."

"She say anything else?"

"Not really. When I walked up to her, she started talking about sept stuff. There's some guy in Washington, D.C., who's like a senator or something."

"Yeah, he's my cousin," Brian said. "He's a big deal, apparently. Maybe he'll run for president someday."

"A vampire? An American president?" Victor laughed.

"Why not?" Brian was annoyed that Victor didn't see the Kahills' full potential. "Peigi says we have more choices than we used to. Like . . . I could go to law school, or be a doctor, someday, if I wanted."

"A lawyer would be cool. Then you could prosecute some of those murderers who keep getting away," Victor pointed out.

"Or we could be soldiers, I guess." Brian pointed at the TV screen. "I would think the sept would need soldiers. You know, to do like Special Forces stuff."

"That would be cool, too." Victor picked up his game controller. "You ready to play again, man?"

Brian reluctantly reached for his controller. This thing about Mary's telling Peigi she needed to talk to him was bugging him. "Yeah. I guess so." He glanced at Victor. "Do you think she'd tell you what she was talking to Peigi about on the phone? Mary . . . if you asked her?"

Victor screwed up his face. "I don't know. Probably not. Mary's kind of a private person. And she doesn't gossip much. Not like some of the other women." He laughed. "Some of the guys."

Brian sat back on the couch and scratched at a spot on his jeans—queso dip, maybe. "I'd kind of like to know. You know? What they were talking about."

"I thought you didn't care about Peigi."

Brian felt a sudden rise of emotion in his chest. It was so strong that a lump formed in his throat, and he couldn't speak. What the hell was wrong with him? He hit the button on the controller to take them to the next screen. "I *don't* care," he said, but he wasn't convinced that was true anymore.

*"You mustn't worry yourself," said the young, blond woman from where she sat in the open window, naked, her long hair falling over her breasts.*

*"I'm not worried," Aedan heard himself say.*

He knew he was dreaming, but all he could do was watch the scene unfold.

*He was lying on his side in a narrow bed, a book in his hand. The words were in French. He could see the woman just out of the corner of his eye.*

*"You'll find him. You'll catch him."*

*"Catch who?" He was torn between the book and what the woman was saying.*

*"There will be a price to pay, of course."*

*"Isn't there always?" He turned his head to get a better look at her.*

*In the second it took him to move, the pretty young woman fell forward, out of the window seat, and hit the floor. Aedan tried to reach her, but he wasn't quick enough.*

*Under her was a pool of blood that was more blood than any human body contained. The blood pooled outward until it covered the floor and he was standing in the middle of it.*

Aedan woke with a start and sat up in the narrow bed in the bedroom in his aunt's house. Still breathing hard, he reached over and turned on the light.

A vampire afraid of the dark? Now things were getting ridiculous.

# Chapter 20

"What's the date today?" Aedan asked, dipping the mop into the bucket and pulling the handle to squeeze out the dirty water. "You know what the date is?"

Dallas was wiping down the last table. They'd sort of found a routine after closing. She'd send all her employees home, and he'd help her clean up before they went upstairs and sent Amanda or Ashley home. Aedan always left before dawn; the whole daddy thing with Kenzie spooked him a little. But the three of them ate dinner together pretty often, before Dallas would go down to thc bar to work and Aedan would take his nightly walks, disguised as young women.

It was weird, but Dallas never asked him where he went at night. And he never told her he was looking for Jay. He never said anything at all about Jay, which had occurred to him tonight, as he was walking down Rehoboth Avenue, as strange. Dallas knew he was working the case with the young women being attacked, but she knew nothing about Jay. About their *personal* history: Aedan's and Jay's.

Sometimes Aedan had to remind himself that Dallas was *not* Madeleine. Sure, they *looked* similar, but the similarities ended there. Madeleine had been younger than Dallas, and far more innocent in the ways of the world. And she had had no paranormal abilities.

Or had she? He thought about the dream last night, the previous dreams. Was it possible Madeleine was trying to communicate to him from the grave?

"It's June fourth. Why do you keep asking me the date?" She flipped a chair up onto a clean table. "No calendars in vampire world?"

Aedan did the math. Teesha's attack had taken place April 24. Three days after the full moon. The next full moon would fall on June 23, and Aedan suspected that Jay would be gone again by the twenty-second, just in time to make it to his hidey-hole before the full moon. A lot of God's creatures were affected by the moon phases. Two phases seemed to be Jay's limit.

That was three weeks away. They were running out of time, but of course there was no way Mark could come out and say that to the state police. He and his team had been doing everything they could think of, but other than adding some patrols in the area, and warning the public to take extra precautions, unfortunately, there wasn't much *to* do without more to go on. It was one of the frustrating realities of police work and Aedan's work. A week had passed since the last attack, since the phone call. Aedan knew another was about to take place. He could feel it.

So if he could feel the impending attack, why couldn't he find Jay on the street? Aedan knew Jay was out there, stalking someone.

Aedan had talked to Kaleigh twice in the last week; so far she'd come up with nothing about a creature that hibernated for fifty years, but she was preparing for her high school graduation on Friday night and said she had "feelers out," whatever that meant.

"You okay?"

Aedan felt Dallas touch his arm. Startled, he dropped the mop to the floor.

She raised both hands. "Sorry."

"No, it's okay." He picked up the mop again. "It's me, not you."

"Let's have a beer. Better yet, I'll take a gin and tonic." She took the mop from his hands and placed it in the bucket. "You grab the drinks. I'll go up and let Ashley know she can go."

He hesitated. "I don't know. I was . . . thinking about going home."

Dallas looked at him. For a second she appeared hurt, but it passed. "Going home?"

"To my aunt's."

She rolled the bucket toward the kitchen. "Is this the beginning of the end?" she asked, suddenly sounding tired. "Of us?"

"No. No, of course not." Actually, he *wasn't* thinking about going back to Peigi's. He was thinking about hitting the street again. He just kept hoping he'd get lucky, posing as a young woman, and meet up with Jay.

"Aedan," Dallas said softly.

He had a feeling she was repeating herself.

"Are you *sure* you're all right?"

He walked past her and around behind the bar. "It's this case."

"You think he'll kill again? Is that what you're afraid of?" She leaned on the mop handle, protruding from the bucket. "The paper said it was the same guy. I've read that serial killers do that. They have to work up to killing."

"He's not a serial killer," he said quietly as he took down a glass to make her a gin and tonic.

She listened.

"He doesn't mean to kill them." Aedan dropped a couple of ice cubes into the glass, one at a time. They made a sharp clink when they hit the glass. "He just got in a rush."

She walked over to the bar and leaned on it, watching him. "You know him," she whispered.

He grabbed the gin. Old Raj. She liked good gin.

"How do you know him?" she asked.

He turned his back to her to pour. He didn't need a jigger to measure the gin. Keeping his gaze averted, he turned back toward her and added a spray of tonic water from the soda fountain under the bar.

"You looked for him before," she said, still in her aha moment. "Before this. Before here. Haven't you?"

"Dallas—"

"Remember, I've *seen* you," she warned. "I've seen some of the things you've seen, through your eyes."

"Just twice," he said hopefully.

"There've been other times," she murmured, holding his gaze. She slid her hand across the bar, palm up, beckoning.

She wanted him to let her in.

He moved his hand out of her reach. He wondered how many times he'd been lax when they made love, or even when he sat down for dinner with Kenzie. They casually touched all the time, like any couple.

How many times had he forgotten to put up a mental wall, or strengthen it?

"Dallas, we agreed I'm not going to give you details of my life or what I do. We agreed."

"Was that what you were doing in France? Trying to find this bastard? And he came here? Did you follow him?" Her eyes narrowed. "Or did he follow you?"

He was pretty sure the phone call to Mark the previous week answered that question. Jay was following him now. Taunting him. How Jay knew he was in Delaware, he didn't know, might not ever know. He didn't care, as long as he caught Jay before he went into hiding again. Aedan slid her drink across the bar. "You mind if I go?"

She accepted the glass. "I don't want you to be anywhere you don't want to be. Even if it's with me." She took a sip of the gin and tonic, still watching him.

"It's not like that."

"No?"

Her lips were wet from the drink, and he wanted to taste them. "No," he said.

She surprised him by smiling. "So, go home, or go wherever the hell it is vampires go after last call." She turned away.

"You sure?"

"I'm sure. I can barely stay in control of my own life. I'm not going to try to control yours." She spun the glass back and forth between her fingers. The ice cubes clinked together again. "Can you walk Ashley to her car, though?"

"Will do."

Aedan waited at the bottom of the stairs for the babysitter, then walked her to her car. They talked about how the Phillies were doing. He waited until she pulled away from the curb in her VW bug and then headed in the opposite direction.

Realizing he'd left his cell phone in his car, he decided to walk the one block over and up to where he'd parked and grab it. Aedan had stopped parking on the same street as Brew because, though he had never met Jay face-to-face, Jay knew what he looked like. At least what he had looked like when he had known Madeleine as a man in his early twenties.

Once Ashley was gone, Aedan morphed into an Ashley-esque woman: jeans, a T-shirt, a tan canvas jacket, and a patchwork fabric bag that hung on her shoulder and hit low on the hip. He passed two guys on the street. One whistled at him as he walked by, but they seemed harmless. A gaggle of women too old to be out this late on a work night poured out of a bar, laughing and stumbling and grabbing each other for balance. On Rehoboth Avenue, where he'd left his car, he walked past several people: an older couple walking hand in hand, more forty-year-old women wrapping up an evening of barhopping. A guy carrying a pizza box and a brown paper bag that looked like it contained a six-pack of bottled beer. He doubted it was Guinness.

He walked a couple more blocks.

Aedan had left his car in front of a caramel popcorn stand. Closed. He reached into his purse for his keys, keeping an eye on the few people still on the street.

Where was he? Where was Jay?

He unlocked his car. It wasn't until he leaned in to grab his cell phone from the console between the seats that he saw the piece of paper on the windshield. His first thought was that it was a ticket. Then, as he stood up, he realized it was a napkin. A napkin from the pizza place where he and Mark had met last week. The place from which Jay had placed the phone call to the police station.

"Sweet Mary, Mother of God," Aedan whispered. He snatched the napkin off the windshield. There was handwriting on it.

**Pizza & Beer! So American!** the note read in elaborate, Old World script. It was signed with a **J**.

"Fuck," Aedan muttered, looking up one end of the street, then down the other.

Then he thought of the guy he had passed not five minutes ago. With the pizza and beer. Pizza from the same place. "Son of a bitch!" Aedan hit the car hard with his fist, which hurt like hell because he had a twenty-year-old girl's fist.

He slammed his car door and ran up the street, to the intersection near where they had passed each other, looking in every direction.

Jay was gone. Of course he was gone.

Aedan stood in the intersection and squeezed his eyes shut, trying to remember what the guy carrying the pizza box and beer had looked like. Damn it to hell! This was what Aedan did for a living! He noticed details. He found people. He watched them.

The problem was, Jay had looked so average that Aedan hadn't paid any attention to him. Aedan had been more interested in the damned beer than the guy.

A car honked its horn, and Aedan's eyes flew open. He threw up his hands. He was still holding the napkin. "Sorry," he muttered, crossing to the sidewalk.

He walked back to his car, so frustrated he thought he might scream.

His phone vibrated in his hand, startling him. *Who the hell* . . .

It was Peigi's home number.

"Hello?" Aedan said, his voice a little higher pitched than his true voice.

"Hey . . . man . . . it's Brian."

"Brian?" Aedan asked, thinking it was awfully strange that the kid would be calling him. "What's the matter?"

"I was wondering . . . are you . . . you planning on coming home tonight?"

Aedan glanced around. There was no one nearby.

Jay was gone. He was sure of it. "I don't know, man. Why?" He walked out into the eastbound lane of Rehoboth Avenue. Once the bars closed, the seaside resort quickly became a ghost town.

"I . . . I don't know, man. Peigi, she's . . ."

"She's what?" Aedan asked impatiently.

"She's pissed. Not at me," he said quickly. "She's out in the backyard . . . throwing fireballs around. I think the corner of the house caught fire, but she used the hose to put it out. I . . . I went outside and asked her what was wrong, but she told me to go back in." He hesitated. "I'm kind of worried, Aedan. About her."

Aedan exhaled. He had a pretty good idea he knew what had happened. The General Council had made their ruling . . . or at least Mary Kay's committee had decided what their recommendation would be. He suddenly felt guilty. He'd been so wrapped up in his own life, in worrying about Jay and playing house with Dallas, that he'd barely spoken to his aunt in the last week. "But you don't know what's wrong?"

"No. We had dinner. Me and her and Victor. She made lasagna. We talked and stuff. She was fine. Then someone called, and she went outside and started lighting shit on fire."

"I'll be home shortly."

"You will?" Brian sounded relieved.

"Yeah." Aedan climbed into his car, morphing back into his own body. Wherever Jay was, he was having pizza and beer. And probably laughing his ass off. He wouldn't be hunting tonight.

"Just stay away from her," Aedan instructed. "And don't let her burn the house down."

# Chapter 21

Aedan saw a giant ball of fire rise high in the sky above Peigi's cottage and then, thankfully, burst into a shower of bright sparks. Another fireball shot into the air as he got out of his car and hurried across the grass to the gate that led into the backyard.

"Peigi?" he called. As he went through the gate, he saw that neither of her neighbors, though their properties were relatively close, appeared to have noticed that sensible Peigi Ross, leader of their General Council, was attempting to set the neighborhood on fire. Or maybe Peigi did this more often than Aedan realized. He wasn't home much.

The lights were off in both neighbors' houses.

"Aunt Peigi?"

Another ball of fire flew into the air, exploding like cannon fire, and Aedan instinctively cowered, covering his head. As the sparks fell from the sky, he closed the gate behind him. He walked around Brian's bicycle, abandoned on the ground near a flowerbed of daylilies that hadn't yet bloomed.

"Peigi!" Aedan shouted above the boom of the next fireball.

"Go to bed," Peigi ordered. She sat on a chaise lawn chair near the shed, dressed in jeans, a polar fleece jacket, and her slippers. A fireball was forming in her right hand.

"You can't make me go to bed, Aunt Peigi," he said with amusement. "I'm a big boy now."

"I can set your hair on fire. Go away. Go back to wherever the hell you've been going every night for the last two weeks."

He sat down on a lawn chair beside her. "What's going on? You scared Brian half to death with your fireworks show. He called me."

"He did?" That gave her a moment's pause, then she started in again.

Aedan didn't know how she did it. She barely blinked, flung her arm skyward, and another fireball flew through the air. This one created a nice arc before disappearing over the fence, hopefully hitting the street, rather than his car.

"Yeah, he's worried about you."

She didn't say anything.

"You want to tell me what's going on?" Aedan asked. "You seem upset."

She threw another fireball into the air, but this one wasn't quite so large. Her anger or frustration or whatever she was experiencing was fading.

"How about you tell me what's going on with *you?*" Peigi countered. "With the HF . . . with a child."

He looked at her through the darkness.

"Mary Hall saw you at the grocery store in Rehoboth," Peigi explained. "She said the three of you make quite the attractive little family." Aunt Peigi could lay on the sarcasm like jam.

He leaned forward in the lawn chair, folding his hands. "One of these days, Mary's gossiping is going to get her into serious trouble."

"I imagine that, over the years, it has," she said quietly. The last fireball had dissipated, until there were just a few cinders that glowed like fireflies in a jar. "Mary said she was quite beautiful."

"Her name is Dallas."

"Pretty name." She sat back on the chaise, stretching out her legs. "Pretty name for a pretty girl. I don't need to tell you the danger a human puts you in. Or you put *her* in. With your job, you don't exactly mix with the best humanity has to offer. This one you're tracking, he's a particularly bad monster. He killed that girl you loved, didn't he?"

Aedan closed his eyes and rubbed his temples with his thumb and middle finger. He wanted to be angry at Peigi for not minding her own business, but of course his business *was* hers. As his aunt and as a member of the Kahill family. And *damn her,* she was right.

Peigi went on. "The one in France."

He hung his head. "Yes. It was just coincidence. He didn't know about me, about what we do. Just bad luck." He pressed his lips together. "But I loved her, and he killed her."

"And you love this Dallas, don't you?" Peigi asked.

"No, of course not. She's human. I learned my lesson."

They were both quiet.

"Maybe," he said.

"Ah, well that makes the matter more complicated, doesn't it? Now, what do you do?"

"How do you mean? Obviously, I'll have to break it off. I've only got another six weeks before I'll be released for work again. It isn't like I'm staying in Clare Point, like this . . . *fling* is going anywhere. I can't wait to get back to work. I love it here, but . . . the job's calling me. Paris is calling."

"You don't find love often," Peigi said. "Hard to walk away from it, even amidst danger." She toyed with the zipper on her polar fleece. "If I didn't love Brian, if I didn't love him so much, still, after all these years," she said passionately, "I wouldn't be in such turmoil over the predicament we've found ourselves in."

Aedan studied her face. "The General Council denied your request, didn't it?"

"Not yet, but it's only a formality. Mary Kay had the decency to call me tonight and warn me." She sounded . . . resigned.

"And you're going to accept that decision, aren't you, Aunt Peigi?"

She let her hands fall to her sides and stared at the dark house. The only light visible, now that the fireworks were over, was the glow from the den that flickered with the TV screen. "What's everyone expect me to do?" she asked. "Sensible, logical Peigi."

"You always do the right thing." Aedan leaned forward, folding his hands. "We can always depend on you to do the right thing. You never seem to struggle with right and wrong the way most of us do. It's one of the traits we all admire most in you."

She got out of the chair. "So, I'll do the right thing." She looked over her shoulder at him. "And I trust you will, too. With the HF." She walked toward the house. "Good night, dear."

" 'Night, Aunt Peigi."

Aedan sat for a long time in the dark backyard before he finally turned in for the night, knowing Peigi was right. He had to do the right thing. He had to break up with Dallas. He had to end it now, before she got hurt.

Before any of them got hurt.

*I prefer the darkness of night, but the gray sky before morning is surprisingly pleasant. And it is nice to do something different, sometimes. Something out of character. It keeps others guessing.*

*Like the note on the vampire's car. I know he is prowling the same streets I am at night because I can feel him, though I do not have the pleasure of seeing him. Perhaps he's not just looking for me, but for his own victims. I laugh at the idea of bumping into him in the same alley, me with my knife, him with his fangs. It is really quite a funny thought.*

*So after leaving the note, I went home and enjoyed my beer and the pizza and the telly. I thought I had turned in for the night, but near dawn I decided to take a stroll.*

*I found her in a parking lot behind a quaint diner.*

Her name was Marsha Pimpton. She was older than the women Jay usually chose; she was thirty-four, divorced, with a ten-year-old son. Jay had attacked her at dawn. A first. Aedan didn't know what it meant. Marsha Pimpton would live, but like the others lucky enough to survive, she would always bear the scars of the attack. No one would look at her face again without pause.

Aedan talked with Mark several times during the day and promised to drop off the note written on the napkin at the police troop. Marsha went into surgery for repairs to the muscles in one of her arms, then to have reconstructive surgery on her nose. The three inch-high letter J carved into her thigh could only be treated with an antibiotic and bandaged; there was no way for the doctors to remove it or stitch it closed, just as they had been unable to remove the signature he had left on the other women.

Mark didn't think it necessary for Aedan to come to the hospital to see Marsha, which actually relieved Aedan. He was already feeling like a failure; time was running out fast, and he was no closer to catching Jay than he had ever been. Aedan wasn't up to seeing another woman brutalized by the bastard.

Aedan stuck around Peigi's house most of the day, just to keep an eye on his aunt. But she seemed her old self. She kept busy with sept business and cleaning out her closets, of all things. All day she carried black garbage bags out of the house and loaded them into her car to donate to a charity. In the afternoon, Aedan ran errands and insisted

Brian go with him; for once, the teen didn't put up an argument.

At one o'clock, Dallas texted Aedan, offering to make him dinner. He texted back, declining. It was early evening before she texted again, asking if he was coming that night. He told her he'd see her after closing.

When Tat left the bar that night, he walked Amber to her car, and Aedan went upstairs with Dallas. She knew something was up. She was restless, and even after he told her he needed to talk to her, she wouldn't sit down. She kept trying to tidy up the apartment, putting laundry in the wash, picking up Kenzie's toys, collecting dirty dishes for the sink.

"Dallas, please," Aedan finally said, grabbing her arm as she went by with an armful of stuffed animals. "I really need you to sit down with me. I need to talk with you." He let go of her.

Dallas opened her arms and let the stuffed animals fall to the floor. She'd stalled long enough. It was time for her to find some balls and say what she wanted to say. Before it was too late. Before the best thing that had ever happened to her walked out the door. She took a breath.

"No, I have something to tell you first. I'm not letting you break up with me," she said, dropping her hands to her hips.

He was so surprised that he didn't say anything.

"I've thought about it, and I've decided," she said. "I'm not going to let you do it."

"Dallas—"

"*I'm* talking right now." She walked around the coffee table and sat down on the couch beside him. "I know what you're going to say, why you're going to say it. You think we should break up now before things get too serious, because you have to leave. Well, I've got news for you; things are already serious. We didn't mean for this to happen. God knows I didn't. But it happened."

"Da—"

"I said I'm talking right now," she interrupted. "I don't want to hear your logic. I don't want to hear your common sense. I love you, Aedan, and I think you love me. So when you go, it's going to break both our hearts, anyway." She took a deep breath for the first time in what seemed like days. It felt good to say what she'd been thinking. "So, until you have to go, be my guy. Let me be your girl. And let Kenzie be your little girl . . . for a little while longer." She shook her head. "I don't understand what kind of connection the two of you have, but I know it's there. And I know she needs you right now." Dallas reached out and took his hand, and the waves of his past washed over her. But they didn't overwhelm her. In fact, she found them comforting.

"Okay," she said in a small voice. "Now you can speak."

After a while, he looked away. Now that she was offering the opportunity, he didn't seem to know what he wanted to say.

He looked back at her. "I do love you, Dallas. Which is why we can't stay together. And I'm not just talking about my job's being a problem; it's more than that." He stopped and then started again. "I'm afraid you could be in danger. Today. Right now."

"Because you're a vampire or because of what you do?" she asked, holding tightly to his hand, refusing to let go of it.

"Both." He nodded. "With my job, I come in contact with bad people, people so evil . . . you can't imagine."

"World's full of bad people, Aedan. You don't have a monopoly on them."

"I know, but—"

"You understand what I'm saying?" She slid closer to him, so that she could look into his eyes. "You're the best thing that's ever happened to me . . . or Kenzie. So you have to go." She shrugged. "So we can't be together forever, so what? Who gets forever? We can be together for the next few weeks, can't we?"

He started to turn away again, but she wouldn't let him. She pressed his cheeks between her hands and rose up on the couch to kiss him hard on the mouth. For a moment, she thought he might resist her, but then he was kissing her back.

He thrust his tongue into her mouth, and she climbed onto his lap, wrapping her arms around his neck. She couldn't get enough of him. She had no unrealistic hope that the vampire would give up his life's work and stay for her, but that didn't matter. All that mattered right now was that he had said he loved her. *That,* Dallas thought, just might last her a lifetime.

Aedan seemed as hungry for her tonight as she was for him, despite his apparent intention of coming over to break up with her. She pulled her T-shirt and bra off, and he covered her breasts with kisses, licking, sucking her nipples.

She straddled him on the couch, his feet on the floor, her knees digging into the indoor/outdoor cushions. She ground her groin against his, stripping him of his T-shirt and kissing his muscular shoulders.

"Dallas," he murmured. "How do you do this to me? Why do I let you do this?"

Feeling Aedan's growing desire for her, she scooted back and tugged at his belt buckle. She unbuttoned his jeans and slid her hand inside, cupping his balls with her hand. He groaned with pleasure and pushed her over and down into the couch. Both seemed to be in a frenzy. He unbuttoned and unzipped her jeans as she pushed his down his hips.

Neither of them bothered to kick off their shoes, Dallas with her jeans around her ankles, him only getting his down to his knees. She was wet and aching for him before he ran his palm over the blond bed of curls between her thighs. Probed with his fingers. Stroked with his tongue.

"Aedan." She ran her fingers through the thick, ginger hair that she loved. "Love me."

"I do love you," he murmured, stretching over her to kiss the pulse of her throat.

"Make love to me." Her voice caught in her throat as she kicked off her jeans. "Please."

"I am—"

She covered his mouth with her hand, actually feeling as if she was in pain, she needed him so badly. "You know what I mean." She reached down to grasp him in her palm and stroke him.

With the faintest smile, he pushed hard into her. She arched her back, meeting him, welcoming him. She moaned so loudly that he covered her mouth with his hand. She laughed . . . maybe she cried. She was so desperate for the feel of him inside her, the fullness he gave her, not just of body, but soul.

Close to orgasm with the very first stroke, she didn't take long to come. Panting hard, gasping, she ran her hands over his bare buttocks, encouraging him to go faster. Harder.

"We running a race?" he groaned in her ear.

She raised her hips forcefully. "This time around? Yes."

As she came a second time, he surrendered, arched his back, and groaned with his own release.

Dallas wrapped her arms around Aedan's waist as he collapsed on top of her. "Let's go in the bedroom," she murmured in his ear when she caught her breath. "And take it slow this time."

*Aedan dropped to the wooden floorboards that were wet and slick with her blood. Her white blouse and pale green skirt blossomed red.* "Mon amour . . ." *He gathered her in his arms, the smell of her blood thick in his nostrils.*

*Her eyelids fluttered, and then she opened her eyes, but he couldn't tell if she could see him or not. There was so much blood on the floor. Too much blood for any human to lose and still live.*

*"Madeleine," he whispered, pulling her close to his chest.*

*"Aedan . . ." Her breath seemed cool on his cheek. "I'm dying."*

*"Non. No." He smoothed her blond hair, smearing blood in it. His heart was breaking. He couldn't lose her. He couldn't bear it. "No, Madeleine. Don't say that."*

*"It's true," she murmured, her voice becoming breathy. Already ethereal.*

*As she spoke, he could feel the light inside her fading.*

*"Save me," she begged.*

*"I cannot." He squeezed her tightly in his arms, trying desperately to think of a way to help her. Knowing he could not.*

*"You can, my love. You are the only one who can. Make me one of you. Give me eternal life."*

*Aedan gritted his teeth. "I cannot. It is against our laws. Against the laws of nature. Of God. It's a curse."*

*Madeleine had been holding on to his arm, but her hand grew too weak and fell.*

*"Dallas," he groaned, cradling her in his arms.*

*"Make me a vampire. I beg of you, my love."*

*"I cannot." Tears ran down his cheeks, mixing with her blood. "I will not curse you as I've been cursed. I will not."*

# Chapter 22

"*I will not curse you as I have been cursed.*"

"Aedan."

"*I will not curse you as I have been cursed!*"

"Aedan? Aedan wake up. It's a dream. It's just a dream."

Aedan opened his eyes to see Dallas leaning over him, shaking him. Her hair fell around his face, pulling him back to the present. Dallas was alive and well. There was no blood. No gaping wounds. No initial carved into her flesh.

"Dallas," he panted.

"I will not curse you as I've been cursed?" she asked. "What the hell is that about?"

He scrambled to sit up, still breathing hard. His heart felt as if it would burst in his chest. "A nightmare," he said.

"Obviously."

She reached out, but he pulled away.

"You want me to turn the light on?" she asked. She laughed aloud. "Okay, that was a ridiculous thing to say. You probably see better in the dark than I do in the light."

He leaned against the wall, because there was no headboard, and hugged a pillow against his bare chest. He was hot and sweaty, but felt cold at the same time.

She sat up on her knees, facing him, naked. She always slept naked, which he adored.

"That was more than a nightmare. That was real. That happened to you."

He stared straight ahead. She had two stacks of plastic drawers that served as a bureau. On top of it, among the pieces of jewelry, socks, and underwear was a vase, obviously made by a child. Kenzie? Or had Dallas made it herself, years ago? "You shouldn't have been in my head," he told her. "We vampires have rules about that kind of stuff. Aren't there rules with people like you?"

"I don't know any *people like me*. And I was trying to shake you awake," she defended. "You were upset. I didn't need to be a witch to know you were reliving something."

He lowered his head, staring at the tangle of sheets across his bare legs.

"I got a glimpse of her," Dallas said softly. "She looked like me."

"This is private," he snapped, jerking his head around to look at her. Before he could stop, his fangs came down, exposing them to her.

She flinched, but not much.

"I'm sorry," he whispered, contracting his fangs. He lowered his head again, embarrassed. It wasn't so much that he was angry with Dallas, but with himself. Maybe with God for putting him in that position with Madeleine. Being forced to tell her he could not make her a vampire, while she lay dying in his arms. Even though he had the power to give her everlasting life, he had denied her.

Aedan glanced up, tentatively, at Dallas.

Another woman might have run away at that point. At the very least asked him to leave. But not Dallas. Not Dallas, because she wasn't afraid of him, not even when he was at his darkest.

"You might as well tell me." She sat down beside him

and leaned on the wall. She pulled the sheet up over her bare hips to her waist, but left her breasts naked to the cool, night air. "I'll see it eventually, you know. The more you try to hide things from me, the more they're right there, waiting to be seen the minute you let your guard down. Which happens more often than you realize."

He squeezed his eyes shut. "I killed her."

"The woman who looked like me?" she asked uneasily.

"Yes."

She shook her head slowly, refusing to look away from him. "No, you couldn't have. I saw her wounds. She didn't die from a vampire attack."

He shook his head. "No, you don't understand. I didn't *kill* her, but I didn't *save* her. I killed her because I had the power to save her and I didn't."

"You had the power to save her?" Dallas repeated, obviously not following.

Aedan leaned forward, pressing the heels of his hands to his temples. "I arrived before she died. As she was dying. I had the power to give her life—"

"You mean to make her a vampire?" she asked.

"Yes." He was shaking, as all the pain of the decision, the torture of it, came back.

"Are you allowed to do that?" she asked, still sounding as if he were telling an incredibly tall tale.

"No," he exhaled. "There are punishments. Sometimes banishments. It depends on the circumstances. But it wasn't that. It wasn't that I was afraid of what the sept would do. It was about right or wrong. But she didn't understand that. Madeleine. She didn't understand that it is a curse to live forever, to be vampire. That it is eternal damnation. She was very young. Nineteen. She didn't understand," he repeated.

"I understand. It's like my *gift* . . . that I see more as a curse." Dallas slid her hand across the mattress to cover his. She was quiet for a moment before she spoke again. "You did the right thing, Aedan."

For a while he just sat there, unable to lift his head. Finally he turned to look at her. "You think so?"

She picked up his hand, turned it over, and kissed his palm. "You did the right thing, letting her die and go to heaven to be with God, or wherever it is we go. It would have been wrong to have made her a vampire."

"She begged me. She pleaded."

"She was young. She didn't understand the burden you carry. She couldn't see it the way I see it. You did the right thing," she repeated. "By making her a vampire, you would have been damning her."

His gaze met hers in the darkness, and he felt a great release. It was almost as if Madeleine was, through Dallas, granting him forgiveness.

Dallas scooted over in the bed and laid her head down on the pillow in his lap. He stroked her hair, pushing it back over her ear.

"I love you, Dallas," he said, so quietly that she wasn't even certain she had heard it.

She closed her eyes. "I love you, Aedan."

"You get my message?" Kaleigh dug a carrot stick into a dish of dip on the table. "The other day? You never called me."

Aedan took a sip from a red and white plastic cup—Kaleigh's high school colors. Her mother had bought all the paper products in red and white. "No, I didn't get your message. You called?"

It was Sunday afternoon, and Kaleigh's parents were throwing a graduation party for her. Aedan felt like he needed to make an appearance. He'd walked over with Peigi and Brian, literally walking between them to keep them from going at each other. The weird thing was, Peigi was perfectly congenial. She said nothing to Brian about the baggy shorts and wrinkly T-shirt he was wearing or the fact that he looked like he'd just rolled out of bed. Which, of course, he had.

Kaleigh crunched on the carrot stick. "No, I think I texted you. The other day." She wrinkled her freckled nose. She was dressed in a yellow sundress. She looked cute—very high school girlish and not very wisewomanish. "I *think* I did." She shook her head. "Things have been crazy. Maybe I didn't. Or maybe it didn't go. I've been telling my mom I need a new cell."

"Kaleigh, try to focus. This is important." He took her arm to move her away from the table and the others standing in line, waiting for Swedish meatballs, crudités, and mini cheesecakes. She grabbed a handful of carrots. He led her off the back porch and into the yard, away from her family and friends. The sounds of the party faded as Kaleigh and Aedan walked to stand beneath an elm tree. "What did you find out?"

"All kinds of crazy things. Did you know there really *is* a Sasquatch thing?" She chewed on another carrot stick. "At least there used to be. Not around here, but—"

"Kaleigh," Aedan said sharply.

She scowled. "I'm sorry, okay?"

He glanced at the pretty two-story house, his gaze straying to Mary McCathal and Peigi in a private conversation at one end of the porch. Something was up with those two. He tried to listen in on what was going on in their heads, but they had both closed their thoughts to others. Almost as if they had something to hide . . .

He looked back to Kaleigh. "Please, hon, just tell me what you learned. I just don't have the patience for this today."

"Fine. I'm getting to it. I couldn't find anything in our library, but I met this girl online, she's from Romania. She calls herself a *strigoi,* but she's a vampire." Again, Kaleigh wrinkled her cute, little freckled nose. "She's like this expert on creatures."

Against his will, Aedan became curious. "You talk to other vampires *online?*"

"I talk to *you* online sometimes, when you're away."

"I'm a Kahill."

She crunched loudly. "I'm allowed to talk to other vampires. Shoot, you single guys fu—"

He snatched a carrot stick from her hand, interrupting her. "Back to the point, Kaleigh. What did you find out about Jay?"

"Cosmina says he's probably a *sleeper.*"

"A what?" Aedan chewed on the carrot.

"It's a stupid name." She waved enthusiastically to someone on the porch and then returned her attention to Aedan. "They're pretty much human, or at least they look human. But they hibernate for years at a time. They come out of hibernation for a few moon cycles, then back they go."

"Back they go where?"

She shrugged. "Cosmina says it's thought that they go underground or in caves or something. They sort of support each other, taking care of each other when they come out of hibernation. Apparently different sleepers run on different timetables. Of course, obviously, Jay's not taking care of other sleepers because he's here attacking women."

"They live in Romania?"

She shook her head and poked him in the chest with her finger. "*Cosmina* lives in Romania. Sleepers are from—"

"Scotland," Aedan finished for her. He hit his palm with his fist. "Damned if Mark wasn't right. It *was* a Scottish accent." He looked at Kaleigh. "Are they violent?"

"She said not generally, but maybe because they're humanoids, they can be, like any other of God's creatures. Maybe he's just a *bad'n.*"

Aedan chewed on that thought for a moment. "I guess that's possible."

"I know that's not much help, but it's all she knew. She

found the information in some accounts of her vampires running into the same sleepers centuries apart."

Brian and Victor and Kaleigh's boyfriend, Rob, came across the lawn toward them, tossing a volleyball between them. "We're getting up a game," Rob said.

He was older than the others and already beginning training with a kill team with the sept. Aedan liked him; he was sensible. A good guy.

"Everyone's a little bored," Rob said quietly. He winked at her. "You want to play?"

"Just a sec." Kaleigh flashed him a smile.

They made a cute couple.

"Aedan?"

"Nah. Thanks, but I'm going to head out. Got somewhere I gotta be."

"Is it that girl Mary saw you with? She's an HF," Kaleigh sang conspiratorially to the guys. "He's gonna be in big trouble."

"Sounds like we spend more time breaking the rules than following them," Brian observed.

"Sometimes," Aedan agreed. He glanced at Kaleigh. "Thanks for your help."

"No problem. Thanks for the card." She flashed him her pretty smile. "And the moola. That's way better than a silly book about the road to adulthood or something else lame like that."

"Have a good time. Behave yourselves." Aedan waved.

The group walked off, headed for the volleyball net that had been set up in the middle of the lawn.

"Hey, Brian," Aedan called. "Can I talk to you for a sec?" He glanced at the porch. More people were arriving, bearing gifts. Peigi and Mary were still standing alone, talking.

"Yeah?" Brian walked back to Aedan and stood in front of him, hands in his front pockets, looking completely awkward.

"Anything going on with you and Peigi I should know about?"

He shrugged his scrawny shoulders. "Not that I know of. Why?"

"I don't know. Have you noticed she's been acting a little strange?"

"She hasn't been riding my ass, if that's what you mean." Another shrug. He looked up at Aedan. "Actually, she's been kind of nice these last couple of days. Maybe she just needed to let off some steam. You know, with the fireball thing?"

"Maybe." Aedan glanced at the porch again. This time Mary and Peigi were both looking right at him. "Okay, well, catch you later."

"Catch you later, man."

Aedan headed in one direction and Brian another.

*What's going on, Peigi?* Aedan telepathed.

*Nothing,* she shot back. *What makes you think anything's going on?*

*I don't like this, Peigi. I'm worried about you.*

*Don't be.* She smiled. *You know I love you, Aedan. As if you were my own son.*

*I love you, too,* he telepathed. *So please don't do anything stupid.*

She smiled at him, again with innocence. *Do I ever?*

"Aedan's coming," Kenzie said. She was sitting at the kitchen table playing with Play-Doh.

Dallas stood at the kitchen sink rinsing off lasagna noodles and trying to read over the recipe in the magazine she'd picked up at the grocery store. She was great in a bar kitchen, but a chef she was not. She'd actually had to ask the guy in the produce section what shallots were. "Yup," she said, glancing over her shoulder. "Aedan's coming for dinner, and then maybe we'll go for a walk on the boardwalk."

"No." Kenzie sat stock still in her chair, her arms stiffly at her sides. She wasn't looking at Dallas, which wasn't all that unusual, but she had a strange look on her face. "Bad man."

Dallas groaned inwardly but made a conscious effort not to let her daughter see her frustration. "We've been over this. You like Aedan. He's not a bad man."

"Bad man," she repeated. "Boardwalk."

Dallas turned back toward the sink, shutting off the faucet. "Kenzie, Kenzie, what's your mama going to do?"

"Die," Kenzie said.

Her voice was so eerie that Dallas spun around, water from her hands dripping on the floor. "What did you say, Kenzie?"

The little girl picked up a glob of blue Play-Doh, dropped it, and began to mash it.

"Kenzie! That's not very nice. We don't joke around about stuff like that. You understand me?"

"Madeleine," the little girl said, pressing her thumb into the middle of the Play-Doh. "Dead."

Dallas felt the blood drain from her face. "Oh, Kenzie, no." She walked over to her daughter and put her arms around her shoulders and hugged her. It didn't matter that Kenzie made no response. Dallas closed her eyes, fighting tears. She'd tried so hard to protect Kenzie, but she was afraid it wasn't working.

# Chapter 23

*I enjoyed my evening. I strolled the boardwalk, eating my caramel corn and drinking a delightful drink called pop, watching the young women in shameful attire pass by. Behaving in shameful ways. But now it is time to get down to business. With so little time until I must sleep again, I cannot dally. Usually I will watch a woman for a few nights. Study her habits. But tonight I am in the mood for something more impulsive. The thought excites me.*

*So many trollops to choose from! How will I ever choose?*

*As the shops close, as the streets become quieter, I begin to study with a knowledgeable eye, looking for an opportunity. She must be alone. Intoxicated would be acceptable. They are usually easy enough to spot. Stumbling. Preoccupied works, too. On the phone.*

*I walk the avenue twice before I choose and begin to follow her. I stay back far enough so that she doesn't notice. She won't notice. She's too busy arguing with someone on the phone. A male voice. Her lover perhaps. She wears a short skirt and high heels that click-clack when she walks. She probably has many lovers. She probably accepts money for sex.*

*Whores. All of them.*

*The streetlights are bright, but there are patches of darkness. It is the darkness I desire. I adore.*

*She turns the corner and looks back over her shoulder. I stop and gaze in a store window. I pretend to sip from the straw in the empty paper cup I carry. She doesn't notice me. I wait until she is half a block away before I begin to follow her again. She is still on the phone.*

*It is darker here, on the side street. Fewer parked cars. No pedestrians. There are no bars on this street. Just shops that have closed for the night. Ahead, I see a patch of darkness on the sidewalk. A street lamp is out. It is perfect.*

*I walk faster. She is speaking loudly into her phone. She calls him a son of a bitch, whomever it is she speaks to. I am quiet, and she is loud. Checking to be sure no one sees me, I sprint two or three steps and wrap one arm around her neck. She cries out. Her cell phone hits the ground and plastic pieces scatter. I cover her lips with my hand from behind and am shocked when she opens her mouth wide and bites me.*

*I cry out, out of surprise more than pain. I am shocked. I am used to being in total control of the situation. She tries to wrench free. They usually struggle some, but not like this one. I pull the knife from my pocket as I drag her toward an alley. There is a trash Dumpster that will give me the privacy I need.*

*But she does not go easily. Not even when she sees the glimmer of the blade. My hand slips off her mouth, and she screams.*

*I raise the knife to her throat, but she manages to sink her elbow into my abdomen. I am so shocked by her attack that I am slow to respond. She twists in my arms, using both fists to hit me. Somehow my arm gets in the air; she pulls it down, and the knife nicks my cheek. It's not deep, the cut.*

*But it burns.*

*It makes me angry that she would do such a thing to me. It makes me want to kill her.*

Peigi stood in the hallway listening to the sound of automatic gunfire, the sound of her husband's voice. She assumed he was wearing his headset, playing online. He played with people all over the world, via the Internet, which really was pretty amazing when she thought about it. There had been a time in their lives when games consisted of wooden dice that Brian hand-carved, and they had communicated with others over any distance by carrier pigeon.

"Yes! Take that, fucker!"

Peigi cringed. She knew it was just a word, a word that had been around since the beginning of time. Nonetheless, she hated hearing it come out of her sweet Brian's mouth.

Who really wasn't all that sweet right now, anyway.

There was more gunfire. An explosion. Another "fucker."

She walked into the den. She'd purposely not put on her robe yet; she knew he hated it. The funny thing was, he'd hated it six months ago at the age of seventy-three, too. As much as she hated to admit it, he was right. It *was* frumpy.

"Hey." She stepped into the den.

Brian sort of nodded in her direction. His thumbs flew over the game controller, and explosives boomed on the TV screen.

"Victor still out?" she asked, just trying to make conversation. They never knew what to say to each other anymore. And that was probably the worst thing about their present relationship. She and Brian had *always* had something to talk about.

"He stayed at Kaleigh's graduation party. I think a bunch of them were going out for ice cream."

"You could have gone," she said, feeling almost shy with him, now that she knew how things were going to go.

How different they would be. "I could have walked home myself. You didn't have to escort me."

"Behind!" Brian shouted.

Peigi startled.

"The guy I'm playing with," he explained, motioning with the controller. "He was gonna get his ass blown off."

Peigi stared at the screen, at something that looked like a remote-controlled car with explosives tied on top. Brian was driving it down a bombed-out street. "What's that?" she asked, squinting to see the screen. She needed her glasses, but she didn't know where they'd gotten to.

"RC-XD. You, like, earn them with kill points. You can send them in to kill people without having to risk your own ass."

She nodded.

"I'm on Prestige 14. 'Black Ops.' Pretty amazing, huh?"

"Pretty amazing." She stood there a moment longer, looking at Brian rather than the TV screen. She wasn't angry with him anymore. In fact, now that she'd been able to let some things go, she could actually see some aspects of his personality that could be appealing. He was cute . . . and he could be kind. He'd walked her home from the party instead of hanging out with the other teenagers.

"I'm going up for a bath, then I'm turning in. Make sure Victor locks the door when he comes in."

"Right." Brian laughed as a soldier on the screen fell dead in a pool of blood on a staircase. "I feel sorry for the poor sucker of a human who accidently tries to rob *this* house. You'll light him on fire, and then me and Victor and Kaleigh and Katy'll all jump on top of him and suck his blood." He bared his fangs with a grin, then quickly covered his mouth with his hand. "Sorry," he said, his voice muffled.

"We don't jump on top of humans and suck their blood," she said, trying not to be amused by his antics.

"Aw! Damn it!" He dropped his controller. "I died. I gotta start over."

"Sorry." She backed through the doorway.

"It's not your fault. I suck on this level, anyway." He picked up the controller again. " 'Night, Peigi."

She smiled as she walked up the stairs in the dark. Even after all these centuries, she still liked the way he said her name.

Aedan eased his Honda into a parking spot next to a state police cruiser and checked the clock on his dashboard. It was one-thirty. He'd gotten out of bed without waking Dallas at one, when Mark called. The state police troop Mark worked out of in Lewes was only a few miles from Brew. It hadn't taken Aedan any time at all to get there.

He morphed as he opened the car door, to a female in her thirties: black pants, black-and-white top, sensible black shoes, and a black briefcase he wore on a strap over his shoulder. He wore his brown hair pulled up on his head in a knot and small, silver hoop earrings. He looked like some mid-level state employee, or a counselor, some sort of professional woman. He made her nondescript on purpose. In the middle of the night, no one would spend too much time wondering why she was here. Not with Detective Karr having just brought in a witness.

In the lobby, Aedan gave his name. Angela Perkins. He said in a professional voice that Detective Karr was expecting him. A minute later, a door buzzed and Mark walked out, offering his hand.

"Detective Karr, nice to see you. Angela Perkins," Aedan said quietly.

"Jeez, Aedan," Mark muttered under his breath, good-naturedly. "I *still* wish you'd give me some sort of warning. I never know who I'm looking for with you. Come on." He adjusted the cinnamon toothpick in the corner of his mouth.

There was the audible buzz again, and then Mark swung open the door. Mark led him down a hall that looked like the hall in any state office: slightly dingy, beige walls, tile floor, fluorescent light. Mark took a door to the right and then entered an interrogation room, which tonight served as an interview room. If the state police had had an "award room," that's where this girl should have been. She deserved an award for what she'd done.

"Kristen, this is Angela Perkins. I told you the state might send someone over, just to go over some things with you."

The woman was in her early twenties, average height, with dark hair and heavy black eyeliner around her eyes. She sipped from a Coke can. "I told the detective I don't need any counseling, and I don't need to go to the hospital."

As Aedan slipped into the chair across the table from Kristen, he noticed that the young woman looked unharmed. The only thing that looked out of place on her was the too-large blue T-shirt she wore that advertised the importance of proper car seat installation.

He guessed that her blouse had been taken for evidence.

He set his briefcase on the floor; there was nothing in it except for his cell phone. "I won't keep you long, Miss Jewel. I know it's been a long night and you just want to get home."

"I want to wash that asshole's filth off, is what I want to do." She looked up at Mark. "You think I could bother you for some of those crackers? I am kind of hungry, now that I think about it. Fighting crime has given me an appetite." She grinned at him.

"No problem. Ms. Perkins?"

"Nothing for me, thanks, Detective." Aedan returned his attention to the young woman in front of him as Mark went out the door. "The detective already told me what happened, but I just want to go over a few things with you, if you don't mind."

"I guess. But can we make it snappy? I really want to go home." She sat back.

"Did you get a good look at your attacker?"

"It was dark," she said. "But I got a look at him, the little prick. I'm going to talk to a sketch artist in the morning. Give my description. Detective Karr said I could go home and shower and come back. He's nice. The detective. He's gonna call my boss, explain what happened, and get me the day off. I work at the outlets. I hate leavin' my boss with no one to cover like this, but like Detective Karr said, this is too important. The police might be able to catch this asshole this time. I cut him, did he tell you? Right across his cheek." She grinned as she motioned with her finger across her cheek.

"You're sure you cut him?"

She took another sip of her soda. "Hell yes, I'm sure. He was bleeding. Got his blood all over my new tank top and jacket. He acted like no one had ever fought him before." She leaned forward in her chair. "What's wrong with girls? Don't they know they're supposed to fight and kick and scream? I screamed. I screamed like he was killing me even though I had no intention of letting that prick kill me. I got tickets to see the Beastie Boys with my girlfriends this weekend. I wasn't lettin' anyone rape me, put me in the hospital," she declared.

Aedan couldn't help but smile. "Okay, so he came up behind you."

"I was on Maryland. That's where I'd left my car. I had dinner with friends at Grottos. We had some beers, but I wasn't drunk. I definitely wasn't drunk." She scowled. "I was on the phone with my boyfriend. It was like eleven-thirty, maybe. He was all pissed off because he heard I went out with this guy, only I didn't."

Aedan wasn't interested in anything to do with Kristen's love life, but he knew from past experience that it was important that he listen to the victim's story the way she wanted to tell it. It was the way to get all the details. And it was *her* story. She had a right to tell it.

"So I'm on the phone with my boyfriend and I sort of hear someone come up behind me. One second my boo is bitchin' me out; the next thing I know, he's got his arm around my neck and I drop my phone. It hits the sidewalk and goes in pieces."

"I thought you called the police from your cell phone."

"I did." She took another sip of Coke. "After the dude ran, I went back, picked up my phone, put the battery back in, and called 911."

Aedan nodded. "Okay, so your attacker is behind you, with his hand around your neck—"

"His arm, like the inside of his elbow." She demonstrated, thrusting her elbow out toward him. "It all happened so fast. I was so scared I thought I was going to piss my pants, but I screamed and I started twisting and kicking and punching. Then, somehow, we were facing each other, and that was when I saw him. Squirrely little face. He looked a lot like that brother on *Two and a Half Men*. You know the show? The guy Alan? He looked like him."

Aedan didn't watch the show, but he'd seen advertisements on TV. He knew what the actor looked like. Sweet Mary, Mother of God, suddenly he had a face to go with Jay's name.

"He got in front of me, and he pulls this knife and starts draggin' me into this alley. I knew who he was. My Aunt Silva read stuff out of the paper to me. What he does to girls. No man is gonna rape me," she warned. "Not without me putting up a fight."

Aedan just sat there and listened, knowing he was at that point in the interview where that was all he needed to do.

"I just went crazy, and I guess it surprised him." She set down the can. "I mean, he was the one with knife. And *he* gets cut? Somehow I got my pepper spray off my bag. I still had my bag. My Aunt Silva gave me the pepper spray. She gave it to all her nieces for Christmas. She always gives us crazy stuff like that. Anyway, I pull the pepper spray off my bag—it's hooked on by the cap, so the cap is off now—and I stick it in his face, and I pull the trigger. I don't know where the knife is by then. I don't care. That stuff sprays out, and he starts yelpin'. I guess I got him right in the eyes, maybe even in the cut on his cheek. He kind of stumbles back, and I turned around and ran. I think he ran, too. I think I heard him running in the opposite direction. I ran out of the alley, grabbed my phone and the battery off the sidewalk, and I kept running until I got to the corner where there was better light and some cars. And I called 911. They sent a Rehoboth cop to get me, and then Detective Karr got me at the police station and brought me here." She raised her arms and let them fall. "And here I am." She took a breath. "Guess I'm pretty lucky."

Aedan smiled at her, thinking to himself that this might just be the break he had been hoping for. "Not lucky. Brave. And tough. You beat him, Kristen. And you probably saved your own life."

The cottage was surprisingly dark and quiet when Aedan arrived home around four in the morning. After talking with Kristen Jewel, he'd chatted with Mark in the parking lot for a few minutes. Mark agreed with him that this might be the turning point in the case. He was going to get the sketch artist's sketch in every newspaper and every storefront in the area. With the cut on his face, he was bound to be recognized by someone. Aedan had then driven back into Rehoboth, just to have a look at the crime scene. He'd walked up and down the block. Seeing nothing and no one of interest, he'd headed home.

Aedan was surprised when he got to the house to find the front door locked. He had to find the key under a flowerpot in one of the flowerbeds. When he let himself in, even the den was quiet; for once, the TV was off. Leaving the key on a table in the hall, he went quietly upstairs. The door to the boys' room was closed. Peigi's door at the end of the hallway was closed, too. He used the hall bathroom and then went to his own room. He stripped and climbed into bed, feeling like maybe he could get a few hours of real sleep, something he felt like he hadn't gotten in weeks.

As Aedan laid his head on his pillow, he felt something under his cheek. He heard a crackle of paper. "What the hell?"

He found a note on his pillow. He read the short note, in the dark, twice, before swinging his legs over the side of the bed and dropping his head into his hands.

"Ah, Aunt Peigi," he whispered, his eyes tearing up. "What have you done?"

# Chapter 24

"God. I'm so sorry about Peigi." Mark slid into the booth across the table from Aedan. "You hear about people *talking* about doing it." He shook his head, pulling a toothpick out of his mouth. "But nobody actually does it. Who's got the balls? She actually bled to death?" he said as if he still didn't believe the facts. "I didn't even think it was possible . . . for a vampire."

"Apparently it's possible if you do it right." Aedan leaned back in his seat at the diner and closed his eyes for a second. His head was so full of the voices around him that he could barely think. Everyone in Clare Point was talking about Peigi Ross, about what she had done. The news would be all over the world, via the vampire network, by tonight. "She cut her carotid artery just right." He drew his thumb across his neck. "Bled out faster than her body could replace the blood." He opened his eyes, sitting up again. "Did it in her bathtub . . . so I wouldn't have a mess to clean up."

Aedan tried not to think about how he had held her lifeless body in his arms. How hard it had been to make the phone call to Gair. Waking Brian to tell him. Brian had been stunned, not completely understanding exactly what she had done or how it would impact them all. He and

Victor and all the teens were gathered at the cottage now; the TV had been silent all day.

Mark folded his hands together and leaned forward on the table. "And the Council is going to let her be reborn?"

"What choice do they have?" Aedan shrugged. "You know the drill. We've all been there. On the third day . . ."

"I'll be there for the rebirth. I promise."

"Thanks. I appreciate it. Someone needs to be there to keep me from killing her again when I get ahold of her."

"Of course, when she's first reborn she might not even remember what she did," Mark pointed out. "Then you're the schmuck standing there hollering at a sixteen-year-old girl who doesn't know what the hell is going on to begin with."

Mark was totally right, which was partially why Aedan was so upset. It might be years before Peigi would fully realize what she'd done. He was angry. He understood why she had done it, but he was still angry with her. Everyone in Clare Point was angry with her, and that anger would come out tonight at the emergency Council Meeting that had been called to decide what they were going to do with Peigi once she was reborn. There had to be punishment. The question would be, how severe?

Aedan motioned toward the front counter. "I ordered both of us an iced tea. I'm having the chicken fried steak. It's the special."

Mark followed Aedan's hand with his gaze. "You can't blame yourself for this."

"Sure I can. She threatened to do it. I should have taken her more seriously." He opened his arms, looking back on the last few days. "But she seemed fine. You know, after she found out the Council was going to deny her request."

"You can't stop a vampire from doing what she's going to do. Not one as stubborn as Peigi."

Aedan sighed. "You're right." He slid a menu across the table. "Maryann said she'd be back to get your order."

Mark picked up the menu. "Any idea what the sanctions will be?"

Aedan toyed with a saltshaker. "Well, obviously they're going to take away her position on the General Council. She actually left instructions on her desk, for all of us. She's put Mary Kay up to be the next head of the Council. Peigi appointed Mary McCathal as her and Brian's guardian until they're of age." He exhaled. "We'll find out tonight what the Council's going to do."

"You think they'll decide tonight?"

Aedan nodded, then looked up, ready to change the subject. "So what's going on with the investigation?"

"Kristen did a super job working with the sketch artist. Jay's picture's gone out to all the newspapers. We've already got uniformed cops passing out fliers at hotels, restaurants, shops." He was quiet for a minute. "You know, there's a good possibility we're not going to catch him this time. He might take off. He's got less than two weeks 'til hibernation, if your hunch is right. He could go home. He could move to another town, another state, another country."

"He's not leaving town. Not on this note," Aedan theorized. "He'll be out there again, stalking. He'll rape again before he goes."

"Yeah, well, buddy, I hate to say this, but it would be okay with me if you were wrong this time."

"Ladies, gentlemen, could I have your attention?" Mary Kay asked in a clear, authoritarian tone. It was her first official night as the new leader of the General Council. "Could everyone take his or her seat so we can get this over with?"

Aedan stood near the display case with the fake coins and real hinges from the captain's cabin of the ship they'd come to America on, and watched as Council members, everyone talking at once, made their way to the circle of chairs. It was a full house tonight. Usually, at least 25 percent of the members were missing on any given night, but tonight, anyone who was supposed to be here, was here. The only person he was expecting who wasn't here yet, was Kaleigh. She wasn't a regular member of the Council, but as the wisewoman of the sept, she had the right to attend any meetings and speak anytime she felt her wisdom was needed. Aedan needed her tonight. He'd been counting on her.

He leaned over to speak quietly to Brian. He hadn't thought having Brian here was a good idea, but Mary Kay had insisted. The kid barely knew what was going on with the sept, yet, and he certainly didn't understand what Peigi had done. Aedan hadn't been able to explain to him why, if she committed suicide, but was going to be reborn, she was in so much trouble. It had to do with the Kahills' special relationship with God and their attempt to be redeemed. Not only was suicide a sin to the Kahills, but the act threatened the eternal redemption, not just of the individual who took his or her own life, but possibly the entire sept's. The sept had to, therefore, hand down a harsh punishment, to set an example to the others as to why they couldn't kill themselves whenever they got fed up with the life cycle they were in.

It was hard for Aedan to grasp the whole concept, so it was no wonder Brian was looking lost tonight . . . and a little scared.

"These are all vampires?" Brian whispered, watching as the Council members took their chairs in the main room of the museum. "Kind of creepy."

"No, not at all. This is your family," Aedan assured him. "They wouldn't hurt you. The Council protects you."

Brian cut his eyes at Aedan. "But they're going to punish Peigi as soon as she's reborn tomorrow night?"

Aedan exhaled. "I told you this would be a lot to take in. You'll come to understand it all, with time."

"Aedan? Brian?" Mary Kay smiled. "Join us?"

As Aedan and Brian entered the circle and sat side by side near Mary Kay, the vampires all got quiet. Everyone was looking at him and Brian, almost to the point of making *him* feel uncomfortable.

*I didn't do this,* Aedan telepathed, making it a general message. *I didn't kill Peigi, and I didn't know she was going to kill herself.*

*But you had an idea.*

*She listened to you.*

*You could have stopped it.*

*You could have told us.*

The thoughts bounced around the room, around in Aedan's head, until he threw up his hands. "Enough!" he declared, coming out of his chair. "You have something to say, you say it out loud so Brian can hear you. You know he can't read your thoughts, and of all of us in this room, he's the one most affected by what you're about to decide." He yanked at the front of his leather coat, trying to get control of his own tumultuous emotions. "So be honorable Kahill men and women and speak up."

Everyone was silent for a moment, in the room and in Aedan's head.

"Well," Mary Kay said, looking from one Council member to the next. "Shall we get on with this distasteful task?" She looked down at notes she'd scribbled on a yellow legal pad. "I did a little research in the library today, and while no one has ever committed suicide that we know of"—she glanced up at the circle, then back at her notes again—"there is precedent."

The back door of the building slammed, catching everyone's attention.

"Sorry, sorry," Kaleigh called. *Sorry I'm late. Teenage drama at the—oh, never mind. You don't need to know that crap,* she telepathed.

A sense of relief came over Aedan. Kaleigh was here

now. She was the voice of reason. She would be the voice of reason for Peigi, who could not speak for herself now.

"Sorry to interrupt." Kaleigh entered the room, grabbed a chair from behind the table where coffee was being served, and dragged it loudly across the tile floor. "Sorry." She offered a quick, cute smile. She stopped near Brian's chair, next to John Kahill's. There was no room for hers. "You mind, John? Could you just scooch over?"

John got out of his chair, and so did three people to his right. Everyone's chair made a screeching sound as they all moved to accommodate Kaleigh.

"Thanks." She plopped down next to Brian and patted his hand.

Brian's face turned bright red.

Mary Kay cleared her throat. "As I was saying, there is precedent."

"There was no beheading," someone said. "I'd remember a beheading."

"Certainly not," someone else answered.

Brian looked at Aedan, his eyes wide. "They could behead her?" he whispered. "But then she couldn't be reborn, right? She could never be saved from the curse, she could never be—"

"We're not beheading her," Aedan said firmly.

"We're not beheading her," Kaleigh assured him.

"What are you going to do to her, then?" Brian must have spoken louder than he intended, because, suddenly, all the General Council members were looking at him.

Aedan sensed that if Brian could have crawled out of the room, he would have.

"Banishment," Mary Hall declared.

"Banishment," someone else agreed.

"We can't have our members thinking they can off themselves whenever they like," John Kahill said, "just because they're having a bad day."

"It wasn't like that and you know it!" Tavia shouted from across the circle.

"How do you know?" Mary Hall demanded. "Did you know she was going to do this? Should you be taking partial responsibility for this?"

"God knows Mary McCathal should be," someone put in. "Why isn't she here? Maybe we should be considering sanctions against her."

"Ladies, gentlemen," Mary Kay said loudly.

"Maybe we should consider beheading her," John said. "That would certainly serve as a deterrent in the future."

Aedan had been looking in Tavia's direction when John spoke. Out of the corner of his eye, he saw Brian move, but the kid was so fast. Incredibly fast for a teenage vampire. One second Brian was seated beside Aedan; the next, he was in front of John Kahill and had the guy by the collar, fangs bared, yanking him out of his chair.

"Brian, no!" Kaleigh flew between them and the room erupted.

Aedan grabbed Brian by the shoulders, and dragged him back. "Easy, easy," he soothed.

"He's talking about Peigi," Brian muttered under his breath, sounding as if he was about to cry. "About my Peigi."

Realizing he was now standing in the center of the Council Circle and that everyone was looking at him, Brian wiped at his eyes in embarrassment. "I'm sorry," he whispered. "I don't even understand what's going on here." He wiped his eyes with his arm again. "I don't understand why I'm so upset."

Kaleigh took Brian's arm and led him back to his seat. "You care because she's your wife," she said softly. "Because you love her."

Brian sank into his chair. "I don't want her to be beheaded."

“We’re not beheading anyone,” Mary Kay announced, using her authoritative tone. “Now, that’s enough. According to precedent, Peigi Ross should be exiled.”

“She should be banished,” someone said.

“Exiled, not banished,” Mary Kay responded firmly. “Banishment is permanent; exile is not.”

Surprisingly, everyone grew quiet.

“For how long?” Mary Hall asked. “Giving her a year or two away from Brian and Clare Point isn’t much of a punishment.”

“I guess you’d make it a life cycle if you had your way, wouldn’t you?” Tavia asked Mary, her tone accusing.

Mary stood up, planting her hands on her ample hips. “No, actually, I think a life cycle would be harsh,” she said, surprising everyone in the room, including Aedan. “I think it would be excessive . . . especially since whatever we do to Peigi, we have to remember that we’re doing to Brian.” She gestured toward the teen. “And he was no part of this.”

“Mary Hall the voice of reason?” Kaleigh whispered. “And who says there are no longer miracles?”

In other circumstances, Aedan might have smiled.

“So what do you propose, Mary?” Mary Kay asked.

Mary Hall took her time, seeming to enjoy her moment in the limelight. “A twenty-five-year exile. That will give Peigi time to think about what she did. We can send her to Lia’s people in Italy. God knows those vampires owe us a favor.”

“Twenty-five years? That’s not long enough.”

“Twenty-five years? Isn’t that overkill?”

“I say fifty years.”

Then everyone was talking at once, again.

“They want to send Peigi away?” Brian whispered to Aedan.

“Yes. She’ll be sent to live with non-Kahill vampires.

She'll be safe, but she'll be allowed no contact with any of us."

"I can't see her?"

Aedan shook his head. "Not for the time specified by the Council. Then all would be forgiven, and she'd be welcomed back into the sept."

"Even twenty-five years seems like a long time," Brian murmured.

"To you right now, sure. To her, for a while, yes." Aedan shrugged. "But it's not so long when you think about the fact that we've been around for fifteen-hundred years."

Mary Kay let the Council members talk for a minute, then she held up her hand. "Ladies, gentleman. We want to get home tonight. Do I have a motion on the floor?"

The remainder of the meeting went quickly. It only took two votes to reach a majority decision, and Aedan soon found himself on the sidewalk, walking Brian home in the dark. Kaleigh walked with them.

"So that's it?" Brian asked.

"That's it," Aedan said. "The decision is final. Peigi will be exiled for twenty-five years."

"Can . . . can I see her? When . . . when she comes alive? Just for a few minutes?"

"No. Because the sentence is immediate. She'll be taken from the churchyard to the airport."

Brian looked at Kaleigh. "I . . . I can't talk to her?" he repeated. He sounded lost.

Kaleigh rubbed his arm. "It'll be okay, Brian. You'll be okay. Time goes by quicker than you realize."

"But . . . where am I going to live? Do I stay in the house? It's my house."

Aedan glanced at Kaleigh in the darkness. "The details have to be worked out, but Peigi must have known this sort of thing might happen. She asked Mary McCathal to take you in. So you and Victor can, you know, hang out."

"She knew this might happen?" Brian looked at Aedan, then Kaleigh. "She knew she'd have to give up her job as the Council leader and would be sent away? I don't understand. Why would she do this?" He sounded close to tears again.

Aedan exhaled, trying to get control of his emotions; otherwise, he would be crying, too. "She did it for you, Brian. For both of you. Because she loves you."

# Chapter 25

*It feels good to be out again, after staying cooped up in the condo for more than a week. Thank goodness I had the forethought to rent through the Internet rather than staying at a hotel where I might have been seen.*

*For days I nursed my wound . . . and my festering anger. I only meant to toy with the vampire, taunt him a little. Then my intention was to disappear . . . and revisit in fifty years. But the vampire has made this personal. He has put a likeness of me in newspapers, on the TV. Even in the mini market, where lowlifes abound in the middle of the night. I will have to wear a cap on my head and keep my eyes downcast so no one will take notice of me.*

*Fortunately, I heal quicker than humans. A touch of women's makeup, and no one can see the gash the whore made. I also resorted to using a bottle of blond hair dye. I know I should go home, to the safety of my lair, but I hate the idea of leaving on such a sour note.*

*And there is the favor to repay for the annoyance the vampire has caused.*

*It took me two days to find his car again. This time I did not leave a note. But I did follow him to see where he goes. Who he stalks. I even went inside one night and had a beer when he was not there.*

*She is pretty, the tart behind the bar. And vaguely famil-*

*iar. It takes some time for me to put two and two together. I recall the tavern wench near Orange and realize how much this woman looks like that one. Then I realize this pretty woman at the bar is the vampire's whore.*

*One more book,* Kenzie telepathed.

"No more," Aedan said. He sat in her bed beside her, legs stretched out. "Your mom said two books. She's the boss, applesauce."

In an unusual display of physical affection, Kenzie slipped her hand in Aedan's. *I don't want you to go. I don't want you to leave us. I'm afraid,* she telepathed.

He set the book on the cardboard box beside the bed that was shaped like a red and blue racecar. *Of what? There's nothing to be afraid of.*

*The bad man.*

He turned to look at her, but she wouldn't meet his gaze. She stared straight ahead at the *Transformers* poster on her wall.

*What bad man?*

*You know.*

*I don't know, Kenzie,* he telepathed, trying not to seem impatient. *You have to tell me.*

It had been a long week: Peigi's suicide and the uproar in Clare Point it had caused, her rebirth and immediate exile. Trying to help Brian understand and deal with everything that was happening. Then there was the way Jay had just disappeared again. Aedan truly feared Mark was right, that Jay had fled. On one hand, that meant women would be safe from him for another fifty years. On the other hand, it would mean they wouldn't be safe in another fifty years. And Aedan would have failed. Again. The sketch they had distributed hadn't given them the results they had hoped for. They'd gotten hundreds of leads; none had led anywhere. Apparently Jay really did look like an ordinary guy, and everyone saw him everywhere: on the boardwalk, in restaurants, at Funland.

*Don't leave us.*

Aedan closed his eyes and rubbed his temples, wondering if it was time to warn Kenzie that eventually, he would have to go. But the truth was, he didn't know when he would be leaving. With Peigi's death and rebirth, everything was unsettled. Mary McCathal seemed set on looking out for the teenagers, but Aedan wasn't sure how he felt about that. Wasn't Peigi his responsibility? And Brian, too? They'd cared for him when he was a teenager.

"Everything okay in here?" Dallas entered the dimly lit bedroom.

"Just finishing up the book." Aedan got out of Kenzie's bed, extracting his hand from hers.

"Give me a kiss good night." Dallas walked over to the bed and leaned over.

Kenzie rolled onto her side, presenting her back to her mother.

Dallas looked at Aedan as if to say, "what's up with her?"

Aedan shrugged. " 'Night, sugar pie."

*Don't go,* Kenzie telepathed. *You'll be sorry if you go.*

*I need more information than that,* Aedan shot back.

Kenzie responded with silence.

" 'Night, sweetie." Dallas followed Aedan out the door, shutting the light off on the way out.

"She seems moody tonight," Dallas commented. She glanced over her shoulder as they went down the hall. "Of course, you do, too. You have been for days."

"I told you." He walked into her bedroom. "I've got a lot going on."

Inside her room, she closed the door. "You could tell me what." Before he could speak, she sat on the bed and brought her hands to her head and said, with frustration, "and don't tell me *vampire business.*"

"I don't want to argue, Dallas." He stood at the foot of her bed looking at her, his hands hanging at his sides. "You want me to go?"

She looked at him for a second and then reached out and grabbed his hand and pulled him toward her. "No, I don't *want you to go*. I want you to tell me what's going on in your life. And I want you to explain to me how all those people are in your head. They're not just people you've met. Some of them *are* you."

"I don't want to talk about it. Not now. Maybe not ever." He opened his arms. "I'm sorry I can't do what you want."

She sighed, and pulled him closer. "How about this? I want you to make hot vampire love to me, then I want you to spend the night and make breakfast for me in the morning. Can you do that?"

He looked down at her and smiled. They were still holding hands. "I can do that."

Aedan wasn't expecting a phone call from Mark. Possibly not for another fifty years. But when his cell phone, in his jeans pocket, lying on the floor, vibrated, he woke instantly.

"Aedan?"

"Yeah?" He held the phone to his ear, still lying in bed beside Dallas, who slept soundly.

"Come now."

"Okay," he said, still not fully awake.

"*Now,* Aedan." Mark's voice sounded strange. Tight.

Aedan sat up.

"His latest victim. She says she has a message for you. From *him*."

"A message?" He got out of bed and pulled on his pants.

"She won't tell me what it is. She's scared to death,

Aedan. He said he'd come back and finish her off if she didn't pass on the message to Aedan Brigid."

"I'll be right there."

Aedan kissed Dallas good-bye and whispered to her that he'd try to be back in the morning for breakfast, that *duty called*. She mumbled something about French toast and rolled over and went back to sleep. Aedan let himself out and walked to his car. It was raining.

As he drove as fast as he could to the hospital in downtown Lewes, he thought about what Jay's message might be. Some sort of farewell? It was still almost a week until the full moon. But maybe this was it: his last hurrah for another fifty years. There was talk of sending troopers to the local airports later in the week, closer to the full moon; but how would Mark explain the significance of the moon to his superiors? And Jay had several choices of where to fly out of: Baltimore, Philadelphia, Dulles, Newark, even JFK. They could distribute the flyers, but it would be like looking for a needle in a haystack with no name and the "everyman" sketch they had of his face.

At the hospital, Aedan pulled up to the Emergency Room doors, morphed into an EMT with red hair and a badge that said Aedan Brigid, and walked inside. He found Mark pacing outside a curtained exam room. "She's bad, Aedan," he murmured. "I'm surprised she can still speak."

"What's her name?" Aedan's gaze was fixed on the curtain.

"Sadie."

Aedan took a deep breath and walked into the cubicle. Like the other victims, she was on an IV as well as having a heart monitor and a blood pressure cuff that wheezed as it took her blood pressure at regular intervals. Her eyes were closed, buried in her bandaged face.

"Sadie?"

Her eyes flew open; they were the prettiest green. She stared at the light fixture over her head, startled.

He walked over to her bedside and laid his hand on her. "My name is Aedan Brigid. I understand you have a message for me?"

She turned her head toward him slowly. "Aedan Brigid?" she whispered, her voice breathy.

"Yes." He squeezed her fingers.

"You know him?" she asked, as if horrified by the very thought.

"Not really."

She swallowed. "I'm sorry."

"What?"

"I'm so sorry." Tears ran from the corners of her eyes to dampen the white gauze on her face. "He said to tell you"—she choked—"he said to tell you, you had made a fine choice. Again."

For a moment Aedan felt so light-headed that he thought he might pass out. Vampires didn't pass out. He felt his fangs vibrate the way they did sometimes when he had to fight to keep them retracted. "What? Tell me again. Tell me exactly what he said."

Mark stepped into the room.

Tears streamed down the battered woman's face. "He said . . . you made a fine choice, *again*. I don't know what it means." She began to cry. "But he said if I didn't tell you—"

"It's okay." Aedan squeezed her hand and glanced at Mark. "Stay with her! Don't let her out of your sight." Aedan ducked out of the curtain and ran for the exit.

# Chapter 26

Aedan didn't know what to expect.

Yes, he did. He was too late. He knew he was too late. That clever fucking bastard Jay had drawn Aedan to the hospital so he could get to Dallas.

He pounded his fist on the dashboard as he drove in the pouring rain. *That fucking bastard.*

Mark called several times as Aedan sped back to Rehoboth, his gas pedal to the floor. No one seemed to notice him. It was as if he were invisible tonight. Like Jay.

He pulled up in front of Brew, closed down and locked up for the night. He didn't have a key. He didn't have a freakin' key to get in the front door!

He ran along the side of the building, then back to the rear entrance, thinking he would kick down the door if he had to. He didn't need a key. The door was open. The lock picked, no doubt, probably minutes after Aedan had left. Jay had set him up.

He took the stairs two at a time. The door to the apartment had been left open as well. He flew through the door, his heart pounding, his chest heaving. "Dallas!"

Kenzie stood in the hallway outside her mother's open bedroom door, as pale as any ghost he had ever seen. He threw his arms around the little girl. She was dressed in the pajamas he had put her to bed in that night: Spiderman. No blood.

*Bad man,* she telepathed.

He went down on one knee and hugged her tightly. "Did he hurt you?"

She shook her head. *I hid.* She was dry-eyed, but her skin was a deathly white. *Momma,* she telepathed. *Save her. You know what you have to do to save her.*

Aedan closed his eyes for a moment, then opened them. "Go to your room, Kenzie," he ordered. "Go to your room, shut your door, and don't come out until I come for you."

*You won't leave me?*

"I won't leave you."

He watched Kenzie go back down the hallway, too-long pajama pants dragging.

He found Dallas lying naked on the floor at the end of her bed in a puddle of blood. "Oh, God. Oh, God," he sobbed, falling to his knees, lifting her in his arms.

She was still warm. But there was so much blood. So many wounds. She couldn't still be alive.

He lowered his face over hers and was surprised to feel her light breath on his cheek. His voice trembled. "Sweet Jesus. Dallas?"

Her eyelids fluttered, then opened. "Kenzie?"

"Safe. Fine."

"He didn't . . ."

Aedan shook his head, fighting a sob that rose in his throat. "She hid. I don't know how or why, but she knew to hide."

"I'm dying, Aedan."

He looked away.

"You have to help me. You have to save me."

It all came tumbling back so quickly. One instant he was in Rehoboth Beach in an apartment over a bar; the next, in a pub in France, hundreds of years ago. Madeleine. Dallas. The same. It was happening all over again.

"Aedan," she cried urgently. She tried to take his arm but she was too weak. "Look at me."

It was all he could do to force himself to look into her dying eyes.

"You have to save me," she whispered. "You *have* to do it. You have to make me a vampire."

He shook his head. He couldn't think. How had he let this happen? This was his fault. Dallas would die because of him.

"Make me a vampire."

"I can't," he groaned. "You know I can't."

She closed her eyes, and for a moment he thought she was gone. He could feel her body letting go.

Then her eyes fluttered open again. "Aedan, please. I'm begging you."

"You said I did the right thing." He wiped at his eyes with his sleeve. He couldn't fall apart. Not now. He had to stay strong for Dallas, for Kenzie. "With Madeleine, you said I did the right thing. In not damning her. In letting her die."

"You . . . did . . . do the right thing," she whispered. She coughed, and blood ran from the corner of her mouth. "For Madeleine. But . . . I have Kenzie." The light in her green eyes was flickering fast. "I would give my soul . . . for my daughter."

Aedan hugged Dallas's body to his, remembering his vow to Madeleine. *I will not curse you as I have been cursed*. But then he looked into Dallas's ashen face and thought of the little girl down the hall.

What was he supposed to do? He groaned in anguish.

If he didn't decide quickly, it would be too late, and the decision would be made for him.

* * *

It was late morning by the time they reached the Philadelphia airport. Aedan took one of Kenzie's hands and Kaleigh the other as they tried to hurry through the ticketing hall without catching the eye of any security guards.

*Hurry,* the little girl telepathed. *He's getting away. We have to hurry.*

She was still wearing her Spiderman pajamas. Aedan hadn't been able to convince her to change out of them. She *had* agreed to sneakers and a jean jacket, which Kaleigh had buttoned up to cover the fact that she was wearing pajamas in an airport.

Aedan had been certain Jay was gone. In all the confusion at Dallas's apartment, it had been a good hour before Aedan had sat down with Kenzie and tried to figure out what to tell her. How. She'd been there in the apartment. She knew what had happened to her mother.

*You're sure he's still here?* Kaleigh telepathed.

Kenzie thrust out her lower lip. *Bad man. He's here.*

*Where?* Aedan scanned the crowd. There were so many people. And there was a flight leaving for Edinburgh in forty-two minutes. He sort of knew the face he was looking for, from the sketch, but he saw no one with a scar on his cheek, and, honestly, everyone looked like Jay now. *Where is he?*

Kenzie halted, so Aedan and Kaleigh halted, all causing a minor traffic jam.

"Over there," Kaleigh suggested. "Want to stand over there?"

Kenzie allowed herself to be led to a spot near the windows. Outside, people hurried past, rolling suitcases behind them. Cars pulled up to the curb, dropping passengers off.

*Where is he?* Aedan asked.

Kenzie pointed to the men's bathroom.

Suddenly, Aedan's heart was pounding. He dropped down on one knee in front of the little girl and grasped her shoulders. How had Dallas failed to tell him of her daughter's very special gift?

Kenzie could not only see a person's past, like her mother, but his future as well. And she didn't need to touch him, either. She had known Jay was in the area before he had come to their apartment. Then she'd *seen* Jay from inside her closet, where she'd hidden when he had come for Dallas. Jay had never realized Dallas had a daughter. A very special daughter.

*You're sure he's in there?*

*He's going to the bathroom, then he's going on the plane. Blue pants. Yellow shirt with buttons. No cuts on his face. Red hat. It has a fancy* P *on it.*

*A "P"?* Then it hit Aedan. *P* for Phillies. *You're absolutely sure?*

*I can read!* Kenzie insisted.

Somehow, Aedan found that he could still smile. He stood up. *You stay here with her. Anything out of the ordinary happens and you walk out with her,* he telepathed to Kaleigh, and Kaleigh alone. *You take her home to Clare Point. Anything.*

Kaleigh glanced around to be sure no one was watching them and then slipped something wrapped in cloth to Aedan. Aedan slid it inside his leather jacket and zipped up just the bottom. He gave Kenzie a wink. *Be right back.*

*Then we go home?* Kenzie telepathed, grinning.

*Then we go home.*

The airport was so busy that Aedan had to morph the first time in the very short hallway going into the men's room. He entered as an elderly, bald man with a cane. As he walked to a stall, he spotted a man at the urinals: blue pants, yellow oxford shirt, red Phillies ball cap. Jay.

There was no one else in the restroom.

Aedan doubted there were cameras directed at the urinals, but just to be safe, he entered a stall, then exited it as a tall, slender Caucasian male in his late twenties. He walked up behind Jay as Jay moved toward the sinks.

Jay, like many of God's creatures, must have had a sixth sense about what was about to go down. Aedan saw Jay lift his head, and their gazes met in a mirror. Aedan saw in his eyes a moment of confusion, then recognition of the moment at hand . . . then absolute fear.

Jay spun around, whipping out a long knife with a jagged blade.

How the hell did Jay think he was going to get through security with that thing? Aedan wondered.

Maybe Jay had known he was never going to get away this time? Maybe it was that sixth sense.

Aedan lunged left, then right, staying just out of reach of Jay's wicked blade. He slipped the ceremonial knife out of his coat and grabbed the creature by his scrawny neck.

There was no way Jay was any match for Aedan's strength . . . or his anger. And Aedan was angry, perhaps angrier than he had ever been in his lifetimes. He was angry for what Jay had done to his life, and the ramifications . . . the pain that was still to come.

Jay struck out wildly with his knife.

Aedan brought his fist down on Jay's forearm, snapping the bone. Jay cried out in pain as the knife hit the bathroom tile and skidded out of the way.

Aedan spun the creature around and drew the ceremonial knife across Jay's throat. He sunk it deep, using brute strength to force the blade through bone, severing Jay's head from his body. Aedan refused to take the chance Jay could be reborn as vampires could; without a head still attached, there was no chance of that.

He let Jay's body fall to the tiled bathroom floor as the head rolled away and hit the wall under the sink. Aedan took a deep breath, calming his pounding heart. But he didn't have time to stand around. He morphed again, ridding his clothing of the blood, and walked out of the men's public bathroom, a short, elderly, dark-skinned man in a porkpie hat, plaid shorts, and black socks and white sneakers. No one checking the camera recordings later would ever be able to identify six-foot-five, red-haired Irishman Aedan Brigid as the executioner.

Aedan put out his hand to Kenzie as he walked by her. *Ready to go home?* he telepathed.

Kenzie looked at Kaleigh, then at the old man whose identity she was well aware of, and grinned.

*Ready.*

So, home they went.

# Epilogue

*One week later . . .*

"Just keep stirring the hamburger," Brian said. "Like this." He stuck a wooden spoon into the frying pan and stirred, then handed the spoon to Victor.

Victor frowned. "You're only a couple of months older than me. Quit acting like you're an old man or something."

Aedan, at the kitchen counter cutting up black olives, met Mary McCathal's gaze. She smiled and went back to rinsing lettuce in the sink.

The kitchen was full of teens; it was taco night, which Aedan had a feeling would become a weekly event. Mary and Aedan were still working out the details with the General Council, but they were pretty certain a couple of teenage girls were going to move into Mary's house. Aedan was going to stay at Peigi's cottage with Victor, Brian, and some other teen boys. In the past, it had been up to individual families as to how to handle the rebirth of a teen, but after Peigi's suicide, most members of the sept agreed it was time to take a new approach. If teens were allowed to grow up together, under adult supervision, while still living near spouses and family members, the transition might be made easier. If nothing else, it was worth a try.

At first, Aedan hadn't been crazy about the idea of being a house mother, but the Council had been so pissed with him after what happened with Dallas that he was lucky he hadn't been exiled, like Peigi. Losing his job had been painful, working as an assistant at Tavia's gym was going to be a pretty harsh sentence, but he could have ended up living with a bunch of Transylvanians or something. So at least he would be allowed to stay in Clare Point. It was only because of the extenuating circumstances, because of Kenzie, that his sentence had been so light.

"How long 'til the burger's ready?" Aedan asked Victor.

Victor shrugged. "How long Brian?"

Brian glanced in the frying pan. "Ten minutes."

The doorbell rang.

"I'll get it!" Katy hollered.

"I'll get it!" called another teen.

"*I'll* get it," Aedan insisted, putting down his knife and wiping his hands on a tea towel. "It's *my* house."

"*Technically,* it's mine and Peigi's," Brian pointed out. "And since Peigi's not here." He stopped and started again. "Since she won't be home for a while, I'm in charge here."

"You wanna try to take me down?" Aedan opened his arms wide, towering over Brian, trying to make light of the moment. "You wanna piece a dis?"

The teen, who seemed to be maturing by the day since Peigi's death, laughed and backed away. "No way, man. I own the house. You're the housekeeper. You answer the door."

The teens roared with laughter.

Aedan threw the hand towel at Brian and walked out of the kitchen. When he opened the door, Kenzie was standing there, holding a plate covered in foil.

*Brownies,* the little girl telepathed, eyes downcast.

"Terrific! You make them?"

*Mom.*

Aedan grinned and let Kenzie duck under his arm so he could lean forward and kiss Dallas on the lips. "How are you doing?" he whispered.

She was paler than she had been before, but she looked good. Most of her wounds had already healed due to her vampire blood, including Jay's signature on her left breast. In a few weeks, she would be unblemished, physically, by Jay's attack. Aedan was unsure how long it would be before the emotional scars faded.

"I'm good." She looked up at him, her eyes tearing over. She kissed him again, stroking his cheek, and laughed with embarrassment. "I . . . I still don't know what to say to you. How to thank you for what you did, for what you did for Kenzie."

He ushered her in the door. Kenzie waited in the hall for them. "Don't thank me yet. This isn't going to be easy. You're going to be making some of the same transitions the teens are going through. We've got a lot to talk about."

"Like the fact that you failed to tell me you're a shapeshifter who can appear as different humans," she whispered. She gave him a light punch in the bicep.

He frowned. "Kaleigh should keep her mouth shut."

Dallas smiled up at him and rubbed his arm where she'd just thumped him. "She's helping me understand how this all works. And I don't care about what you did and didn't tell me. You gave up a lot for me, for us. Your job, your—"

"It doesn't matter."

"It *does* matter." She grabbed his hands, looking into his eyes. "You play this off however you like. I know how much your job in Paris meant to you. Kaleigh said it could be lifetimes before they let you go back to work."

He shrugged. "I'll get fit working at the gym."

"Aedan, this is serious." She searched his gaze.

"I'm not worried about me. I'm worried about us," he confessed.

"What do you mean?"

He looked down at the pretty, bright carpet at their feet. "I just . . . I hope you . . . don't come to hate me."

"Hate you? How could I ever hate you? You sacrificed so much for us."

He shook his head. "But I cursed you, Dallas. You can't forget that. We can never forget it." He lifted his gaze to meet hers. "And with time, you're going to realize how . . ." He stopped and started again. "I just hope you don't come to hate me for what I did. For making you a vampire."

"I could never hate you," she breathed, lifting up to press a kiss to his lips. "Never."

*We'll see,* Aedan thought, his heart heavy. *We'll see in a hundred years, a thousand.*

Then he leaned down and kissed Dallas again, lowering his mental barriers and letting her see who he was, who he had been.

"I love you," she whispered, trembling. "And . . . and I know we can't marry, but I think we could become a family."

Kenzie slid her small hand into Aedan's. *We're already a family,* she telepathed.

Aedan laughed, and Dallas looked at him and then her daughter. "I don't know what's up with you two," she said suspiciously. "But we're going to have a talk. *Very* soon."

Aedan put one arm around each of them and led them into the kitchen to meet the rest of his family. He wasn't like Kenzie. He didn't know what the future would bring, but tonight he felt as if he had, at last, come home.

Have you read all of the Clare Point Vampire novels?

Take a trip to the Delaware beach town populated
with vampires, and get to know
the Kahills from the beginning.
Don't forget your SPF 100. . . .

## ETERNAL

*Centuries ago, the shipwrecked vampire clan known as the Kahills came ashore on the sleepy Delaware peninsula of Clare Point. In* Eternal, *V. K. Forrest introduces readers to the ravishing, undead Fia Kahill, an FBI agent who's in danger from a vampire-slayer—and the one man she must resist but can't. . . .*

FBI Agent Fia Kahill has just learned her cousin Bobby McCathal is dead. His body is found burned, and his head and hands are missing—the unmistakable calling card of a vampire-slayer. When more vampires' corpses surface, Fia knows it's only a matter of time before the killer catches up to her. But that's not her only worry. She's been assigned to work with FBI Agent Glen Duncan, who is the spitting image of Ian, the man she once loved—and the man who betrayed her. . . .

Four hundred years ago, Ian used his relationship with Fia to infiltrate the clan and kill as many of them as he could. Fia promised herself she would never make the mistake of loving a human again. With the murders in Clare Point escalating, Fia has no choice but to trust Glen even as her promise is becoming more difficult to keep. Fia wants Glen like no other man she's ever desired—and before she knows what's happening, she is deeply immersed in a forbidden love affair. But this time the consequences could be far graver than Fia ever could have imagined. For a killer has her in his sights as his next victim. . . .

## UNDYING

*The Kahill vampire clan has lived among humans for hundreds of years in Delaware's peaceful village of Clare Point. In* Undying, *V. K. Forrest introduces readers to Arlan, a fierce member of the clan who must fight his desire for a love most forbidden. . . .*

As part of the Kahill clan's special operations "Kill Team," Arlan is devoted to ridding the world of its most depraved human members. He's been asked by fellow clan member and FBI Agent Fia Kahill to assist in one of her investigations: the notorious Buried Alive Killer case. Arlan agrees to meet with one of Fia's key informants, Macy Smith, but he's completely unprepared for his response to the young woman. Blond, petite, and achingly beautiful, Macy is everything Arlan could want in a woman—and it's clear the attraction is mutual. Although Arlan once vowed he would never again let himself fall in love with a human being, he surrenders to his overpowering desire for Macy. . . .

Soon, Arlan and Macy keep mysteriously crossing each other's paths, even in Clare Point. In Macy, Arlan can sense a loneliness that reminds him of his own and a vulnerability that tugs at his soul. But Macy is a drifter with a past far darker than even Arlan can imagine. And when the Buried Alive Killer strikes again, he learns that Macy has a deep connection to the case—one that will put her in the crosshairs of the killer if Arlan can't find a way to protect her. . . .

## IMMORTAL

*For centuries, the Kahill vampire clan has lived quietly among locals and tourists in the tranquil beachfront village of Clare Point. In* Immortal, *V. K. Forrest weaves the unforgettable tale of Fin, a Kahill clan leader who discovers that the woman he loves may harbor a secret too dark to comprehend. . . .*

Magnetic, fearless Fin Kahill has dedicated his life to ridding the world of its most vicious serial killers. Fin is used to roaming the earth freely—not getting stuck in sleepy Clare Point. But when the clan needs him close by, Fin agrees to take a summer job on the town's tiny police force. He expects little excitement—until he meets Elena, an ethereal Italian beauty.

As Fin struggles against his feelings for Elena, the peace in Clare Point is shattered by the inexplicable murder of a tourist. The young man's throat has been cut, his body eerily posed. When the killer strikes again, Fin wonders if a member of his own clan is responsible. The only one he can turn to is Elena, but he knows that falling in love with a human can be a deadly mistake. Yet just as Fin edges closer to solving the murders, he discovers Elena may not be exactly who, or what, she appears. . . .

## RAVENOUS

*Welcome to the quiet coastal town of Clare Point, Delaware, where the Kahill vampire clan has made its home for centuries . . . and where one vampire's love for a human woman could put their entire world at risk. . . .*

As a member of his clan's Kill Team, Liam McCathal helps rid the world of undesirables. It's the perfect job for a vampire of his talents—except that lately, Liam is getting a little *too* good at it. Which is why he's back home to "cool off," when Mai walks into his antique store and changes everything.

Liam's not in the habit of making friends—least of all with beautiful, exotic human females. But something about Mai ignites a spark he hasn't felt in over a century. When Mai's uncle is killed and her father threatened, Liam takes on a ruthless crime boss and puts every vampire in Clare Point in danger of discovery. Because Mai's father has secrets, too, and Liam is edging ever closer to losing his reputation, his clan, and the woman he would do anything to protect. . . .